THE CAUSE

THE CAUSE

by

Jane Mann

Vinca Press

British Library Cataloguing in Publication Data
A catalogue record for this book is available from the British Library

ISBN 0-9549093-0-5

Typeset by Amolibros, Milverton, Somerset
This book production has been managed by Amolibros
Printed and bound by T J International Ltd, Padstow, Cornwall

ABOUT THE AUTHOR

Jane Mann was born in Sevenoaks, Kent but spent most of her childhood in Devon. After gaining a teaching qualification and degree from Exeter University, she went out to Hong Kong, where she worked as an Education Officer, teaching English to Chinese students. While in Hong Kong, she travelled extensively in the east and made lasting friendships. Here she met her husband, Ray, and started writing. An adventure story she wrote, *Chang Fook and the Viper*, was published by OUP and used as a reader in schools there.

Returning to England, she got married and settled in a rural community in Buckinghamshire where she has raised her family – two daughters and a son. Her work continued as a lecturer in further education and later as an examiner for three exam boards.

Concerned about pollution and the way we treat other species, she has been active for many years in a number of environmental organisations. She is particularly interested in animal rights issues, hence her focus on the conflict over vivisection in her novel, *The Cause*.

Her knowledge of undercover and vivisection procedures has been gained from research into relevant film and written documentation. The precise setting, the actual plot of her novel and all its characters are fictitious.

For those who have dedicated their lives to
alleviating the suffering of animals, and
especially for the animals themselves.

Rosy

Thanks for giving me a great
factual book about NVDA. To
return the compliment here is a
work of NVDA fiction

Tim

16/6/24.

ONE

I wasn't sure what to make of Mark Stanton when we first met. It was a sultry June evening, heavy with the past week's heat wave and impending storm. Sweat soaked my T-shirt as I climbed the hill to the building where he was to speak. I felt wary, on edge.

It was a grim-looking Victorian building with high, barred windows and flaking, brown paint. Two men, dressed in black trousers and sweatshirts, stood like guards on either side of the rust-hinged doorway. One wore a black balaclava hiding his face. The other looked at me intently for a moment and then waved me inside.

I was in a narrow hallway and confronted at once by two large posters fixed to a crumbling, cork notice board. One showed the mangled body of a beagle with a raw scraped neck, a slit open stomach and broken legs; the other a monkey clamped in an elaborate, metal instrument with iron bars wrenching back its neck and contorting its limbs, its eyes caught in a wild, uncomprehending expression of despair.

It was the eyes that got to me. They were like a human's, suffering, demanding action and I wanted to act, get that monkey out of that clamp and away from the torture.

Then I stood back, remembering my resolution that I wasn't going to get involved without facts and knowing for myself. I had to be sure, not swayed by emotion, by a mere picture that could play tricks. "Doubt everything," my father had once said.

Ahead of me in the hallway, I noticed three other women dressed, like the men outside, in black and I wondered if it was some kind of uniform. I felt uneasy again, wishing I'd stayed at home and not given in to Steve's persuasion.

Then Steve was there, to my relief, coming towards me in the usual green tracksuit he wore, swinging his arms in the bear-like way he had, his smile tentative.

"Mark's about to speak," he said. He took my arm, gently leading me into a dimly lit room with one of the high barred windows I'd seen from outside, the bars starkly silhouetted from inside against a greying sky.

The room was small, more a committee room, but there must have been at least thirty people there; youngish, mostly in their twenties, with alert, determined expressions in their eyes, cramped together in rows of hard-backed, folding chairs. All of them except Steve and me were wholly or partially dressed in black. I persuaded Steve into the two remaining chairs in the back row, hoping I wouldn't be noticed and could make a quick exit.

Then the door opened behind us and Mark came in, deftly edging past the chairs to the table in front. He was a lean, compact man with an air of suppressed energy, giving the impression as he moved of being ready to act, yet trained, in control of his body.

Like the others he was dressed in black, in tight-fitting trousers, T-shirt and high boots. Unlike the others he had thick, black hair swept back off his forehead so his clothes seemed to be a natural part of him, not imposed.

There were no preliminaries. Speaking without notes, Mark launched straight into his theme on the need for continual action:

"Words mean nothing," he said, "without action. It was action that closed down the notorious primate farm at Monkton. It is our action now that will close down our next target, the laboratories of Draco Life Sciences.

"We don't know everything yet that goes on in these laboratories. We do know beagles are injected with noxious chemicals and monkeys are cut up while still alive. We know kittens, only a few days old, are blinded in one eye and put in head frames while their heads are injected with dye. Then they are killed and their brains dissected."

As he spoke, Mark looked around the room. He had deep blue eyes that focused on each person in turn, giving a sense that one mattered, had to listen. It was all part of the method he had cultivated, I realised later, as was the compelling quietness of his voice. You could have heard a pin drop as the audience strained to listen.

I knew then he'd noticed me. There was no smile, no surprise, no obvious sign of recognition, just his deep blue eyes looking into mine. I had a strange sense for a moment of being drawn into an underwater world where there were just the two of us, swimming free from the heat, the mustiness and gloom of that crowded room. Then, as if resisting, Mark was asserting again the reality and brutality of facts, speaking, it seemed, directly to me:

"Every year 180,000 animals are killed at DLS; dogs,

cats, rabbits, rodents, monkeys. If an animal moves at DLS, they experiment on it. If it breathes, they kill it. All animals at DLS end up as non-survivors."

He gave further statistics, then made the point that most of the experiments were pointless because of the differences between species, making it impossible to extrapolate results from one species to another.

"Experiments such as those carried out at DLS are totally useless, owing to these differences and in fact hold back progress," he emphasised.

With relentless logic, Mark continued his indictment and, as I looked round the hall, I could see, could feel he had carried his audience along with him. They were no longer an audience, more a group united with him, with the cause. Despite my reluctance to come, my doubts about being there, I could feel myself being drawn into their empathy. It did seem wrong, the suffering pointless. But how much, I wondered, of his speech was slanted? How much was he driven by the intensity that showed in his eyes? How much did he know of what happened inside the labs if he hadn't been there himself? I felt I wanted to find out more, know for myself, be sure.

Mark closed his speech with practical suggestions for action. Demonstrations, vigils, letter-writing to shareholders, urging them to withdraw their investment; telephoning the company itself to block the telephone lines and fax machines, the targeting of the bank financing Draco. It was a carefully devised strategy for practical effect. And I admired Mark for it. He was obviously dedicated and had managed to combine general purpose with detail. So often people with a cause speak eloquently enough but slip up on the implementation, or lack vision and general oversight to give purpose to practicalities. Mark seemed to harmonise the two in a way that was unusual.

I was tempted, when he'd finished speaking, to go with the others and say I'd help. But something held me back. A natural caution perhaps. I liked time to think, to decide for myself. I'd never been one to commit myself spontaneously. Or perhaps it was just apprehension of what was involved, what I might be drawn into; the violence that so often erupted from demonstrations. Whatever it was, when Steve went to talk to him, I turned instead to the exit door to the hall.

Here a table was laid out with leaflets, with dates of demonstrations and graphic pictures of cats with clamps on their heads and throats slit open. I hesitated for a few moments, then picked up a couple of leaflets and made my way past the posters of the tortured monkey and dog to the exit.

I was about to slip outside, feeling I wanted to get back home to think things over, when I heard Mark's voice behind me.

"Don't go. Come and have a drink with us."

I felt his hand on my shoulder and, as I turned, his eyes, even more intensely blue in the subdued lighting, focused on me in direct appeal.

Behind him stood Steve, looking awkwardly tall, hovering from one foot to the other in the hesitant way he had when he wasn't sure of my reaction.

"I'm sorry." The words came without thinking. "I'm afraid I've got work to do."

"Steve tells me you're a teacher."

"For the moment, yes." What else had Steve told him,

I wondered. I hoped he wasn't manoeuvring behind my back to get me involved.

"You're looking for another job then?"

"I'm trying, let's say."

It struck me then how little time I had left, barely a month, before my present contract ended. All the more reason to get back, I convinced myself, to fill in some of the application forms.

"A new direction or the same?"

"I'm open to new ideas. So long," I added pointedly, "as they pay the bills."

"You're interested though in helping." It was more a statement than question.

"When, if, I have the time," I qualified, ready to reach down into my usual rag-bag of excuses. But the deep blue eyes regarding me were not dissuaded.

"One always has time if one wants it," Mark stated matter-of-factly. "It's the need surely that counts and gives perspective?"

He was right, of course. The need was there. It was insufferable sentient creatures should be treated merely as objects and tortured even if some of the facts might be exaggerated. And I knew in the end it would be difficult to resist being involved. Partly it was the catalogue of cruelty Mark had just outlined. Partly, it was Mark himself; the inner strength and conviction he exuded through his eyes, his lean, fit body and dark hair.

Whether he was attracted to me, or viewing me simply as a recruit for the cause, I couldn't tell. I felt at that moment I had to get away from him, to resist the influence he was having on me.

As another woman came up to him, I seized my

opportunity and without committing myself, abruptly said goodbye and left.

Back at home, I tidied around and tried to concentrate on filling in application forms but kept thinking about Mark, what he'd said, and our encounter. The points he'd made about vivisection were all new to me. I realised I'd never really thought about what went on in research laboratories. It struck me afresh how little I knew, how little I'd tried to find out or contributed beyond my own concerns. I'd undertaken the odd bout of fundraising for Oxfam and letter-writing for the Friends of the Earth but it hadn't added up to much. I kept thinking of the horrible clamps on the heads of the kittens and the pain pointlessly inflicted on the beagles, monkeys and other creatures. Yes, they were different from us in many ways but still aware, intelligent and feeling. I kept thinking of Mark himself and the touch of his hand on my shoulder.

It was midnight by the time I had completed the two application forms. They were both for teaching posts in two colleges of further education within travelling distance of Horton. I really didn't hold out much hope for them. I'd tried already six other posts, from all of which I'd been rejected without even an interview.

It was partly, I knew, my own fault. I'd given up a relatively secure post with long-term prospects at Ashmead College far too readily when I'd discovered I was pregnant. The pregnancy had gone to my head as well as body and I'd felt I couldn't cope. I just wanted to hide with the baby in peace. I didn't want all the hassle of planning, marking and challenges from awkward students whose problems I knew I couldn't solve.

Then totally out of the blue Simon left. I knew I should have read the signs of his affair with Sara. They were there in his absences, his mobile calls and withdrawal. But I was too preoccupied with being pregnant and too unthinkingly dependent on Simon for his goodwill and support. When I had my miscarriage two months later, I was devastated. I felt as if a vital part of me had been taken away, that I was imperfect, incomplete. I yearned all the time for her, my baby girl, almost perfectly formed but too small, too young to survive.

For weeks I stayed inside, not wanting to go out. If it hadn't been for Steve and Carol, I doubt I'd have spoken to anyone at all. It was Carol who, through a contact, helped me get my present part-time job at Royston, another college, when my money finally ran out. It was Steve who'd helped me in so many ways with practical plumbing problems and the like, saving me money, energy and time.

But I knew I couldn't go on trying to make ends meet on part-time contracts and depending on Steve to help me out. I needed a proper job with money to pay for the upkeep of the house and more. Fortunately I didn't have a mortgage. The house, a terrace built in 1900, had been bequeathed to me by my father when he died but a great deal needed doing to it. The brickwork was basically sound but the window frames were all rotting, all in urgent need of repair and replacement. I suspected there was also wood rot in the timbers of the lounge and in other places as yet unseen.

As I lay in bed thinking of the house and Steve, I felt guilty I'd walked out of the meeting without waiting for him. He'd been so good to me, so kind. But it was too late to ring and apologise. I was afraid of disturbing his mother whose nights were already fragmented with her cancer and pain. Then just as I was going to sleep, the phone rang. It was Steve.

"What did you think of him then?"

"Mark Stanton, you mean?"

"Who else?"

"Does it matter what I think?" I didn't want to voice a judgement. I didn't feel I could. Mark had unsettled me in a way I couldn't explain, especially to Steve.

"I think it may do, yes."

"What do you mean?" I had a curious sense of trepidation.

"I think Mark would like you to help with a project he has in mind for the holiday."

"What kind of project?"

"That's for him to explain, which he'll do if you're interested."

"You're the intermediary, you mean?"

"I said I'd ask you first, yes."

"I might be interested," I said cautiously. "It depends on how my applications go and whether I've got work to prepare."

"When will you know?"

"In a month or so."

"I'll suggest he rings then. How would that be?"

"Fine." By the end of the month I reckoned Mark would have found someone else and I wouldn't have to be involved. The thought, oddly, prompted both relief and regret.

"Meanwhile, how about coming to the demo Mark's organised for Saturday at DLS," Steve suggested. "There's a minibus going so you wouldn't need to worry about transport."

"Are you going?"

"As long as I can get help for Mother, yes. Everyone is. It would give you a good idea of the size and strength of the movement, Kate."

"Would it?" I felt I'd already had that at the meeting, a reluctance to be more immediately involved. Demos, like meetings, were not, I was sure, my scene. They usually meant trouble or at least the troublemakers took over, I told myself, as I selected scenes I'd seen of stones and broken glass and scuffles on TV. Then I was aware of Steve's silence and remembered. "I'm sorry I didn't stay and wait for you."

"It doesn't matter," Steve's voice held its usual calm. "You're free to do as you want and only join when you're ready for it. Mark knows that. He understands."

"He doesn't know me, Steve."

"No, but he knows the movement. He knows how people feel."

"And he's effective, you think?"

"He's the engine now and driver, Kate. We couldn't manage without him. He's one in a million, totally committed. But he doesn't expect everyone to be the same."

"Doesn't he?"

It was characteristic of Steve to see the best in others, to be generous about their achievements and underestimate his own. It was one of the reasons I liked him, yet perversely, one of the reasons I doubted. Could one really be totally committed and was anyone, when it came to the point, indispensable? How, anyway, on a

10

practical level, did Mark find time for all the activities he organised? What did he do for a living?

"He understands," Steve repeated, "and that's what's so good about the movement. People join because they want to, because they really believe in it, because it's right. It's where our roots really lie, Kate, the link we have way back with other creatures."

"You really believe that?" It was the most heartfelt tribute I'd heard Steve pay.

"Yes, I do, and I think you will come to believe it too once you've gone into things and seen what really happens."

"Maybe."

I was moved by Steve's words but the future seemed suddenly uncertain again, a grey expanse. Like an unseen furry presence, the heat closed in, draining, drawing me back to the past. I felt I wanted to hide, an intense longing to have my unnamed baby back inside me again.

In a way I couldn't define, I sensed Mark Stanton as a threat.

TWO

The storm broke the next day, lashing out with its fists of wind and rain until nightfall. It cleared the air but brought down tiles from the roof, exposing the timber, and broke two windows. I had little time in the next three days to think further about Mark and the planned demo. A builder had to be found and the mess sorted. I had my temporary job and endless more application forms to complete before deadlines.

Then the day before the demo, I had simultaneously three rejection slips in the post. I felt completely fed up and had a sudden desire to chuck in teaching altogether and do something quite different. When Steve rang and asked me if I was going on the demo, with a sense of relief and without thinking, I agreed.

Steve dutifully collected me the next morning in his van and we joined a minibus going to the demo from the station. I felt tense as we clambered inside, wondering what I was letting myself in for but the atmosphere on board was friendly and relaxed. I recognised some of the faces that had been at the meeting and Steve introduced me to Gemma and Karl. Gemma was a robust, no-nonsense woman, with short, dark hair and a resolute chin, who'd been an anti-vivisectionist, she told me, virtually all of her life. Karl was quite different with dreamy eyes and long, fair hair with bits of twig and grass in it as if he'd been sleeping rough. The rest were a broad cross-section of people, not one type as I'd feared, though most like myself were in their twenties, I guessed. There was no sign of Mark.

The talk was mainly of animal rights issues, the present campaign and the future. Karl asked me what I'd done in this connection and I had to admit to being an 'ignorant, but interested, novice'. "It doesn't matter," he said encouragingly. "The fact is you've joined us and got started." Despite my very limited credentials, I felt I'd been accepted.

After two hours' travelling, we stopped at a lay-by on a minor road in flat open country. As we stepped from the minibus, Steve pointed out the Draco building for me across the fields about a half a mile away. It was at the back, he explained, where the animals were kept.

It was a bright, sunny morning with a clear blue sky with hardly a cloud in sight yet the effect, as I followed his gaze, was of greyness: block upon block of identical outbuildings, constructed of grey slabs of concrete with rust coloured sheet steel roofing. None of them appeared to have any windows but a few had chimneys, incongruously tall and grey, against the skyline. All round the compound was high razor-wire fencing, reminding me, with the chimneys, of a picture I'd once seen of Auschwitz. I felt uneasy, chilled.

The place repelled me but in a strange way also attracted, made me feel I wanted to break through its defences and find out what went on there.

I was trying to work out how someone could get into a place like Draco when two coaches and another minibus arrived. I saw Mark step from the minibus with a pile of skull masks in his hand. He was dressed all in black again, in calf-length boots, tight fitting jeans and T-shirt, accentuating his leanness, dark hair and blue eyes. On his T-shirt was a white logo of a beagle with a massive collar round its neck and the words "CLOSE DOWN DLS".

His arrival was the signal to gather round.

"Just a few words before we set off." Mark called for attention, holding up the skull masks. "No compulsion, but if you want to help make an impact, then wear one of these. They'll also help you to avoid detection. The police have taken to videoing us in a big way recently. They're out for evidence. Don't give it to them. Which leads me on to what we can achieve today. The police, we've just learnt, have set up a cordon right around Draco. It's unlikely we'll get into the grounds without arrests and confrontation. I suggest we leave the grounds for the next time when they don't have prior warning and we keep this essentially to a peaceful protest outside. We can still make our point and get reported for it in the press which is what we want at this stage."

"You're not telling me we've come all this way just to stand pussyfooting outside," a disgruntled voice behind me suddenly challenged. I turned to see a thickset, bearded man with a shock of long black hair glaring at Mark.

"I wouldn't call it pussyfooting to make our point," Mark replied, "and we will make our point when everyone is gathered outside. I'll be suggesting exactly what individuals and groups can do to get this place closed. Essentially I feel we have to give encouragement today, ideas for action. What we don't want is confrontation with the police giving us a bad press. You yourself can speak, Jake, if you've a point to make."

"I'll have that. Don't you worry."

"Right, let's go and get as near to the buildings as we can. The coaches and minibus will leave at six but you can come back to them at any time. There'll be stalls with veggie food along the way."

The group around me shifted and I found myself standing next to the bearded Jake. There was a strong smell of decaying flesh coming from the black plastic sack he was carrying. I didn't like the smell or the look of him at all and moved away to be near Steve.

As Mark gave me a skull mask, our eyes met briefly: "Glad you came," he said, then moved on to the next group.

Steve and I put on our skull masks and joined a couple with billboards on their backs with enlarged photos of helpless cats clamped and outstretched, with their stomachs slit open, in metal instruments of torture.

Despite our lurid appearance, there was almost a carnival atmosphere with people laughing, joking, whistling and even singing as we walked towards Draco along the lane. More people soon joined us from other buses, coaches and cars. Most were not disguised as we were but dressed simply in conventional outfits or new-age free flowing garments with gothic jewellery and exotically coloured hair. There was an amazing range of ages from babies-in-arms and six-year-olds holding their fathers' hands to silver-haired pensioners being pushed in wheelchairs. I felt moved, a sense of wonder that so many diverse people were amicably united in a common cause.

We reached the end of the lane and around me the mood became more sombre and subdued. I could see two rows of policemen guarding the razor wiring and several on horseback with a further reserve overseeing the extension of the lane leading past Draco's main gates. We were clearly not going to be allowed to get anywhere near these.

There were rumbles and mutterings of dissatisfaction as we were increasingly crowded together in the narrow lane. I became aware of a helicopter circling above, of the police in the front row looking wary and apprehensive as we bunched like a growing amoeba towards them. It was at this point Mark climbed on a tree stump, his head and shoulders above the crowd, and started to speak.

"Friends and supporters, I want to thank you all for coming today. Your support is proof, if any were needed, of what the public think of this evil place and that they want it closed."

"Close down DLS," a woman shouted. Her words rippled like a wave through the crowd until everyone chanted, echoing her. It was some time before Mark could make himself heard.

"There was never any point in animal experiments," he continued, "because most other animals, as we know, react differently from us to drugs and disease. This has been shown time and time again by the mistakes made. Today there is even less justification. We now have computer modelling, stem cell research and other techniques that more enlightened firms and academics are using. There is no excuse at all for the torture of animals by Draco. Why do they do it then? I'll tell you why. For greed which puts money and profits before all moral considerations, for the sense of power it gives them over the vulnerable who cannot help themselves.

"Because they cannot help themselves, we must help. They depend on us and we must give our help freely. How can we do this? By coming here, as we have today, to show our solidarity. By contacting shareholders by letter and phone to tell them what goes on here. By shaming those who work at Draco by our vigils outside. By phoning DLS numbers to make known what we think and blocking their lines. All these actions will help and any others you can think of to bring this place down. Remember the animals need us. No one else will help if we do not. Resolve to act today. Don't pass by on the other side. Help close down DLS."

Again came the refrain chanted even louder now by the protestors, uniting them in common cause and feeling.

As Mark climbed from the tree stump, immediately Jake, the bearded man, took his place and swung into action literally with the black plastic bag he'd been carrying. He swung it around and around his head, and shouted, "You've heard the words, now you'll see what really goes on in there."

As our eyes focused on him, he stopped swinging the bag, undid the hessian rope binding it and plunged in his hand. He paused a moment, for effect, then drew out the mangled body of a beagle. There were gasps from the crowd, murmurs of anger. A couple of women nearby had tears in their eyes as they turned away and I knew how they felt. The eyes of the beagle had been gouged out, the head slit open and the intestines were protruding from a cut in its underbelly. What was most overwhelming just then nearby was the smell, the cloying sickly smell of flesh disintegrating. From where I was standing, I could see maggots already burrowing in the open head.

Suddenly a silence fell on the crowd as Jake held the body up higher with his left hand, pointing at it with his right.

"This is what the scum inside are doing," he shouted, "and who's protecting them?" He pointed directly with his right hand at the nearest police guarding the razor wiring. "These scum here. They're no better than the scum inside. In fact they're worse. They're protecting a rotten system. Big business, that doesn't give a damn about anything! About its workers, its animals, welfare, the environment! Nothing except making money! They're fascists guarding a corrupt system. Look at them. How contemptible can you get, to guard a concentration camp of torture, to condone the torture of thousands of animals like this mangled beagle?"

"Scum bags! Shit!" someone shouted and others joined in.

I looked across at Mark who stood beside Jake. He was frowning with a concerned, edgy look in his eyes, clearly worried about the way things were going.

As I watched, I noticed two men in black masks sidle behind, keeping him like bodyguards deliberately, it seemed, within a defined range and distance. One was tall and thickset, dressed like Mark in black, with ice-blue eyes and black bushy eyebrows streaked with grey, showing through the eye-slit of his mask. The other also in black, was shorter, slighter, with shifting brown eyes. Neither of them bore any resemblance in build to the people I'd met on the minibus or along the lane and I wondered who they were and whether Mark was aware of them. Were they bodyguards or did they have some other purpose? They were each carrying something grey in their hands but I couldn't see exactly what it was.

As Jake's speech came to an end, he paused a moment on the tree stump, holding the beagle's broken body still higher. For a moment I thought he was going to fling it at the police. To my relief, Mark in an adroit move took the body from his hands and passed it in the sack to Steve. He clambered onto the tree stump again, arms outstretched with the intention of calming the crowd after Jake's outburst. As he did so, I noticed the tall, masked man close in again behind and nod to the shorter man. As Mark raised his arm, they too raised theirs.

The next minute I saw two large, grey stones flying towards the police. One landed between two of them in the back row near the razor wiring. The other hit one of the younger front row policemen square in the face.

I saw him flinch in surprise. Blood spattered from his cheek. He raised his hand to feel it dripping onto his yellow jacket.

There was a stunned silence. Then a ripple of concern ran through the crowd. A woman near him started to cry. One of his colleagues with a first aid box ran to his aid.

I saw Mark look round, perplexed, from the tree stump, trying to assess who could have thrown the stones. But the two masked men had slipped deftly away in the moment of diversion, back through the crowd to the hedge beyond.

As Mark hesitated, the police, who had been guarding the lane leading to the main gate of DLS, closed in surrounding Mark and the group around him. There were shouts of protest and dismay.

I had a split second of choice. Then in a surge of anger, I pushed through the hedge, holding on to my skull mask, and ran out into the field behind, where the two masked men had made their escape. I heard someone shout behind me. It may have been Steve or the police. I couldn't tell. All I knew was the two men had deliberately sought to wreck a genuine and well-intentioned demonstration and I was determined to find out who they were and where they'd gone.

There was no sign of them as I stumbled over tufts of grass sodden by recent heavy rain. Then as I reached the end of the field and climbed over a gate leading back into the lane, I saw them running ahead towards a Land Rover parked further off.

So far I was fairly sure they hadn't realised I'd followed them. It was too much of a risk, though, I thought, to challenge them on my own. None of the others had caught up with me as yet and there was no one else in sight. I decided to pretend I was walking to another car, intending to get a closer look at them and get the Land Rover's registration number.

As they reached the vehicle, the larger man whipped off his mask. He had sparse, tufted, grey hair and a lined, discontented face. Then his ice-blue eyes were looking at me and I knew he'd guessed I'd followed and had seen them throw the stones.

He hesitated briefly then climbed into the driver's seat and started the engine. Quickly I took out the notebook I always carry with me and scribbled the vehicle's number.

As I wrote, the Land Rover reversed suddenly at speed towards me. I was completely taken by surprise and leapt out of the way only just in time. It came to a halt and the shorter man climbed out of the passenger seat and came over to where I was standing.

He was still wearing his mask. I was more confused than afraid that his eyes were so prominent, his face hidden. They were eyes still darting, now from the road to me and back up the road again—hard eyes like beads that had lost their lustre. Assessing the road was clear, suddenly he lunged and snatched the notebook from my hand. Gripping my shoulders then, he sent me reeling into the hedge. It was a holly and hawthorn hedge. The thorns stabbed through my T-shirt, scratching my neck, face and arms. It was painful just to move. By the time I'd extracted myself, the man had climbed back into the Land Rover and they'd driven away.

I took off my skull mask, desperately trying to recall the numbers and letters of their registration plate but all I could remember was a B, an H and a 3.

Shaken, I sat on the verge, trying to make sense of what had happened. My skin burned from all the scratches but I was conscious more of an inner fear that the two men might return and try to run me over again, that they were dangerous in a way I couldn't yet understand and perhaps wouldn't. It was obvious they intended to undermine Mark's efforts, but why and who were they?

I could feel my heart still racing, had a desperate need to talk and get back to the others.

To my relief, as I struggled to my feet, I saw Steve

coming along the lane towards me with Gemma and Karl.

"Whatever happened to you?" Immediately concerned, Steve got his first-aid kit from his haversack and started wiping my worst scratches and applying antiseptic.

I tried to explain about the two masked men. I still couldn't remember the numbers and letters of the Land Rover's registration.

"It'll come back," Steve tried, as he always did, to reassure. "I think we should tell the police what you've seen. Mark's got a problem, trying to explain what happened. He didn't see who started it."

We went to Draco's razor wiring and I told the police what I could of the two men and their actions and gave the letters and numbers I could remember. I'm not sure how much they believed me but it was written down and Mark and the group around him were let off with a caution and allowed to go home.

Over a Tannoy, the police then ordered everyone to leave the area. The demo had effectively been scuppered.

I didn't have any opportunity to talk to Mark until we reached the lay-by where the coaches and minibuses waited. He asked me to describe the two men in more detail. Eyes, eyebrows, build and tufted grey hair, it was a sketchy effort but Mark said he'd do his own investigation.

"You don't know who they are then?" I probed.

"Not yet, no, not for sure, but thanks for what you did. I'm sorry you were hurt."

"They're dangerous, aren't they?" I persisted. I sensed he knew more than he was saying and I was still angered by what the men had done. They'd had no compunction about running into me, or running me over. It would be difficult to prove, of course. There were no witnesses. It was a dilemma I suspected Mark had encountered before. But if he was worried, he didn't show it.

"They like to think they are," he said, "but they won't defeat us. Our cause is just and in the end we'll succeed."

I looked at the people streaming now like a defeated army with despondent faces back down the lane. Then I looked into his eyes. They were deeply focused, deeply blue and determined and I believed him.

"Stay with us," he said. "I'll be in touch."

Then he turned, urging people to get into the minibus and coaches. A few minutes later we left the grey slabs of concrete and chimneys behind.

THREE

I awoke late the next morning to a persistent ringing on the front door bell. I stumbled downstairs to find Carol on the doorstep, dressed casually in jeans but immaculately made up as always, her blond hair shining.

Carol never calls without a reason and my immediate reaction was one of panic I'd forgotten something.

"It's all right. Nothing urgent." Her nails glinted in the sunlight as she waved a reassuring hand. "I thought I'd better bring you the last few exam papers so you can get on with them." She picked up her briefcase and we went to the sitting room where my application efforts of the previous evenings were still strewn about over the desk and chairs.

"Looks as if you've been busy. Any luck so far?"

"Not yet."

"I'm sure it'll come." With an encouraging smile, Carol deposited a pile of papers on the desk. "Sorry I didn't get them to you earlier. I called on Wednesday evening but you were out."

"Yes, I was at a meeting."

"A meeting? It doesn't sound like you. What kind of meeting?"

I hesitated, wishing now I hadn't mentioned it, but I didn't feel I could brush Carol off. She had been very good to me, had helped me get a foothold again on a job. Although at times I resented her organised and organising manner, I knew she could be relied upon and trusted.

"It was about vivisection mainly, the need to treat animals better."

"Animal Rights, you mean?"

"I suppose you could say that, yes."

Carol shook her head with one of her knowing, sceptical smiles. "I should think twice, if I were you, about getting involved with Animal Rights."

"Why? Surely improving the lot of animals is a worthwhile objective?"

"I don't doubt the objective. It's the methods I don't like."

"What do you mean?"

"The direct action. The violence. Only yesterday, I've just read in the paper, they stoned a policeman at some demonstration or other."

"One or two maybe," I said defensively. "The majority, I'm sure, are law abiding and peaceful."

"They should control the firebrands then. That fur shop burnt down two months ago in north London, wasn't that by Animal Rights? And their leader, what's his name, Mark something?"

"Mark Stanton."

"I read somewhere he was convicted for arson some years ago in the States. It's fine if they keep to conventional methods of protest," Carol was on her high horse now, "but once they go for direct action, then the anarchist elements take over. No, I shouldn't have thought it would help your cause in looking for a job, getting involved with that. You aren't seriously thinking of it, are you?"

"I haven't decided anything yet."

"Well, don't. That's all I can say. Anyway, I didn't come to talk about Animal Rights. Apart from the exams, I came to ask if you'd like to come this evening for a drink. There's an architect, Alan Masson, who's just moved in to old Mrs Ashbourne's house at the end and we're inviting him to meet the neighbours. He seems a nice chap. I think you'd like him. He's divorced apparently but no children."

I could feel Carol already going into matchmaking mode. Cautiously I asked, "Who else is going?"

Carol reeled off the names of several couples and singles who also had terraced houses in the street. There would be safety in numbers and I accepted.

One had to hand it to Carol. She made a great effort for people and communal affairs generally. Despite having two children and Robert to look after plus a full-time job, she always seemed to find time for other people as well. If anyone in the street could be called superwoman, it was Carol. How she managed in reality I don't know. The children were now six and eight years old and both at school but it must have been a strain keeping up with all their activities out of school after a day at work.

I imagined it was a matter of organisation. Carol was a planner at heart. She always looked ahead and mapped out her time, utilising all the stray moments, which most people would use to relax in or waste. She also had what appeared to be total support from her husband, Robert. I wasn't sure quite what he did for a living. I knew vaguely it was some kind of medical research but into what exactly, and where, was never made clear. A quiet man, Robert rarely talked about either himself or his work. His hours, however, appeared to be flexible for he was always at hand when needed to collect or take the children to school or do the cooking. If Carol was superwoman, then Robert could well have qualified for super house-husband.

"Good," Carol responded, genuinely pleased, by my acceptance. "It's time you got out again and had some social life, met new people. I know Steve comes round to see you but he's not really in your league, is he?"

"What do you mean, my league?"

"Well, he doesn't have your professional qualifications and intelligence for a start."

"He may not be qualified but he's a good man, Carol, good in the true sense. Not many men would look after their mothers as he does, and he's genuinely honest and sincere."

I was probably misleading Carol in the way I defended Steve but her snobbishness sometimes got to me, the way she overrated IQ and qualifications, as if they were all there was to life. I wasn't in love with Steve, as she feared. I liked, rather than loved, him and in so far as I saw a future, it was of friendship, no more. Perhaps that's what Carol couldn't understand, that it was possible to just be friends with a man.

"He's looked after his mother, that's true," Carol conceded, "but he could have made more effort with the rest of his life." She picked up her briefcase, slightly exasperated, I suspected, and made for the door. "Well, I must be on my way. Good luck with the marking and applications and see you this evening, six-thirty. Try not to be late. Alan apparently has a meeting at eight."

"Right."

I made myself a large reviving black coffee when Carol left. I was still tired, on edge and Carol's disapproval hadn't helped. We didn't see eye to eye on many things but her views were representative of quite a large section of society. They had to be taken into account when considering the animal rights issues.

I had virtually to force myself to do the marking she'd brought and after four hours, then filling in another application form, felt I had to get some fresh air.

I decided to go for a walk and call in on Edith Hobbs, Steve's mother, on the way home while he was out at work on his gardening job with the local town council. It was the only job Steve had been able to get and he enjoyed working outside; but it wasn't well paid and the hours were long which created difficulties in caring for his mother. A nurse called morning and evening and a catering firm brought lunch, but there were long hours between when she was lying or sitting alone.

Not that she ever complained. Her eyes, a gentle grey like Steve's, reflected a remarkable acceptance of her fatal illness and she seldom judged others' actions.

A nurse by profession, she had helped my father in innumerable, practical ways before he'd died and I was very grateful to her. She was one of those rare people who literally do dedicate their lives to others; her husband through his long illness, bereaved neighbours or children needing care. Whoever came her way, whether in her professional life or otherwise, she'd always found reserves of energy, concern and time when the need was there.

Now the need was hers and I was shocked to see how much she'd changed since my last visit. Her face had become gaunt, a parchment colour with visible grooves of pain; her body so thin, she seemed shrivelled in the huge double bed. She was no longer the comfortable, comforting person who'd treated my father but fragile, vulnerable herself now, like a leaf that could any moment be blown away.

The cancer in her throat was too advanced now for her to speak with any ease and she was heavily drugged which also made talking a strain. We sat in silence mostly while she showed me some photos of Steve and I could feel her trying to tell me what she couldn't articulate, that she loved him and recognised what a good son he was. Then, unable to resist the drugs, her eyes closed and she slept.

I sat by the bed for about an hour, feeling an inexpressible sadness at what was happening to her. Suddenly, all my efforts to get a job, even the teaching itself and the marking seemed trivial. I began to realise how Steve must be feeling, remembered from my father's illness; the helplessness that comes when you've done all you can but it has no effect, the need to find significance.

Perhaps, I reflected, it was why he had taken up the cause of the Animal Rights Movement. The need to assert the claims of life of the vulnerable and abused against those of death, which death itself and the powerful exerted. Increasingly, as I sat there, Carol's judgement both on Steve and the movement, seemed harsh, lacking insight.

I returned home not at all in the mood to go to her party, but knowing I would not be forgiven if I didn't.

I drifted round the house, trying to get myself into a more convivial state of mind. I must have fallen asleep, as I lay on the bed, for when I was next aware of the time it was already seven. Seizing a long skirt and a loose fitting black top, the nearest clothes I could find that didn't need washing, I quickly dressed and brushed my hair. There was no time to put it up as I usually did for a party.

I was about to leave, knowing I was already in the doghouse with Carol, when the phone rang. Irritably I picked up the receiver to tell the caller to ring later. I must have sounded snappy for there was a brief pause, then I heard the voice I'd both longed for and dreaded.

"Hello, Kate, Mark Stanton here. I hope this isn't an inconvenient time for you."

"It's not ideal."

"Right, I'll get to the point. Steve tells me you'd be interested in helping with a project?"

"Yes, but not yet, I told him."

"That's fine. It wouldn't be yet. Things take some time to organise, preliminaries I mean."

"Yes, I can see that."

"I was wondering, therefore, if we could get things going, if I called round this evening."

"This evening!" I felt at once nervous, on edge at the thought of seeing him again so soon. I needed space, time to adjust to the prospect and to avoid him guessing how much he attracted me.

"It wouldn't take long, just a few minutes. How would it be if I called, say, in half an hour?"

"I'm going to a neighbour's for drinks. I won't be here in half an hour."

"When will you be back?"

"About nine."

"I'll come then."

"Yes, but do you know where I live?"

"Sure, Steve told me."

"I see." What else did he know? What a fool I was. What was I letting myself in for?

I went to Carol's, apologising for being late, but I could see she wasn't too pleased.

All the other inhabitants of the street she'd invited were already gathered in groups on the back lawn. Most of the women wore, as she did, short closely fitted summer dresses. I felt both conspicuously late and ill-dressed as the eyes turned. I wanted to run back home. Only I knew I wouldn't. I didn't have the nerve and Carol had other intentions.

Thrusting a glass of wine into my hand, she took my arm and led me straight to Alan Masson who was talking to Robert.

"Alan, let me introduce our latecomer, Kate Wilson. Kate's a colleague of mine and she's in the process of having to make some difficult decisions."

"What kind of decisions?" Alan Masson asked with polite interest. He was a cool, good-looking man, very photogenic with a classic straight nose, broad forehead and wavy, light brown hair. But his hazel eyes, I sensed, were rather wary as he looked from Carol to me, then back to Carol again.

"About a job mainly," I replied.

"And whether to join a certain organisation," Carol intervened. Alan didn't take up the prompt this time and she continued, "Kate's not sure whether to join the Animal

Rights Movement. I've suggested being careful. Wouldn't you agree, Alan?"

"If there's a risk of going to prison, then, yes, I suppose I would."

"There you are. Words of wisdom." Her mission accomplished, Carol turned to dispense drinks and advice elsewhere. Robert, meanwhile, discreetly took himself off to chat with one of the secretaries renting the house next door.

"Sorry," Alan smiled, "I was rather forced into that. I don't know much about the Animal Rights Movement, except it does seem rather revolutionary in its tactics sometimes."

"Aren't revolutionary methods sometimes necessary if you're going to get somewhere?" He looked so cool, complacent. I had a sudden urge to argue.

"I don't think they do, I mean, get somewhere," he answered, unfazed. "That's the problem. I feel it's important to take people along with one or there's a backlash."

"Surely though, where there's suffering we should try to stop it here and now," I persisted, "and there is pointless suffering with all the experiments being carried out on cats, dogs and primates especially. I don't see why this should be extended until we've taken everyone with us. We'll never do that."

"No," he agreed, then qualified, sceptically shaking his head, "but one can't be optimistic about changing attitudes. People are deeply conservative when it comes to change. It's a matter of evolution in my view, not revolution, and sudden change. More bite-sized pieces, stage by stage."

"We'd still have slavery if that was the case," I countered and was beginning to enjoy the challenge of arguing my case, when Alan Masson looked at his watch and said he had to leave for a meeting with a client.

"But we haven't really resolved the issue, have we?" He raised his eyebrows, regarding me for a moment with slightly bemused interest. "Perhaps you'd like to come to dinner some time with Carol and Robert to continue the discussion."

"Thank you." I wasn't too sure I wanted to now. Carol would determine the agenda and I had an uneasy feeling from Alan's expression he was a bit of a chauvinist and would not take my views and the issues seriously.

When he'd gone, I hovered a while looking at Carol's well trained shrubs and borders. Robert, I noticed, was still talking to the secretary from next door and appeared to have given up his dutiful role of playing waiter and helping Carol. He was looking unusually animated for Robert, his eyes and balding head shining in the evening light. As had often happened before, I thought how little I really knew him.

As soon as the next group of guests started leaving, I thanked Carol and slipped away.

I hurried home, hoping to have some time to myself before Mark Stanton arrived but although well before nine he was already waiting on the doorstep. He was dressed casually in jeans and a green army jersey but had the same alert air of readiness as at the meeting, as if any minute he might spring into action. His eyes, in the evening light, were the same intense blue.

"You got away early then?" he smiled.

"Yes." I unlocked the front door and led him to the

sitting room, wondering where he lived himself. I couldn't imagine him attached to property or wanting to own things.

"Sorry about the mess." I started to clear away exam papers and application forms strewn across the settee, desk and chairs but he told me not to bother, that he was used to the floor. So we sat on the stained remains of an old Bokhara carpet.

He sat compact and upright, his legs neatly crossed, his back straight in front of my father's grandfather clock. He looked at me intently then as if trying to assess me, sum me up and I wondered what my father would have made of him and my initiation into the movement for that is how it seemed—an initiation. I felt again the attraction experienced at the meeting and demo, tinged with wariness and apprehension.

"I had a sense at the meeting you were sympathetic," he said, "which is why I think you're the right person to help us."

"Help in what way?"

"Briefly, we need to get someone inside Draco Life Sciences, DLS for short, I mean as an employee."

"To do what exactly?"

"To find out more about the abuses, to photograph them if possible, to get to know the routine and above all the security system. We're planning to make DLS an unviable operation."

"How?"

"Partly by destroying the records, partly by releasing the animals when the time comes. At the same time there will be continuous pressure on shareholders to cut the financial lifeline to DLS."

"So you want someone to go to work there for a period, get all the info, then on a certain day there'll be an organised break-in."

"That's the gist."

"And you're visualising me as the employee, is that it?"

"Yes, yes, I am."

I was amazed how confident he sounded and, without really knowing me, that he should disclose his plans. I presumed it was a trust based on his knowledge of my friendship with Steve but the whole idea still struck me as preposterous.

"But I have no scientific training, no lab experience. There's no way I'd be accepted even if there were a post vacant. I haven't the credentials."

"Not all the jobs are in the labs," he replied, unruffled. "There are also jobs looking after the animals themselves. Animal technicians they're called."

"I haven't the experience for that either," I protested.

"You don't need it. It wouldn't show if you didn't have it, and as far as applying goes the experience can be fabricated."

"But I'm not free in any case. I'm still teaching and applying for jobs."

"You're free in the holiday though, aren't you," Mark persisted, "which most people are not? That's when they'll need people to cover the holidays and you wouldn't necessarily have to stay more than three weeks. You could probably get all the info we need in that time."

"If they didn't see through me."

"They won't see through you if you don't want them to." Mark had switched from the conditional as if it was already feasible, a reality. One by one my objections were being scaled away. "It's all a matter of will power and planning," he continued. "One has to defeat these evil bastards by outwitting them. If it means acting and being underhand, then that's what has to be done. One never gets anywhere writing letters and appealing to their better nature. There's no better nature when it comes to making money from animals. They're scum, Kate, and one has to use all the wiles one can think of to bring them down."

"Why me though? There must be others in the movement with far more commitment and experience of these things."

"There are others but they're too well known on the animal rights lists, whereas you are not."

"Not yet," I said, sceptical still.

"It's all in a good cause. That's what you need to remember. That's what matters, to stop all the suffering and pain that achieves nothing anyway. We need to give animals back the respect they deserve."

I could feel myself slowly, inevitably slipping into his will, to my feeling both for him and the animals suffering but I needed to be more certain.

"Yes, but there are still things that worry me." I hesitated, then blurted, "You set fire to a fur business, didn't you, and you've been convicted of arson in the States."

"Who told you that?"

"Carol, a friend of mine."

"Well, take it from me it's just not true. It's one of those rumours spun by the local newspaper, *The Herald*, for their own ends because they had shares in the firm. We did break in but the fire was an accident caused by faulty wiring which they conveniently blamed on us as a scapegoat."

"And what happened in the States? Is that also untrue?"

I knew at once from his hesitation it wasn't. I felt more than anything then I wanted the truth from him, that I wanted him to be honest, that being honest mattered more than his actions.

Perhaps the way I thought got through to him more than I expected.

"No," he said at length, "it's true. I was convicted."

"You went to prison then?"

"For six months, yes."

"What did you set fire to?"

"It was a slaughterhouse. I went to work there to find out what went on." There was a tension suddenly in his eyes and the muscles of his cheekbones. "Some of the animals were slit and skinned while still alive. Everything was geared to saving money, everyday a hell for the animals. No one did anything about it. If anyone protested about the abuses, they were sacked. I set fire to the office on my last evening when I couldn't stand it anymore. It seemed all I could do. I think you would have felt the same if you'd seen what I saw."

"There are no regulations then?"

Mark gave a deeply cynical laugh, "There are minimal rules yes, but they're inadequate and flouted all the time. The fire was to draw attention. I can't pretend it stopped the machine functioning. After two days they were back in business with a vengeance, but the issues were raised in the press and the courtroom. A seed was planted that has grown. A few more people are protesting now but it all takes time. That's the problem. One's up against big business. Whatever the cost in animal pain and suffering they are out to make money. One has to make dramatic gestures to get noticed. Few people otherwise listen. That's why I resorted to arson in the States. It would be better if more rational means could be used to get attention, but they don't work."

"No, I can see that." I couldn't get out of my mind Mark's picture of the animals skinned alive. The excruciating torture of a knife cutting relentlessly at one's flesh and not being able to escape in any way. The thought of it was unbearable.

As Mark talked, I felt his anger and understood why and how he'd acted and saw it was justified. The idea of working at DLS no longer seemed preposterous but something I could in fact do, needed to do, to know for myself the real situation.

"Would you be willing to try for a job at DLS?" Mark looked across at me in the growing darkness. He was willing me certainly but also respecting my right to decide.

"Let me sleep on it," I said. "I need some time. I'll let you know in the morning."

I offered him a drink but he said he had to go and I wondered if he had a girl friend and what she was like. It was difficult to imagine him in a context not allied to animal rights.

In the doorway he took a newspaper cutting from his pocket. "I'll leave the job advert for you just in case and thanks again for what you did at the demo. You helped me out of an awkward situation. I hope you'll stay with us and use your powers of observation inside." For a moment our hands touched and he hesitated. I had a sudden desire to kiss him and draw him back with me into the house. Then he was gone and I was looking out at a darkened sky.

FOUR

I had no second thoughts as I'd expected. I slept better that night than I had for weeks and as I looked at the advert Mark had left me the next morning, I knew I would apply, that it seemed the right thing to do. The advert, however, was very brief. 'Animal Technician required for holiday period, preferably with experience. Apply by letter with CV to Glensen Recruitment, 20 Hart Street.'

The CV I'd prepared for teaching would rule me out immediately and might even arouse suspicion as to my motives for applying. I decided to ring the agency and ask them what exactly they were looking for. A sharp voice at the other end of the phone told me they wanted people "used to handling animals competently" and who were hard-working and knew how "to get on with the job". Experience in zoos or kennels would be useful. She then urged me to get in my application as soon as possible, as the closing date was in four days and the starting date the 15th July.

It was the day after my present contract ended. Mark had been wiser than I'd thought in looking ahead, I reflected.

I was trying to think how to reconstruct my CV to make it more appropriate when Mark himself rang.

"What's the verdict then?"

"I've decided to try," I said.

"You have?" Mark sounded surprised, then relieved. "Thanks, Kate. You won't regret it."

"Won't I?" I was to remember his words many times later, but for the moment it was the practicalities that mattered. I asked him for some plausible names of kennels where I might have worked and a reference I could use. He gave me the name of a Mrs Shepherd in Wales and said she'd vouch for me. He suggested questions I might be asked at an interview. To my surprise then, he said he was going to be away for three weeks in Europe lobbying but would get in touch when he returned.

"Any problems – you can contact me by e-mail but no give-away details or names." He gave me an address, and then said he was sorry but he had to go.

I felt oddly in limbo as I put down the phone. I wanted to see Mark, be near him again, not be told things from a distance. Then I remembered what Steve had said about his dedication. Perhaps that's what it meant. Absence, being elsewhere, working away and I wondered again whether he had a girl friend.

Reconstructing my CV was a bit like doing a crossword. I had to make all the pieces fit especially dates as I was reducing my age and qualifications. I added the name of the kennels Mark had suggested under experience and wrote a letter painting myself as efficient and unsentimental.

I didn't expect to hear for some time, if indeed at all,

41

so was surprised to receive a letter three days later offering an interview at Glensen Recruitment the following week. By luck, it was an afternoon when I didn't need to attend the college and it gave me time, with Mark's suggestions, to work myself into the role of a twenty-two year old kennel maid seeking fresh employment. It was a bit like the role-playing I'd done in the past with students and I enjoyed in a perverse way the challenge of diluting my accent and asking myself awkward questions.

I felt nervous all the same when, a week later, I found myself in the cool, blue, carpeted office of Glensen's. A sharp-faced, middle-aged woman with glasses and a jacket to match the carpet stared at me from behind an executive desk.

The blue was soothing, but the words as she read out the job description were not soothing at all. The job, as Mark had known, entailed working for Draco Life Sciences in their animal testing labs. The job of the Animal Technician was to tend the animals for their feeding, exercise and cleansing and handle them for the testing.

"These tests," she peered at me over her glasses," are ordered by the various medical and commercial companies and are carried out by the Lab Technicians. As an Animal Technician, you follow the instructions of the Lab Technicians to aid them in their work with the tests."

"I see." I wanted to ask what tests, what animals and what rights the animals had in the process but, as Mark had warned me, to ask anything of this kind would be to put the whole plan in jeopardy and give the game away.

"It's a demanding job, which requires a certain amount of detachment. I'm sure you understand that. You cannot become too emotional and involved." Her thin lips curved round the word emotional, isolating and dismissing it as an aberration.

"No, of course not," I concurred, forcing a smile.

"Good." She put down the job description, seemingly relieved and scanned my CV. "Tell me," she asked, "what made you decide to leave the kennels in Wales?"

I trotted out some prepared clichés on wanting to widen my experience and invented family members I wanted to be near. She asked me what I had gained from my experience in Wales.

"I learnt how to handle dogs and understand their needs," I said.

"What do you think their needs are, Miss Wilson?"

I thought of Brandy then, the dog I'd had as a child and the need she'd had for companionship, a stable home, trust, being part of the pack and heard warning bells again. These were not needs to mention with their "emotional" connotations and I answered in as remote a voice as possible about the basics of food, drink and shelter.

She then asked what societies I belonged to. I'm not a joiner by habit and I could truthfully say none but she wasn't satisfied and wanted to know if I had ever been on a demonstration.

I feigned surprise and in a pathetically self-righteous voice said I didn't believe in them.

"You haven't had anything to do with the Animal Rights Movement then? You haven't been to any of their meetings?"

"No, of course not," I lied.

She peered at me over her glasses with suspicion but I held her gaze and suddenly she was straightening them, smiling and saying she'd have to check my name of course on the Animal Rights lists but if all was well, I could start at DLS on 15th July. I would get £200 a week and a letter of confirmation within three days. The interview was over.

I returned home with an odd sense of elation. I didn't want the job, far from it, but felt in a small way I'd taken control at last and passed a test. Not one significant in itself but which might open fresh possibilities, free from the constraints of the past, to do something more meaningful and challenging with my life.

I straightaway e-mailed a cryptic message to Mark with my news. I didn't expect an immediate response, but when a couple of weeks had passed without reply, became concerned. Steve could shed no light on the overall plan Mark had in mind for my investigation at DLS nor the equipment I was meant to use. Nor did he have much idea, it seemed, about Mark's activities in Paris, which made me wonder how much Mark consulted the others and how democratic the movement really was.

Then late one evening, three days before my teaching contract ended and I was due to start at DLS, a woman with a French accent rang, calling herself Marie and saying Mark had been detained after a demonstration in Paris but was due to be released on the 18th and would be in touch then. Abruptly she rang off and I was unable to trace the number.

I shouldn't have been surprised by Mark's detention. I'd already had indications he was internationally known and likely to be sought by the authorities but it threw me into a state of apprehension about the assignment at DLS as I realised I'd been depending on Mark for direction and the practicalities of the photography.

"You'll manage," Steve tried to encourage me. "You can feel your way for a couple of days, then Mark will be here to help you. He'll come. Don't worry. He always comes in the end if he says he will."

"You've got great faith in him, haven't you?"

"He doesn't let people down," Steve asserted simply, "if he can help it."

Perhaps it was the woman's voice that had got to me. Perhaps it was the fear, more real and imminent now, of my pretence being exposed. Perhaps it was just the simple fact Mark was not around as I'd expected him to be.

As I stood in front of DLS with my bicycle three days later, I felt on edge and alone.

Approached from the front, DLS presented a rather different facade from the back we'd seen at the animal rights demo. Set well back from the road, it had its own exclusive driveway leading to a pair of black iron gates, electronically operated, with a disc for each car. Close to them, inside was concrete concourse for parking, and directly opposite a gleaming white office block of speckled white concrete and extensive smoked glass which I learned later was reinforced and virtually unbreakable.

In the shadow of the office block to the side, I could see some of the dreary outbuildings of grey concrete for the animals. More hidden from view, they were not so dominant, but there was no escaping the high razor-wiring which extended all around the premises from the entrance gates and I felt again the same strange mixture of curiosity and repulsion that I'd experienced at the demo. I wanted to turn around and cycle home. I also wanted to break through the defences and find out what went on behind them. And hadn't I earned the right now to be admitted? As a car drove up, opening the gates electronically, I slipped through with my bicycle.

There was no sign of a cycle shed, so I pushed my bicycle to the nearest outhouse and leaned it against the wall. As I bent down to padlock it, I heard a prolonged, muffled whining sound coming from inside, then a voice barked close to me.

"What are you doing here?"

I looked up to see a man dressed in a grey security outfit, glaring down at me. He had bulging muscles and suspicious eyes.

"I've come to work here. I'm expected," I explained.

"Where's your card then? What's your name?" He continued to glare at me.

"My name's Kate Wilson. I haven't got a card."

He consulted a piece of paper then from his pocket and said, "You can't leave your bike there. It'll have to go at the back of the compound."

He led me across the concrete concourse, past more windowless outhouses to a small shed where there was one other bicycle.

"Most people come by car," he said with disapproval, though whether this was directed against cars or bikes, I wasn't sure.

"I see."

There was still a wariness in his eyes. I noticed he had a baton attached to his belt and wondered how many other security guards there were prowling about.

Things didn't look too promising for Mark's proposed break-in and I decided to put on a conciliatory act to try and win him over. Exaggerating my thanks to him for showing me the shed, I asked what entrance to use, at which he directed and accompanied me to the main office block.

There was a pad of numbers outside which he pressed too quickly for me to note with any certainty though I got the first two, a 9 and 8. Then the glass door opened and we walked across a marbled floor to another glass door with yet more numbers which he pressed and I found myself in a well carpeted reception area facing a woman with short, blond hair, immaculately made up, and dressed in navy and gold.

"Kate Wilson! Says she's working here."

The woman nodded and the security guard gave a mock bow and withdrew through the glass doors to the concrete outside.

"Please take a seat, Kate." The woman smiled. "You'll be starting in the dog unit, Section 18. I'll get someone to show you around."

She picked up the phone and a few minutes later a man wearing a white medical jacket and thick, dark rimmed spectacles came into reception and introduced himself as Tony Brown. He was overweight, rather flaccid looking, with plump fingers that he extended in a cold, half-hearted handshake.

"So you've come for the holiday period then?" His lips curled as he spoke with a hint of scepticism.

"Yes, that's right."

"So what do you normally do?" He emphasised 'normally' with more than polite interest.

"Kennel work mainly but I'm in the process of changing areas."

"I see. Well, I'd better show you round then, hadn't I?"

He led me along a corridor linking the main office block to the outhouses, explaining that everyone used the same main entrance and I'd be given the entry code before leaving that evening. There were strict codes of secrecy, he warned, and it would be instantly changed if there was any suspicion of it being passed on. Was he just warning me generally or already suspicious, I wondered. I felt increasingly the need to be on my guard with him.

We passed ten outhouse doors marked with numbers. He told me there were thirty in all and I would be in 18. As we passed number 11, I asked him what was inside.

"It's the breeding section," he answered tersely.

"How many litters do the bitches usually have?" I asked.

"Ten or eleven. It depends on how fit they are."

"What happens to them after that?"

"One or two go to homes organised by the staff. The majority are put down."

"And the puppies?"

"If they're a conforming product we use them for our tests. If they're NCP we get rid of them."

"What does NCP mean?"

"Non-conforming product."

"What's an example of a non-conforming product then?"

"A stumpy tail, heart murmur, having one testicle."

"So these go to homes then?"

"If someone will have them."

The way Tony Brown talked of the dogs as 'products'

was chilling and it seemed ironic that the only dogs ever likely to leave DLS alive were deformed. I was even more nervous by the time we reached Section 18.

So far the soundproof doors had been closed and I hadn't been aware of much noise. As Tony Brown opened the door to 18, it hit me then, a cacophony of howling, barking, whining and screeching, punctuated by the clanging of iron.

"It's all right. You'll soon get used to it."

Tony Brown ushered me into an office packed with filing cabinets with three small labs leading from it, each with shelves and cupboards stacked with medical and testing products, weighing machines and various instruments I couldn't yet decipher. He introduced me to a pale young man with a crew cut and an even paler-faced woman, both, it appeared, lab technicians like Tony, though of more junior rank. I was then taken down some steps to the pens from which the noise arose.

Never had I seen such a cheerless, miserable place. There were no windows, no prospect to the outside world. The only light was from harsh neon strip-lighting. The immediate effect was of being confined in a prison underground. A concrete corridor ran down the centre with concrete pens on both sides, sectioned and divided by thick, rounded, grey metal bars, in each of which were groups of beagle puppies or adult dogs alone.

As Tony Brown led me along the corridor past the pens, it struck me at once the enormous difference in the way the dogs reacted. The puppies at once pushed to the bars to greet us, seeking attention, wanting to play. The older dogs, penned in alone, cowered at the back of the pens when they saw us or plodded backwards and forwards in nervous, fearful movements. Some of them were bandaged and wearing large head collars but there was nowhere for them to shelter or hide away from the glare and no objects to play with, nothing to distract them. All they had, it seemed, was the concrete, scattered with some sawdust.

I asked Tony Brown where they slept at night.

"Here, of course. They've got sawdust," he replied.

But most of the sawdust I could see was sodden with urine and faeces and some had blood in it.

"How often can I change the sawdust?" I asked.

"Once a day. One shovelful per pen and you exercise them here in the corridor for one hour a day, no more. The food's over here." He led me to a recess where sacks of dried pellets were stored.

He then showed me how he wanted the dogs picked up for the tests by lifting one of the puppies by the scruff of its neck and supporting it beneath the ribcage. It was a method I wouldn't have known and was relieved by his demonstration that I hadn't been exposed.

Everything else though depressed me deeply, the setting, the dogs themselves, the way they were treated and Tony Brown's attitude. I wondered how I was going to stick it out. I wanted to open the soundproofed door and let the dogs out onto the grass outside, into the fresh air and sunshine. How many of the older dogs, though, would make it? Some of them looked not only cowered, but ill, visibly shaking.

"Right now." My tour was over and Tony Brown was bent now on extracting some value from me. "I want you today to give them all a health check. We have some important tests to do tomorrow."

"What sort of tests?"

"There's a toxicity test for a Japanese company and a chemical injection test for liver diagnosis."

"I see." It struck me then what a waste it would be if I couldn't film the tests. How though without Mark could I get the right equipment in time? "What do you want me to check?" I asked, trying to hide my agitation.

"The usual, whatever you did at the kennels. Teeth, paws, ears, nose. Just tick here." He pointed to the record sheets at the end of each pen.

I noticed the dogs had numbers not names, numbers in their thousands. I wanted to both shout and cry at the implied destruction, but Tony Brown was looking at me with scepticism and I had to control my feelings and act, not whimper.

"Is there anything special you want me to note?"

"Any discharge from the ears or nose. Otherwise, I'll leave it to your common sense and experience." There was a hint of mockery as he curled his lips over the word "experience" but I decided to ignore it and appear as efficient and detached as possible. Fortunately his mobile phone rang and he disappeared back to the office and I was left to get on as best I could.

It was a very long tortuous day. I didn't really know what I was doing and looking for but was afraid to reveal the full extent of my ignorance. Tony Brown should have explained more fully and shown me what to do, by way of training, to make me more competent. If I hadn't been undercover, I would probably have sought help more openly.

As it was, I had problems with practically every dog. The puppies were friendly and didn't mind my touching and checking them but wouldn't keep still. They kept wriggling, licking me and wanting to play, which I found difficult to resist. Most seemed to be reasonably healthy, so I ticked away on the positive side of the chart, hoping for the best. Some of them, though, the weaker ones, to my concern, had bite marks inflicted by the other dogs. One had open raw wounds on its hind legs and haunches but when I went to the office to let Tony Brown know, he merely shrugged and told me to make a note and he'd tell the vet.

"It often happens when they're crowded together," he commented, as if nothing could be done about it.

The older dogs alone really distressed me. They didn't want me to handle them at all and kept backing away. It took me ages with each one to check ears, nose, paws and teeth. Most, it seemed, had other parts of their bodies troubling them. One literally could not stand, she was shaking so much and her hair was standing on end. There were stains of blood from her faeces and urine all over the sawdust in her pen. Her eyes had the same uncomprehending despair I'd seen on the poster at the meeting. Only this was worse. It was real. In front of me an innocent, once trusting dog, tortured. I wanted to cry out myself with despair.

It was beyond my actual brief but I decided to write down all the physical symptoms in the hope that someone, an inspector perhaps, would see. I doubted whether it would do any good but I felt I had to do something, a rising anger that was increasingly difficult to disguise.

I felt totally drained, physically and mentally, by the time my working day was over and I pushed my bike back through the iron gates. The prospect of the tests the next day filled me with dread.

FIVE

I was disappointed on returning home to find there was still no message from Mark either by e-mail or phone. There was a note though from Steve in the letterbox, asking me to visit. My immediate thought was his mother had taken a turn for the worse, so I went straightaway.

To my surprise, Edith Hobbs was propped up against her pillow, looking gaunt, still and pale, but no worse.

"It's Mark," Steve explained, taking me into the kitchen. "He's left a parcel for you."

"Mark? You mean he's been here?"

"He came a couple of hours ago but you weren't home."

"But surely, I mean, where is he now?"

"He's got to lie low for a while he says."

"But he was supposed to show me what to do," I protested. "There are tests being done tomorrow." It was probably the accumulation of what I'd seen that day but I felt, by not waiting, Mark had let me down.

"I'm sure he will as soon as he has the chance," Steve tried as ever to reassure me. "Perhaps you'd better see what's in the parcel."

As he spoke there was a crashing sound suddenly from his mother's room. We rushed in to find the scattered remains of crockery and glass from her tray on the floor. It wasn't a major problem. Steve soon cleared the mess but his mother was very distressed by what had happened. There were tears of helplessness streaming down her furrowed cheeks and Steve wanted to comfort her. Gently he moved her to the centre of the bed, repeating there was nothing of value broken, that she had no need to worry. It was as if their roles were reversed. She was the child now in need of reassurance and it reminded me afresh how kind and patient Steve was. He was not only a good son, but he'd make a good father. He held her hands until her crying ceased, then gave her medicine and read some of her favourite poems until she slept.

I waited awhile, then, feeling I was intruding, went to the kitchen and opened Mark's parcel. Carefully wrapped in bubble plastic inside was a compact mini video recorder and the smallest video camera I had ever seen in the shape of a black button. Both were brand new with a packet of instructions and a guarantee. I'd never used such a camera or recorder before and wondered how I'd manage. It was obvious the button camera could be fixed to my clothing in place of a real button but how the camera worked in conjunction with the recorder I'd no idea. Then I noticed with the guarantee a folded piece of paper with my name on in upright, angular handwriting.

"Dear Kate," I read, "I'm sorry to have missed you and not to have been around when you started at DLS. I'll get in touch with you as soon as I can. Meanwhile I hope you can make sense of the instructions. All the best and thanks for what you're doing. Mark

"PS. Could you please check how many night staff there are usually and security guards and where specifically the main computer records are?"

There was no telephone number, no address and I had the sense again of being left in a void as I examined the equipment. The instructions were highly technical and in very small print. I was still bewildered, when Steve, having settled his mother, came to my rescue. Together we went through them step by step, working out the process of how I'd film the tests the next day and what clothing I could use which would not be conspicuous. It wasn't as complex as I'd supposed once I'd discussed it with Steve. We decided I'd wear a shirt with a large chest pocket for the recorder with a black cardigan over it, through the top buttonhole of which I'd fix the mini camera, which could be attached then to the recorder. The white, protective jacket we had to wear for the job could be discreetly left open just below the button. How noticeable would it be though to anyone on the alert? How likely was a black cardigan at the height of summer in a place already warm?

"It'll be fine. It'll all work out. You'll see." Steve put his arm around me as I left.

He'd helped me and I was grateful but can't say I shared his confidence. I was still uneasy about Mark's elusiveness and apprehensive about what I was letting myself in for. Could I pull it off? Suppose I was caught in the act of recording? Tony Brown with his scepticism was hardly likely to be content with a mere reprimand and DLS, as an organisation, no doubt had its plans for dealing with infiltrators like myself. Returning home, I wondered whether to jack in the whole project.

Then I thought of the dogs, the one especially that had been so miserably shaking with blood all over its pen, and knew I had to go through with it.

I got up early the next morning and fixed the camera with its fake button through my cardigan buttonhole and placed the recorder attached by wires through a transmitter in my shirt pocket as planned. I had a tape inside which could record for an hour each side.

I cycled to DLS to see if I could assess, as Mark wanted, the number of guards usually on duty through the night. As far as I could see, there was just the one guard who'd accosted me the day before, his muscles still bulging, his eyes suspicious but at least he wasn't barking at me. Forcing a smile, I asked him what kind of shift he'd had.

"Quiet," he said, without expanding.

"It must be a bit lonely for you on your own here all night."

"I'm not on my own," he said.

Again, he didn't elaborate. I'd have to get the number of guards by observation or other methods. Here was one guard though I didn't doubt would use his truncheon, if he had the chance, and enjoy it.

Having memorised the code, I got through the main office entrance this time without a hitch. Passing the receptionist, I looked around to see if there was any indication of where the main computer room was, but all the doors leading off the reception area were closed and I couldn't think of a plausible reason for asking where it might be.

To my surprise, Tony Brown was already at his desk in the office of Section 18, scrutinising some figures.

"An eager beaver this morning, I see." He gave me one

of his sceptical smiles. "Well, since you're here, we may as well get started."

He explained to me we were going to do the injection tests for liver diagnosis on six dogs for each of the next three days with a blood test following every hour.

There were forty pens altogether, two for the puppies, ten for toxicity tests, ten for skin tests and eighteen for injection tests for liver diagnosis. The dogs for testing needed their own pens. Two were already free which meant we needed to release four more. Four dogs that had completed their tests had to die.

"You can come and help me choose." Tony Brown proceeded to lead me down to the pens where the usual cacophony of barking, whining and howling greeted us.

He walked up and down then, along the central concrete corridor between the pens, looking at eight dogs and their records. His casual scrutiny reminded me of the same film I'd seen of Auschwitz where the guards marched up and down similar concrete corridors, casually choosing inmates for the gas chambers. The gift of life, its evolution, all the nurturing, the wonders of being and the mind, eliminated by a glance or a word, of no importance.

Tony Brown stopped twice hesitantly in front of the dog that was shaky. Tess, I'd called her in my mind, though of course she had only a number. I stood, in terrible confusion, as he assessed her. She looked so ill, so frail. I felt I wanted her released from suffering, that a final injection would be a relief. At the same time I desperately wanted to save her, to take her home with me and give her some comfort and reassurance, even if her life might not last all that long.

"She hasn't finished her injections yet," I said.

"So I notice. I wonder if she'll last that long."

He moved on and eventually chose four others. Tess was saved but for what?

One by one, I carried the four selected dogs to a small lab off the main one, which I later heard was called "Death Row". Here each of them was given a lethal injection of anaesthetic, to which they succumbed almost instantly. Two of the bodies were kept for "further investigation". The others were unceremoniously dumped in yellow plastic bags to be collected, I was told, for the incinerator. I hadn't been wrong in associating the chimneys with Auschwitz.

As I swept out the abandoned pens, ready for the unsuspecting puppies to be injected, I wondered again how I was going to stick another day, let alone three weeks. I realised, to my dismay, I'd forgotten to film what I'd just witnessed. How could I have been so stupid, so wrapped in myself, to forget my purpose? I felt under my white uniform jacket the recorder still in place and the mini-camera primed behind my cardigan button. All I had to do was to switch them on. It wasn't that easy to fumble with my clothing with Tony Brown nearby and I needed to be sure I was about to film and record an important sequence and not waste the tape.

"Heh! You don't need to scatter all that sawdust," I heard Tony just behind me. "One shovelful is enough. This isn't the Hilton, you know."

"Sorry, I forgot." I forced a contrite smile.

He told me then the order of the dogs he wanted. "We'll start in five minutes," he said.

"Right." I waited three minutes, then went to the toilet

and switched on the recorder and camera. As quickly as I could I took the first dog for the injection. He was the largest of the puppies, a calm, reasonably passive dog with trusting eyes. In the lab Tony Brown put him in a sling then told me to hold his head and lower front legs, to all of which the puppy submitted without protest. His leg was shaved and the injection was administered. The leg almost immediately swelled up and the dog vomited, some of it splashing, to Tony Brown's annoyance, over his jacket. But it was more the puppy's eyes that disturbed me. The trust had gone and they were rolling in fear. As I returned him to his pen, he cowered at the back of the pen instead of seeking my hand and licking me as before.

The next dog was smaller, a bitch, and Tony Brown, despite the shaving, couldn't find a vein and started cursing. "She's too small! Why do they send in these damned dogs that are too small?" He plunged in the needle, nevertheless, and the dog yelped, then squirmed and struggled. "I still haven't got it." The needle plunged in again.

This time the dog let out an eerie scream like that of a child. I felt for a moment that I was literally holding a child, a creature vulnerable, helpless, that didn't understand but which felt in the fabric of its nerves and brain the same loneliness and sensitivity to pain that humans feel.

All the more shocking then seemed to me the torture, the fact that by being there I was complicit in promoting it. And for what? There was no guarantee, as Mark said, that any of the research was relevant in helping people.

It was all for money, for gain. I wanted to punch Tony Brown, swear at him for swearing at the dog, for blaming it for something over which it had no control. It was only knowing the hidden camera was doing its work that kept me going and under control. Would it all be captured though as I wanted? I wasn't sure I'd always stood in the best position for filming.

The door leading to the pens had been left open and the screaming puppy had been heard by the other four waiting their turn and had its effect. None of them wanted to come with me up the steps. Each of them cringed in fear as I collected them and tried to run away.

When eventually we'd finished the six allotted for that day, Tony Brown said we deserved some sustenance and made some coffee. "What a bunch," he whinged. "They get worse and worse."

Again I wanted to hit him. He had no sympathy at all for the dogs. They were just commodities, objects, and I wished I could inject his leg to see how he'd react. I threw away the coffee when he wasn't looking and went to the toilet to check my tape. As I'd guessed, I'd used up a whole side on the injections and had to turn the tape over. It took me longer than I thought trying to see what I was doing in the dimmed light and I dropped it. As it rolled towards the next cubicle, I heard Joanna, the other lab technician, push the door open. Hastily I grabbed the tape before she saw it, but it was a near thing.

"Are you all right?" She peered at me as I emerged to wash my hands.

"Yes, I'm fine."

"But you're not too happy about the injections?" Her eyes were wide with forced concern and I wondered, with alarm, how much I'd unconsciously given away. Or had she been sent by Tony Brown to probe?

"It's part of the job, isn't it?" I wanted to push her back, push her away.

She looked disappointed a moment, then said cheerfully, "You'll soon get used to it. I felt like you did when I started. Look at me now. I've been here two years and it's just routine. I don't let it get to me."

"Do you have a dog yourself?" I asked.

"Oh yes." She told me, her eyes shining with enthusiasm and obvious affection, about two spaniels she owned, about their walks, the time she spent with them and the way they slept on her bed.

My question, to my relief, diverted her but her enthusiasm and answer disturbed and puzzled me. How could she so separate the dogs she lavished affection on at home from the dogs she helped to torture here? Were they not all of the same species, capable of the same response, of communication and pain?

I felt despair as she talked, for if she could so clinically differentiate, how many others in the system would do the same and keep it going?

The next few hours working with Tony Brown were even worse. The blood of the six injected puppies had to be drawn every hour. After their first experience, they were in no mood for testing of any kind. It was heartbreaking to see them cringe, whimper and change from lively puppies to cowering adults within a few hours. I tried to stroke and talk to them as I carried them backwards and forwards to their pens but there was very little time to spend with them with all the other jobs I had to do. In between cleaning pens, feeding and exercising, I had to help Tony Brown administer capsules for the toxicity tests and apply cream for the skin tests.

Tess, the beagle I was especially concerned about, was now in her twenty-fifth day of taking capsules for the toxicity tests and I could hardly bear it seeing her shaking so much and vomiting as Tony Brown forced a capsule down her throat.

"Couldn't she have it later?" I asked but he forced down another, saying he couldn't keep coming back just for one dog. It would invalidate the test. I asked him then how strong the dose was compared to what a person was ever likely to take.

"It's probably ten times stronger," he admitted to my surprise, "but then we have to be sure."

Ten times stronger! I couldn't believe it. Tess was going through all this suffering, vomiting, shaking, for a situation that would never, in fact, arise!

I was close to giving the game away then, I felt so angry. I wanted to ram those capsules down Tony Brown's own throat and see him shake and vomit too. Then I noticed him looking at me curiously, with his eyes screwed up in scrutiny. Just in time I reined myself in and followed him in silence to his next victims.

The 'skin dogs', as they were called, were not in such extremis but were suffering all the same. We had to give them a daily application of anti-psoriatic cream for thirty days. This also had to be fitted in between the blood tests and there was little time to stop and reassure the dogs. The cream was applied to a shaved area on their backs that was then bound with plaster and they also had to wear head collars to stop them from scratching and pulling. They were now in their twentieth day of the cream treatment and had extensive sores on their backs and blisters which were clearly distressing them. I asked Tony

Brown if they were given painkillers but he dismissed the idea, saying it wasn't necessary, that the sores were only a minor discomfort. I wondered then at the number of psoriatic creams on the market and why we had to have more.

How I got through the day without erupting and revealing myself, I don't know. It was a real strain constantly hiding my feelings, but knew I had to if Mark was to achieve his objective. I couldn't afford to give anything away. Yet every hour seemed worse, more traumatic for the dogs. They were in desperate need of protection, yet had none.

Back at home, I couldn't stop thinking of them. Every few hours I woke during the night, wondering what I could do to get them out. It was a dream of course. Most of them were too ill, or too cowered, to get far and survive, but it was a dream that kept me going, kept me filming and thinking of Mark.

There was still no follow-up message from him, but what I'd seen in the past day had brought me closer, nearer to his view. I understood now his anger, felt it as my own. If only, I thought, he would come and I could talk to him. Was he really lying low or was there someone else? He had to come sometime to collect the tapes and camera, but when? I wondered how long I could go on working for Tony Brown without exposing myself or being exposed.

I could feel Joanna, particularly, watching me during the next few days. These followed a similar pattern to the first as we tested the next twelve dogs. I filmed everything possible until the tapes ran out.

I tried to focus then on the other two requests Mark had made regarding the guards and computer room.

Arriving early on the fourth morning, I saw the suspicious, muscular guard talking to another of a similar build beside a small outbuilding near the main electronically operated gate. It appeared the building was their base and they weren't operating in the main office block at all. The second guard ironically had a dog, an Alsatian, attached to his left hand on a leash. It looked strangely passive and subdued for a guard dog as if it sensed what it was guarding and reacted. Dogs are remarkably sensitive to their surroundings. It didn't mean though it would remain passive with a break-in of the type Mark envisaged.

Finding out about the computer room proved more of a problem. I had no reason, no excuse for exploring the main office block and, with Joanna watching, wasn't inclined to reveal myself with probing questions.

On Friday then, the last day of the liver diagnosis tests, an opportunity unexpectedly fell my way. A Home office Inspector visited in the morning. I had been looking forward to this as a chance to make known some of my concerns but, to my consternation, the official didn't even set foot inside the pens to see the dogs. He just talked in the office to Tony Brown who showed him records of the tests and told him the main ones were now complete. It was frustrating seeing an opportunity to draw attention to the suffering of the dogs pass by but it had one fortunate result.

Brown was in a good mood after the visit, from which he'd managed to escape unscathed. He was anxious to get away for a long weekend in Paris.

To my surprise, at four o'clock he said he had to go and, while Joanna was in the lab, asked me to take an envelope containing some records upstairs to an office on the first floor to save him time. I decided not to mention his request to Joanna in case she followed. I slipped away later, when Tony had gone, while she was on the phone.

I had my excuse now for exploring, but was uneasy as I opened each door on the first floor, naively pretending I'd got the wrong room. Eventually, I found the main computer room next to the office I was legitimately seeking. I was about to go downstairs, pleased with my discovery, when below me on the stairs I saw two men coming up towards me. One, the younger, had thick wiry black hair; the other, by contrast, was balding and suddenly from the balding head I recognised Robert. I knew from Carol he worked in some kind of medical research, but not here at DLS.

The implications hit me at once like shrapnel. My whole cover would be blown if he noticed me. Turning, I retreated in haste back along the corridor past the computer room to some toilets I'd noticed at the end. I locked myself in a cubicle for at least twenty minutes, fearful any minute someone would come knocking, wanting to know who I was and what I was doing there.

The whole situation had taken on a new dimension of danger. Once Robert knew I was working in DLS, Carol would tell him I was sympathetic to the Animal Rights Movement and my kennel maid credentials totally fake. I was sure he hadn't seen me at the top of the stairs, but he may well have noticed a retreating figure and how long could he continue not being aware of my presence in the same building? I still had another two weeks to go and any minute we could meet and the whole project blow up in front of me. Once they knew I was undercover, the security codes would be changed and Mark would never get inside.

My heart was thumping still with fear as I left the toilet and made my way downstairs to the office of Section 18.

"Where ever have you been?" Joanna demanded.

"Tony asked me to take some records upstairs."

"It doesn't take half an hour." Her eyes wrinkled again with suspicion.

"I had to go to the toilet. I've had a stomach upset," I said.

"We've got a toilet here." She still wasn't satisfied. If she could have ripped off my clothes to search me, she would have done it. "Oh by the way, Tony asked if you would clean out the pens again before leaving, to last the weekend."

"Sure." She'd made it up, I was sure, but I was only too glad to get away to the dogs. They were even more distressed and I wondered, as I cleaned out Tess's pen again, how long she could last. She could hardly stagger to the pellets of food so I took them with some water to her to the back of the pen. I sat with her as long as possible, stroking her as she rested her head on my knee. I felt a terrible hypocrite, wanting to help her yet being part of the system of torture, and resolved, if she survived until Mark's break-in, I would take her home.

Cycling home that evening, I reflected with apprehension again on the fact of seeing Robert. By arriving early and leaving late I could possibly elude him for the next two weeks but it was still a hit-and-miss business. Why had he got involved in such a filthy trade? What exactly was his role and how much did Carol know? Did she in fact know at all or was she just turning a blind eye?

As I cycled on my last stretch past their house, I saw Robert getting out of his car with his briefcase. He gave a brief nod of acknowledgment in my direction, neither more nor less than usual. He stopped to talk to his neighbour, the secretary whom he'd spoken to at the party. I sensed she'd been waiting and saw her hand him an envelope. Then Carol was at the front door calling to him and he went inside.

SIX

Back at home I found a note from Alan Masson asking me to dinner the following week with Carol and Robert. The thought of facing Robert at such close quarters after all I'd seen at DLS did not appeal and I wondered how to get out of it.

Not wanting a cooked meal, I made tea and toast and sat on the sofa in the front room to read the rest of my post. It was all bills and junk mail apart from two more rejection letters for the teaching posts I'd applied for—nothing to inspire hope, and I began to fear I'd be working permanently at DLS just to make ends meet. The thought appalled me.

In a mood of depression, unintentionally I drifted off to sleep.

It was getting dark when I awoke and I had the eerie sense something in the room had changed. Momentarily too dazed with sleep to focus, I then saw the silhouette of a man framed against the window. I knew it wasn't Steve. He was too still, but, I sensed, watching.

In a cold sweat, it came to me. The man who'd taken my notebook at the demo had tracked me down. My one thought was to get out of the room and house as fast as I could to Steve.

Grasping the cushion I'd been leaning against, I hurled it as hard as I could at the figure and dashed for the door. I heard something fall as I wrenched the door open, then ran into the hall.

I had just reached the front door when a voice called, "Hey, hold on! There's no need for histrionics."

I stopped with my hand on the latch, knowing instantly who it was but was too fired with fear to be pleased. Angrily, I turned back to the sitting room and switched on the light.

Mark Stanton stood in the middle of the room, holding the cushion I'd flung. He was shaking his head with a quizzical, slightly patronising smile.

"What do you mean, no need?" I demanded. "You gave me a real fright, standing there. Do you realise that?"

He looked slightly surprised by my reaction, then still smiling, said calmly, "I obviously miscalculated. I didn't realise you'd overreact."

"Overreact! Christ, you could have been…"

"Could have been who?" He stopped smiling and frowned.

"The man at the demo. He took my notebook. I thought he'd found me, broken in." I could feel my heart still racing with fear. "How did you get in, anyway?"

"The back window. It was open."

"You came the back way?" He'd scaled the high wall running the length of the terrace houses; difficult to get a grip on at the best of times. "Is this your usual mode of entry, creeping in the back when people are asleep?"

"Not usually, no."

"But you thought you could with me?"

"I didn't want to draw attention to myself."

Suddenly Mark turned off the light and went to the window. I followed and saw him look along the road to a Land Rover parked under a street light near Carol's. I couldn't see the number but there were two figures sitting inside it, facing our direction, as if waiting.

"You mean…" I looked at Mark, back to the figures, then at Mark again.

"They've got your address, yes, but they're after me, not you. I saw them parked, which is why I didn't come the front way."

"They didn't see you then?"

"I don't think so, but they'll no doubt do some prowling."

So my fears were real after all. The two men were a threat and all too near. "Why are they so keen to get you?" I pressed. "Who are they?"

"I'll tell you later. I want to hear first what you've been doing at DLS." Mark glanced again at the road, then closed the curtain.

I switched on the standard lamp, then, taking his cue, went to all the other rooms in the house and drew the curtains. When I returned, Mark was sitting cross-legged on the Bokhara carpet beneath the lamp. As I joined him, he looked at me silently, then laid his hand on my arm.

"I'm sorry I frightened you," he said. "I should have thought. And I'm sorry I've taken so long to get back to you about DLS. I dare say you're annoyed about that as well."

It was true I'd been disconcerted by his absence. I'd wanted to discuss things and get help, but I didn't want to admit it now.

"You obviously had reasons, other pressures," I said.

I noticed then in the lamplight Mark had stains of bruising around his left eye, as if someone had punched him. Both eyes had the same brightness but he looked more vulnerable now, tired.

I felt I wanted to caress the side of his face, stroke the bruise away, an unease at the same time that there was too much I didn't know, that he was still in some way a threat.

"How did you hurt your eye?" I asked.

"Paris, one of the guards at the vivisection place there."

"He gave you quite a thump."

"Nothing compared to what some people took."

"What do you mean?"

"Marie's husband, Pierre, got a fractured skull."

"Marie? She's the one who phoned, wasn't she?"

"So you got the message then?"

"Yes, yes, I did." I hesitated, confused, ashamed now of my suspicions. I'd judged too soon about Marie and his absence. "I'm sorry about what happened."

He shrugged. "It's all part of the job. You have to expect it now."

"The violence you mean, or prison?"

"Both."

We were silent for a while. Then I asked him what it had been like in prison but he seemed reluctant to talk about it, more interested in knowing how I'd got on at DLS.

I told him about the practicalities, that I'd finished the tapes and had the code for entry. I spoke about the computer room and the guards, all of which he seemed pleased with. Then I made coffee and handed him the tapes to get them developed and he asked me about the experiments. I described the puppies and their reactions, Tony Brown and my dislike of him and Tess, how I felt about her. It was a relief to be able to talk at last and I could see Mark identifying with my emotions, particularly about Tess. She was a symbol of what he was fighting for.

"If she's still alive for the break-in, we'll get her out," he asserted. "It's precisely for her and every dog like her we have to destroy the place."

"How do you mean destroy?" It was too vast a word, I thought, too ambitious. How could one destroy a place like DLS with all its defences and varied, scattered buildings?

"By making it dysfunctional."

"How?"

"By wiping out the records for a start."

"Disabling the main computer you mean?"

"It's one of the objectives, yes."

"Don't you think they'll have contingency plans?" They weren't fools, I thought, when it came to their business interests.

"They may well have. It'll set them back all the same while we try to reduce their financing."

"How will you do that?"

"By getting at the shareholders."

"But their names are secret, surely?"

"Usually yes, but we've a contact now in the city who's given us their names."

"A sympathiser, you mean?"

"There are more than one thinks."

"It must be quite a risk though—for him I mean."

"If you care, you have to take risks."

"Will the shareholders respond though?"

"Some already have and sold their shares which the company has been forced to pick up."

"But not all?"

"There's obviously a load of bastards out there who don't care how they make their money as long as they make it."

"Wouldn't it be better then to press for legislation, put more pressure on MPs?"

"We've been writing to MPs for years. It's an ongoing operation but it hasn't got anywhere, at least not yet. Just as we seem to get somewhere with a more sympathetic government, they get diverted by other pressures. It's no use expecting much of MPs. Animals simply don't count for most of them because they don't have the vote. It would be better, I agree, to have legislation, a more rational debate, more rational methods but it doesn't work that way. One has to make a physical, visual impact, get the media on board, make a noise and waste police, money and time. That's how we closed down Treetops, the Primate Farm; that's in the end how we'll close down DLS."

As Mark talked on, quietly confident of his words, I gradually came to absorb his view, to feel, despite my misgivings, he was right, that he'd reached his view on rational grounds from his knowledge and experience of the cause.

We made our plans and I felt I'd crossed a line, that I'd become part of the movement, needed, operating.

The break-in had already been fixed for the following Saturday, eight days ahead and Mark had organised the help of fifteen members; the core membership whose silence he could trust. The first aim was to disable the computer so as to scramble or wreck the company's records. The second was to rescue as many of the primates and dogs as possible.

"We need to know," Mark said, "where the primate cages are. Could you find out this week and also where the back exit is? If reinforcements arrive to help the guards, we could get cut off from the front. We also need to make a hole in the razor wire that's concealed ahead of going in. Can you think of a place where there are bushes not scanned by CCTV?"

"Not offhand. I've had no chance at all to explore the grounds."

"How about the lunch hour?"

"I can try if I'm given time." I told him about Joanna and her watching me, then what concerned me more, the prospect of Robert seeing me. "I've got to keep a low profile if I'm to get through the next two weeks."

"Yes," Mark admitted, "I can see that's a problem. In that case, why don't we go and look tomorrow evening when it's dark? We'd get an idea of how the compound works on Saturday with guards."

"You and me, you mean?"

"Why not? My father lives a couple of miles away. We could set off from there and walk."

"Would your father mind my turning up?"

"Mind? Why should he? I live there too. At least it's my base."

"I see." I wondered what his father made of Mark's lifestyle and his devotion to the cause. Not many parents would sympathise, I thought. "Fine, I'll cycle out. What time?"

"Let's say eight. We'll get there then as it gets dark."

He wrote an address at Youlton, a village I passed close to on my way to DLS. "It's down the lane to the right here." He drew a rough map.

I folded it carefully and put it in the top drawer of my desk by the window then drew back the curtain a couple of inches and looked along the street. The Land Rover was still there with the two figures inside. Quickly I drew the curtain closed again.

"They're still there, I take it?" Mark asked.

I nodded. "Why are they so determined? You still haven't told me. Who are they?"

"They're part of the hunting mob, basically. They're angry because of a video I took of them killing a stag in a hunt and over a court case. Craig, the larger one, was put inside for six months for assaulting me and another saboteur."

"So they're out to get you?"

"They're out to get both me and the movement, but they won't succeed."

"Getting you? What does that mean? What specifically are they trying to achieve?"

"To provoke me into a fight, getting witnesses for assault, getting me into the clink if they can, for revenge."

"Do they know where you live?"

"No, they don't, at least not yet. I always divert when I leave Horton just in case," Mark looked at his watch. "I'd better go before they start prowling around the back."

"There's no need if you don't want to."

Suddenly, I wanted him to stay the night and make love to me. I wanted to feel him close, part of me, his body naked with me on the bed upstairs.

I saw him hesitate as if he knew what I was thinking, feeling. He looked at me for what seemed an eternity then said, "I'd like to stay, but it's best I give them the slip while they're still in front, unaware. I don't want to risk their seeing you with me. I don't want you involved. Don't, whatever you do, open the door to them."

"How will you get back?"

"I've got my father's van two roads away."

I followed him to the back door, "How long were you here," I asked, "before I woke?"

"An hour or so."

"Why didn't you wake me?"

"Because you looked so peaceful. I didn't want to disturb you, break the spell. The sleeping princess with her hair spread out."

"You're mocking me."

"No, you have lovely hair."

He paused a moment, stroking back my hair down to my shoulder, then leaned forward and kissed me, his tongue deep in my mouth. He ran his hand down my arm, then drew back.

"I'll see you tomorrow," he said and was gone, climbing over the wall at the end of the garden and out of sight.

I went to the sitting room, switched off the light and looked out onto the street again. The two figures, to my relief, were still in the Land Rover. Mark had successfully evaded them. As I thought about it, I knew his decision to go had been right. I couldn't stop wanting him, all the same, wanting him to kiss me again. I was still wide awake some two hours later when I heard the Land Rover drive away. They'd gone, but for how long?

As I lay awake thinking of Mark that night, I began to

realise the enormous risks he'd taken on in his life, risks that made him, in a perverse way, all the more attractive. He lived on the edge and I began to feel a sense of being there with him.

SEVEN

I cycled to Youlton early the next evening, afraid of being late. Mark's father's house was the last of four flint stone cottages down a narrow lane off the main road. It was a traditional cottage with small leaded windows, a slate roof and climbing roses over white-washed walls. What struck me instantly was the beautifully tended garden, with an abundance of flowers of every colour, shape and scent. Hollyhocks, antirrhinums, sweet peas, sweet williams, wall flowers, begonias, all the flowers my father had grown and as I pushed open the wrought-iron gate and their scents wafted on the breeze, I knew I would feel at home here.

There was no answer as I rapped the brass knocker on the front door. I propped my bike against a water butt and went around the side of the cottage to the rear garden. Again, I felt close to my father in the handiwork displayed as I surveyed the rows of onions, leeks, carrots and runner beans, climbing almost visibly, it seemed, up bamboo sticks.

I could see no sign of Mark, but in a greenhouse to the west of the garden, bathed in the last slanting rays of the sun, I saw a grey-haired man bending over a tray of tomato plants. I knew at once, as he straightened and extended his hand to greet me, he was Mark's father. He had the same slight frame and high cheekbones; the same blue eyes, only they were more subdued than Mark's, sadder, I thought, less determined and sure.

"You must be Kate."

I nodded. I couldn't think for a moment what to say. I felt overwhelmed by the pervasive smell of tomatoes, the furry warmth enclosing us, the strangeness of seeing an older version of Mark.

"Mark's on the phone. He said he'd find us when he's finished." He smiled, a kindly, gentle smile that made me immediately warm to him.

"I like your garden," I said. "You must give a lot of time to it."

"A fair amount." He smiled again and handed me a tomato. It was small and firm with a fresh subtle taste, far beyond anything found in a large store.

"Does Mark enjoy gardening?" I asked.

"He never has time." Mr Stanton shook his head in a way I wasn't sure how to interpret. He talked calmly, quietly but with underlying concern, "He's always on some campaign, or planning one, or trying to earn a living between."

"How do you feel about it, his campaigning, I mean?"

"How do I feel?" Mr Stanton paused a moment, looking surprised, as if no one had ever asked such a question. "I want Mark to do what he feels is right for him. He has, I'm sure, a good cause. There's too much suffering for animals in the world, but there's also too much violence over the issue. Sometimes," he shook his head again, "I wonder if he'll come back from these demos he organises.

And there's his career." Mr Stanton looked sadly down at his tomatoes. "He's nearly thirty and should have established himself by now. He's got a degree in languages, a qualification in translation and interpreting but no time, with all his campaigning, to make use of them."

"He works though, doesn't he?"

"He gets telephone call jobs and the like to keep him going but they're fill-in jobs, not a proper career. What position will he be in when he's forty or fifty? He has a base here, but what'll happen when I'm gone?"

"You feel he's sacrificing too much?"

"It's all right for someone much younger or older but for his age, yes, it's too high a price to pay. I think someone else should lead now, take the risks he has and give him time to establish himself."

"Is he your only son?"

"Yes. Since my wife died, he's all I've got."

I stepped out of the greenhouse, again unable to think what to say. I could understand his fears for Mark's safety. I was still unnerved thinking of the men who'd thrown the stones at the demo. But I couldn't see Mark following the more secure, conventionally structured career his father obviously wanted for him, or drawing an old age pension. I could only see him, as he was now, alive with purpose, wanting action. Wasn't that what mattered ultimately, to be alive, fully engaged and working for something one believed in?

As I thought of Mark, I saw him coming towards us from the house, switching off his mobile phone and I knew from the intent look in his eyes he was too engrossed in his belief, and action, ever to surrender them to safety.

"Right, we'd better be off then." He said goodbye, putting his arms around his father's shoulders with affection, telling him not to wait up but, from all his father had said, I suspected he wouldn't really sleep until Mark returned. It struck me his father, as a parent, had in many ways a raw deal, knowledge without being able to affect the outcome; he'd be far happier not knowing what Mark was doing.

"He worries about you, doesn't he?" I said as we set off along the lane, then across a patchwork of fields towards DLS.

"It's particularly since my mother died."

"You never had any brothers or sisters?"

"No, my mother couldn't have any more children."

"I can understand in a way how he feels with those men pursuing you."

"He doesn't know about them. They haven't located me here yet so I'd rather you didn't say anything."

"You're not in the phone book then?"

"No."

"Let's hope they don't find out." The thought of the man with a belly and tufts of hair lying in wait outside the cottage alarmed me. "It must be a strain for you."

"I try not to think about it," Mark said. "If I kept worrying, I'd never do anything and there's just too much now to do."

"How did you get involved?" I asked.

"It started with our cat being savaged by the local hunt some thirteen years ago. The hunt moved on and just left her lying there, so I followed them. I saw then what they did to the fox itself. It was being ripped apart while still alive. The whole idea of a quick bite to the neck is a total myth. I joined the saboteurs then. Through them I got to know about other animal rights issues. I began to discover all the abuses in factory farming, animal transportation and vivisection, which are even more cruel than hunting. And you? What made you come to our meeting?"

"It wasn't from any experience like you had. I came, to be honest, because Steve asked me to."

"Is Steve your boyfriend?"

"No, we're just friends. He's been very good to me over the past year and I owed it to him." I don't know why, but having started, I felt a compulsion to tell Mark about Simon, my miscarriage and general mess I'd made of teaching and how Steve had given me so much support.

"Do you have any regrets?"

"For the baby, yes, but not Simon." Looking at Mark, as he strode ahead on the narrow path through a cornfield, I found it difficult to recall Simon's voice, even his features. It was as if a whole era had been wiped out by Mark's presence. Tentatively, I asked him if he had a girl friend.

He was silent for a while, then spoke in a quiet, measured tone as if he'd been carefully thinking about the subject for some time.

"I don't really find time for girl friends, Kate, at least not those who want commitment. I can't really commit myself the way I live and it's what most women want, isn't it? They want you there, not absent, away on a cause."

"Can't they be combined sometimes?" I asked. His words seemed to be warning me off. They weren't what I wanted to hear.

"Not often I think." He turned and looked at me. "It's

not just the commitment. It's the whole idea of possessiveness I don't like in most relationships. People thinking they own each other and can determine each other's lives. Sometimes you see them, couples doing everything together but you get the feeling it's because they think they ought to; that they have to act and look like a couple. It's too limiting. People should be free to express themselves, devote themselves, give themselves to what they believe in, without obligation all the time."

"Some people are more dependent than others though, aren't they?"

"Isn't that all the more reason to encourage independence? No one should live off another or feel they have a right to."

"It's not the same though with children. One's bound to be more dependent if there are children."

"I agree with children, yes. There's a genuine obligation then, but is it right to have children now? Is it the right moral choice?"

"It's in our genes surely, a necessity, a driving force, not one you consciously choose."

"In a world already overpopulated? I don't think so. We can hardly, as it is, support and feed the people already here."

"That's a matter of fairer distribution surely."

"Partly, but the resources are also diminishing, especially water."

"So you don't want children then?"

"Children are a self-indulgence, let's face it. One may want them but they drain one's energy and time for other things."

It was getting dark as we talked. Absorbed, I didn't

notice the turnings we took or direction. I just followed Mark and suddenly we were at our destination. Across a field in front of us lay the now familiar outline of DLS against an ashen sky.

Whether it was the sight of DLS or what Mark had been saying about commitment and children, I don't know, but I felt an inexpressible bleakness at that moment, a sense I shouldn't be there, that I'd made a mistake in coming. There was no future with Mark. His words made that clear and hadn't I had an intimation of it from Steve? Yet as we stood looking at DLS, our arms touching, despite his words, I wanted him and as he took my hand, I thought, even if only temporarily, he wanted me.

"I suggest we keep together," Mark said. "We'll go and observe the guards' hut and main entrance first and see how often the guards scout round. Then we'll work our way around to see how many CCTV cameras there are, and lights, and where we'll cut the wire."

Mark drew out two black cotton facemasks from his pocket and slipped one over my hair. "Just in case they get you on CCTV. If anything goes wrong, run back here and wait for me. Then we'll make for the wood. There's a place there we can hide."

I found it hot and stuffy with the facemask on but the eye and mouth holes were large and I could breathe reasonably and see. Quietly we edged our way forward until we could hide behind some hawthorn edging the path that ran alongside the DLS razor wire perimeter near the entrance. Nervous, my muscles taut, I waited to see what would happen.

For thirty minutes, as we crouched waiting, nothing moved. Then exactly on the hour, the door of the hut opened. A security light immediately illuminated the compound within the razor wire fencing and the two guards I'd seen in the week strode out to make a tour of the fencing. The door was ajar and I could see the flickering lights of a television screen, presumably the way the guards killed time through the night. While the lights were on, Mark located through his binoculars the position of at least four CCTVs strategically located just below the roof line of the main office block and two of the outbuildings. After ten minutes the guards returned to the hut and five minutes later the security lights went out and the door of the hut closed. I could just see the muscular guard looking out of the hut window, perhaps checking to see if the lights stayed off.

We waited to see the whole process repeated with the two guards emerging again on the hour. Satisfied, as the lights faded again, Mark led me to the north side of the razor wire. He located the position of two more CCTVs and where the lighting cable would have to be cut and dismantled. It was difficult to find a place where the wire could be cut ahead without observation. All the places close to bushes were near to lights or CCTV.

"We'll just have to take a risk the night before with the lighting," Mark decided and he chose a place where the approach to the razor wire was most obscured by elderberry and hawthorn.

As we were about to retrace our steps, suddenly the Alsatian of the second guard, which had kept silent all evening, started barking in the compound close to where we were on the other side of the wire. The guard immediately shone a torch in our direction. As I threw myself face down to hide in the long grass below, a stone clattered down from my foothold. Whether the guard could see me I didn't know, but he'd certainly heard. He shouted to the other guard, then we heard them discussing what to do and realised I was, as yet, unseen.

"I'm sure I heard someone," the guard with the dog said.

"It could have been a fox or badger. The wire's not broken."

"I think I'll have a scout around all the same."

There was a pause as they shone the torches again. I realised then the bushes had obscured their view. There were no triumphant cries of discovery, but Mark was worried. As they turned to the hut, he pulled me up from the long grass.

"Let's get out of here. He's obviously going to bring that dog round."

We ran for all we were worth across the field not stopping until we reached the wood. Then Mark took something from his pocket and threw it back behind us.

"Just something for the dog if it gets this far."

"It's not poison, is it?"

"No, of course not. It'll make it feel a bit queasy and put it off following."

"You think of everything, don't you?"

"Not enough. It's going to be a problem cutting that wire ahead and surprising the guards before they use their mobiles."

"What will you do with them?"

"Tie them up. There's not much else we can do with them. We'll need to know though if there's a back entrance and where the primate cages are. Can you find out this week?"

"I'll do what I can."

"Thanks."

He paused and we could hear the dog barking again, closer, "Come." He took my hand. "If we get across the stream, he'll lose our scent."

We stumbled through some undergrowth, making our own track. Periodically I could hear the dog barking again, then silence.

"I think he's had his dose," Mark said. We pulled off our facemasks and he switched on his torch. "Be careful here. There're a lot of exposed roots. We're near the stream."

I heard water surging over stone, like the clinking of glass, and felt the ooze and slip of mud beneath my feet. Then, by the light of the torch, we jumped over the stream onto the opposite bank. We walked alongside the stream until the bank rose higher and opened between the trees onto a patch of moss and grass.

"We'll wait here until we're sure. They won't find us here," Mark said.

He sat with his legs over the bank, took a carton of fruit juice from his jacket, extracted the straw and handed it to me. It was too warm to be refreshing. I was glad of it all the same. I drank about half and handed it back to him.

"Have you known this place long?"

"Since I was at school. We used to come here when we played truant."

"So you were a rebel from the start?" Unable to resist, I touched his thick black hair, stroking it back from his forehead.

He turned then abruptly, putting down his drink, and

kissed me. It was an awkward kiss. His legs still dangled over the bank, and our shoulders were contorted but his tongue reached back into my mouth with an urgency I shared. As he drew back, I touched his jeans, felt the stiffness between his legs.

"It's been a long time," he said as I stroked him. "I may not last."

"It doesn't matter."

We stood up without speaking and helped each other undress. I lay back on the moss and grass.

I felt the evening coolness for a moment, then the heat of his body fused with my desire and I opened my legs to him.

He entered slowly, as if afraid, holding the breath of his seed. Then he kissed my breasts and I felt him surge inside, filling me so that our flesh seemed joined. He gasped and I felt him shudder, the spilling of his semen and I was in a primitive sea, drowning with love for him.

When I rose to the surface, Mark was lying on his back to the side of me, looking up at the stars.

"Thank you," he said as I turned to him. More quietly, to my surprise, he added, "I hope I haven't harmed you."

"Harmed?"

"I didn't take any precautions."

I hadn't taken any either. I hadn't even thought about it, which was strange for me. I'd always been careful, and after what Mark had said about children, should have been especially so. I should be worried now, I thought, but I wasn't. All I could think of was having him inside me again, feeling him close, being part of him.

And so we made love again on the bank of moss and grass by the stream until dawn broke and the insects got the better of us. Slowly then, in the weak, cool sunlight we retraced our footsteps across the fields to Mark's father's house where we found him deeply asleep in the armchair where he'd waited.

We hadn't slept at all but I didn't feel tired; more as if I'd woken from a long deep sleep and everything was waiting to be freshly felt again and seen. The flowers at the cottage seemed more intense in their colour as if they'd recognised what had happened and given their blessing.

It was only later at my house, alone again, I remembered the chill of Mark's words about commitment and wondered with apprehension about the outcome.

EIGHT

The sun was already high in the sky, throwing dusty shafts of sunlight through my worn yellow curtains when I woke the next morning. I thought immediately of Mark and wondered what he was doing.

We'd made no specific date or time to meet again. He'd said he would contact me when the film was developed and confirm the final arrangements for the break-in on Saturday. I knew instinctively he wouldn't want to be pinned down and pressured. I'd have to be patient and fit in if I wanted to see him.

I couldn't stop longing for him all the same. I wanted him with me now, close inside me, our bodies united as one as we'd been by the stream.

I got up eventually to keep myself occupied and did my usual weekend chores of cleaning, gardening and sorting food and shopping. All the time I was waiting for him to telephone or knock on the window, or walk through the back door.

About mid-afternoon, whilst I was ironing, the phone rang, jolting me into a state of anticipation. I rushed to pick up the receiver, only to hear, to my disappointment, the voice of Alan Masson whom I'd met at Carol's.

"Hello there." His voice was more persuasive than I remembered. "I wondered if you got my note."

"Your note?" Everything went blank for a moment. I knew he'd written but I couldn't recall what about.

"I asked you to come to dinner on Saturday."

"Oh yes, I'm sorry! I should have phoned straightaway. I'm afraid, no. I've already got plans for Saturday."

"That's a shame." He sounded genuinely sorry. "How about Sunday for lunch then?"

"With Carol and Robert, you mean?"

"That's the idea. We were going to continue our discussion, if you remember."

"Oh, yes."

"You can come then?"

I couldn't immediately think of another plausible excuse and said yes.

"I'll see you about twelve then."

"Right."

"And can I tell you something? I thought you looked stunning with your flowing hair and that skirt you wore to Carol's. Will you wear it again?"

"If you wish."

"Good! See you on Sunday then."

No sooner had I put down the phone than Steve rang, asking if Mark had got in touch. I told him he had and we'd reconnoitred the DLS perimeter but didn't elaborate. Steve told me Mark had asked him to be one of the core group for the break-in on Saturday. I could tell from his voice he was proud to have been asked but was concerned about his mother.

"Perhaps you could get that friend of hers, Dorothy, to sit in for a while," I suggested.

"Yes, I'll try and arrange something."

"I hope you can." Steve was the kind of person Mark needed, strong and reliable, unlikely to lose his head and dedicated without a personal axe to grind.

I was just going to bed when, as I was least expecting it, Mark himself rang.

"Sorry I didn't call before, I've been trying to get things organised for Saturday."

"How's it going?"

"We still need more homes for the dogs we rescue. Otherwise fine. I thought you'd like to know, there's some really good footage we can use on the tapes you filmed."

"Use how?"

"For a half-hour tape we'll offer to ITV. We'll need to discuss the cuts and sequencing and what the narrative should be. I was thinking it could, perhaps, be your voice, your commentary and you could even appear, when you've left DLS, of course."

I wasn't so sure about fixing myself irrevocably on tape for all to see but readily agreed to go to Youlton. Mark explained he was working late on Monday and Tuesday and suggested calling at his father's house on Wednesday on my way home from DLS.

"They're all coming over at nine o'clock for a final check on the arrangements for Saturday," he said, "but it'll give us time to run through at least some of the tapes."

"Yes."

Abruptly Mark rang off saying he'd three more calls to make. Nothing was said about what had passed between us and I was left feeling more uncertain, than reassured, by his conversation. Was it all in the past already for Mark?

I slept badly that night but, from habit now, was at DLS early next morning. There was no sign, to my relief, of Robert's BMW in the car park, which meant I could probably evade him for another day.

The two security guards stood outside their hut without the Alsatian. Was it permanently off the scene, I wondered? There were implications and I wanted to know, but it was clearly unwise to draw attention to myself. I pressed the keypad and hurried inside to try and get the information Mark wanted on the back exit and primate section before Joanna appeared.

I found the exit without difficulty. It was at the end of the corridor used for the dog unit at Section 18 and consisted of a couple of sliding doors operated by an exit pad. Two men wearing grey overalls were loading some empty cages into a lorry and from the way one of them pressed the keypad, the code appeared identical to the one I already knew. Difficult as it was to get into DLS, once in, one could at least get out.

The primate section was not so easy to find. It was at the end of a maze of small grey passages and I had a distinct sense, from all the closed doors, I was trespassing on forbidden territory. I didn't know what I expected to find. I had no preconceptions, only a sense of dread from what Mark had described and my experiences already at DLS.

There was no one around so I pushed open the final white door of the passage and let it close behind me. It took a few minutes to get used to the gloom. I could hear rustling, scraping and a low-pitched kind of moan.

Then as my eyes adjusted, I saw, ahead of me, stretching the length of a long rectangular hall, row upon row of small box cages, stacked one upon another. Each housed a huddled macaque monkey or baboon. The smell of urine and faeces and sickness, mixed with the stale air, was overpowering.

Two macaques were picking at banana skins; one clutched the bars of its cage, looking out with its large human eyes, as if in anticipation. Most were huddled at the backs of their cages, eerily silent for such social creatures.

I was overwhelmed with the misery and mental anguish conveyed by their isolated, huddled forms. How could anyone confine another social creature like this for torture and one so close to us in form and genes?

I felt I wanted to run forward and release them all straightaway; at the same time a helplessness, knowing with my head it wouldn't work, that I had to hold my fire.

Then from behind the door slightly ajar to the left of me, I heard someone shouting, "Keep still, you bloody bastard."

I thought for a moment it was someone shouting at me as a trespasser but as I looked around, there was no one in sight, no one behind me. Then the swearing was repeated. Curious, I turned and pushed the opened door wider.

It opened onto a small lab. In the centre was a steel table on which lay a macaque monkey strapped down on its back with a technician wearing a white overall bent over it. He was trying to clamp a tube onto the monkey's penis but the macaque, despite the straps, was still managing to struggle and move both its penis and head. I could see from the technician's clumsy movements he was neither experienced, nor in tune with the animal's feelings and predicament. As the tube fell down, presumably for the second time on the floor, he lunged at the monkey and punched its face.

"Stop bloody moving or I'll finish you off for good, you bastard!" he yelled.

A movement of mine alerted him and he swung around and saw me. His eyes were a confusion of aggression and guilt.

"What the hell are you doing here?" he demanded. His fists were clenched and I thought briefly he was going to give me the same treatment he'd inflicted on the monkey.

I felt, as I'd done with Tony Brown, I wanted to hit out and expose him. But something, Mark perhaps, held me back.

"I'm sorry." I forced a smile. "I obviously came to the wrong place."

"Do you work here?"

"Of course."

"You didn't see anything. Okay?

"Nor did you see my wandering."

He frowned, and then nodded. I turned and made my way back through the maze to the main corridor. When I reached Section 18, I went straight to the toilet and was violently sick.

Fortunately Tony Brown had not yet arrived and Joanna was preoccupied with a computer problem. I sat for a while and then went down to see how Tess was doing. She was still shaky and could hardly walk but she wagged her tail on seeing me which lifted my spirits. I was determined to try, if I could, to make her last and get her out. As I was giving her some food, Joanna came to say

Tony was delayed by a strike in Paris and would be late; we'd have to complete the day's tasks ourselves.

She told me to clean out the pens, feed the dogs and do a health check on the puppies that had had the liver test the previous week. I could help her then with continuing the toxicity and skin tests.

The work was familiar to me now but I still couldn't shut off my emotional sympathy as Joanna claimed, and appeared very well, to do. The toxicity and skin tests affected me worse than before.

Joanna was more competent than Brown in the way she handled the dogs but also more brusque and detached. Even more than with Tony, it was a conveyor belt with the dogs essentially commodities, mere objects of experiment.

In an effort to keep Tess alive, I asked Joanna if she would like me to administer some of the toxicity tablets whilst she dealt with the engineer who'd come to repair the computer. She gave a doubtful grimace and then agreed, but I could see her watching me as she went up the steps to the office. Reluctantly, I gave the tablets to the allotted dogs but Tess's I slipped into the pocket of my overall, while Joanna was out of sight. It was such a relief not to have her vomiting, as she usually did, but I pretended she had.

In the lunch hour Joanna told me she'd heard from the security guards two people had tried to get into DLS at the weekend.

"One was a woman." She gave me a sideways glance, close to accusation.

"Did they catch them?" I asked innocently.

"No, but they got them on CCTV."

"Really?" Nervously I wondered which CCTV it had been. It didn't bode too well for Saturday if we'd provoked greater alertness in the guards.

"She had long brown hair apparently, like you."

I felt I was being cornered and decided to go on the attack. "You're not surely suggesting it was me, are you?"

"Wasn't it?"

"Why should I want to break into DLS when I'm already here?"

"I don't know. You tell me."

I worked myself into a state of indignation, which seemed quite convincing, even to myself, "I've nothing to tell you. I work here because I need the money. I'm not keen on it but no doubt I'll get used to it, as you say. That's all there is to tell." I turned my back on her and was pretty certain she was convinced, but she wouldn't be again if a second incident occurred.

As I thought through the strategy for the impending break-in on Saturday, I became more concerned and doubtful about its feasibility and likely success. Did Mark really know what he was up against? In a way I think he did but I wasn't sure. Deep down I was worried it would all go wrong and he'd be arrested or hurt. I kept thinking of his father waiting all night for him, asleep in his chair.

It seemed as if months had passed by the time Wednesday dawned and I was cycling away from DLS to see Mark at Youlton. Tony Brown had returned from Paris in a bad mood, his liaison not having lived up to expectations. He had turned his disillusion on Joanna and myself and, of course, the dogs. I was compelled to stay late to do extra jobs on Wednesday. It was already past six when I finally escaped and decided to take a short cut through back lanes to Youlton to save time and avoid the traffic.

I was nearly there when I noticed a car parked ahead on the grass verge by a farm gate. With surprise, I suddenly realised it was Robert's BMW.

My first instinct was to turn around and cycle to the main road for fear of his seeing me in the area but I'd already drawn up alongside. It was then that I saw Robert was not alone but in the back seat with a blond. The woman had her arms around his neck and was drawing him down on top of her. They were too intent on each other to notice me, but there was always the chance they might. I cycled quickly on, turning, I hoped, before they were aware, into the lane leading to Mark's father's cottage.

NINE

Mark was waiting for me with his father in the garden. "I thought you'd forgotten." His intense blue eyes were fixed on me, probing.

"I wouldn't forget." I stared back at him.

"No one followed?"

"No, why?"

"You seemed concerned as you rode along the lane. You looked back over your shoulder."

I told Mark then about Robert and what I'd seen.

"Do you know who the woman was?"

"It was probably the secretary who lives next door to him in my road."

"And his wife doesn't know?"

"I doubt it."

"Good. You've got your bargain card now if he sees you at DLS and asks questions."

"I suppose so."

It hadn't occurred to me to use this new information to manipulate the situation, nor did it appeal. But I could feel myself on a learning curve now where one had to use whatever means one could to outwit the opposition.

"By the way," I mentioned then, "we were caught on CCTV last Saturday."

"Recognised, you mean?"

"Not exactly, but Joanna had a dig about the woman's long hair."

"As long as they haven't increased security for Saturday." Mark's eyes darkened momentarily in concern. "Did you find the exit and primate section?"

"Yes. The exit's easy enough but the primate section's a bit of a maze." I explained to Mark the circuitous route. I couldn't help telling him about the rows of cages of dejected macaques I'd seen and the technician's assault.

Mark put his arm round me then. "I know how you feel," he said. "I feel the same. It's the reason I'm in this business and why we've got to get them out."

But his words only seemed to accentuate in my mind the problems we were up against.

"I'm not sure we're going to be able to, Mark. Most of them, the dogs especially, are already too ill and weak to be moved."

"We'll get out those we can." His words were calm, matter-of-fact but his eyes were strained by thinking of the scope and practicalities of the operation. He wasn't happy about it, I could tell, for he was a perfectionist in his way, in his war against cruelty. He wanted to be sure, to succeed in outright terms, to have DLS closed for good, not lingering; not for his own sake or image, but for the sake genuinely of the animals and to give inspiration for further action. It was this, his dedication, his real love and concern for the animals themselves, that drew me close to admire, and, yes, love him. At the same time, I could feel the mechanics of the organisation, like the wedge of a third person, taking his time and pushing us apart.

"I'd like you to stay if you could," he said, "to hear the general plan for Saturday when the others come at nine."

"Sure."

"The core group will go in on Saturday when the security lights go off after midnight and deal with the guards and dismantle the lights and CCTV. I want you to take them to the main computer room and sections for the primates and dogs. You'll hear all about it later but I'm relying on you absolutely for the code to get us in. Is there any chance it's been changed?"

"Not to my knowledge, but I'll double-check tomorrow. I'll make sure I have to use the keypad myself."

"Good, let's have a look at the tapes while we've time."

He led me into a small room off the dining room used as an office. It had a computer, printer, TV and video recorder and shelving stacked with bundles of paper. We sat on a bench facing the TV and Mark explained his friend had transferred the tape to VHS to enable us to see it more clearly to edit.

Much needed cutting. There were many wasted sections when I'd been with Tony Brown and turned or bent awkwardly, showing parts of an overall or dog's leg.

To my surprise there was also some effective footage showing Brown's blunders in administering the liver toxicity tests and the dogs' suffering, particularly that of Tess. I wasn't altogether displeased by my efforts. My main regret was I'd got nothing of the horror of the macaques or the "death row" injections.

Mark asked me again if I'd consider telling the story from my view when I'd finished at DLS. I still wasn't sure and told him I'd think about it but I'd be willing to write a script. We looked through the tapes again and decided on the obvious parts to cut. Mark seemed to relax more then, perhaps because we were looking back on a past achievement, rather than an uncertain future. He thought I should continue working at DLS for a few days after the break-in so as not to arouse immediate suspicion.

"They'll probably sack you anyway if we're successful, if there's nothing to do."

"What then if we're successful?"

"We'll tackle the other bio-tech companies using animals."

"And then?"

"The destruction of this country's slaughter houses."

"You don't believe in thinking small, do you?" It wasn't just a big undertaking, but overwhelming. He wanted to take on another whole industry, one both determined and well organised.

"They're worse in their way than the vivisectionists, Kate. More invidious and people don't want to know."

"Have you worked in a slaughterhouse in this country?"

"Not yet but Philippa has."

"Who's Philippa?"

"She's the one organising the transport for the dogs to their new homes on Saturday. She's coming this evening."

"I see."

"She's not a girl friend if that's what you're thinking."

"I wasn't," I lied.

He looked down as he rewound the video, his hair tousled as it had been beside the stream and I couldn't resist him again. "I've just missed you," I said, rumpling his hair.

Mark was silent a while then abruptly he turned, looking at me intently. "I've missed you too," he said.

"But I thought…" I was taken by surprise. I couldn't take it in after all he'd said about commitment.

"You thought you were alone, you mean?"

"I don't know. I don't know what I thought, except I want you." I was throwing myself at him but didn't care. All I wanted at that moment was to go to bed with him, be with him, feel him close inside me, snatch what few minutes I could of his time.

"They'll be here in less than an hour," he warned.

"It doesn't matter."

He hesitated, then caught my mood of desperation and suddenly was kissing my neck, my face, my hair and undoing my blouse buttons, my straps and kissing my breasts. Taking my hand then, he led me without speaking upstairs to a small room with a single bed. It was cool and white, as if designed to chill and calm our desire.

We threw off our clothes and as I stood beside the bed, Mark ran his hands all over my body, lingering over my breasts, the small of my back, my inner thighs. Then he was massaging with slow, gentle movements between my legs till I cried out for him to come inside. He lifted me on the bed and I felt him glide effortlessly inside, wait a while, as I hovered tense with expectation.

He started to move with a slow, then faster rhythm, penetrating each time deeper as if to search the source of my lubrication; each time swelling, filling me yet more, until I felt we were joined and could not be parted.

I heard him gasp, felt his warm juice spilling, then an intense all-absorbing joy, radiating through my heart and head to the edges of my being. Behind my closed eyelids, a deep glow. Still the glow lingered as I opened my eyes on the cool white walls.

Mark was lying beside me, as if asleep, with one arm flung back on the pillow. There was no intensity, no straining on his face now, only calm. I lay across his chest, wishing I could stay there forever.

Then, down below outside the cottage I heard the sound of a bike being wheeled up the garden path; a clank of metal as it was laid against the wall, then an impatient banging of the doorknocker. Mark opened his eyes.

"Have a look, will you, and see who it is?"

Reluctantly, I slipped off the bed, went to the window and looked down to the front door. A thick set man, dressed all in black, with long black hair, a beard and a rucksack on his back stood looking aggressively at the knocker as he was about to rap a third time. It was Jake, the man who'd swung the beagle's body and challenged Mark at the demo. I made no move to catch his attention but suddenly he looked up and saw me. His eyes widened in surprise, then he gave me a come-on smile, cupped his hands over his mouth and shouted, "Tell Mark it's my turn now." I heard a crude guffaw as I turned back to the bed. I hadn't been conscious until then of being naked; it had been natural with Mark. The outside world was intruding and I resented it.

"It's Jake," I said, "and he doesn't look too pleased."

"Jake never looks pleased," Mark smiled resignedly from the pillow. "We'll have to let him in all the same."

"Is he part of the team?" I asked, hoping he wasn't. I

hadn't liked the look of Jake at the demo and he appealed even less now.

"An essential part," Mark replied to my dismay. "He deals with the electronics and not many can do that."

"He was pushing it a bit far at the demo though, wasn't he?"

"It's a risk you have to take with him because of the contribution he makes." Mark slipped off the bed and into his trousers and shirt.

"As long as he's not a danger." I was thinking of the cause but Mark assumed I meant to me.

He kissed me as I finished dressing. "He's all right. You'll see. Just don't get into an argument with him. That's all."

I held onto Mark then, not wanting him to go but could hear other people arriving by bike and car. His tension returned as he became impatient to get on with the meeting. As we closed the bedroom door behind us, I wondered when we would be alone together again.

Downstairs in the sitting room of the cottage, some fifteen people had gathered. I recognised most of them from the demo, Karl and Gemma in particular. Gemma introduced me to Jenny, a lovely, lively girl with long fair hair. Jenny got me talking to Pete and Martin and Philippa. I had the impression Pete and Martin were second-in-command to Mark. Pete was a straight-talking, down-to-earth person, the practical type who will put his hands to the grinding work. His steady blue eyes were reliable, sure. Martin, by contrast, was more intellectual, intent on analysis and ideas and he certainly looked the boffin with his glasses, angular face and rumpled hair.

It was Philippa whose appearance intrigued me most. She had jade green earrings in her nose, a flowing Indian garb and jet-black hair streaked with green, closely shaved at the sides of her head but leaving a central panel which was tied with jade green ribbon at her neck. Mistakenly, I expected her words to flow to match in some green ether beyond my comprehension but, like Pete, to my surprise, she had a very real grasp of the difficulties involved in transporting the animals out of DLS, which was her sphere of operations.

The group were again all friendly and accepting, except Jake who hovered on the edge of the circle in his black attire like an Elizabethan malcontent. I noticed him looking at Mark a couple of times with a rather jaundiced eye as if he had some personal grudge. As I passed, he made a further crude comment about the window and I decided to avoid him if I could and was glad when Steve arrived.

Mark got on then with the meeting's agenda.

"Right. We're definitely set now for Saturday night. This is our chance at last to do something positive for the animals incarcerated in DLS. Remember, if you have doubts, they have no one else to help them; to get them out. They are totally dependent on our efforts and we have to make these work." Mark paused, then continued, "We meet at eleven at the two lay-bys at the end of the west lane to DLS just before it joins the 302. No vehicles are to go initially any nearer at this time. Philippa, Jeremy, Sue and Steve will be bringing the vans to the DLS compound after twelve-thirty when we've dealt with the guards and lighting. Meanwhile, the rest of us will walk the half-mile to DLS. I advise everyone to wear black or dark grey and use black facemasks until after we've immobilised the CCTV."

"Where's the initial break-in point to be?" Jake asked.

"Just below the bushes on the north side opposite the first outhouse. I'm planning to cut the wire on Friday night so we'll have a clear run for Saturday."

"Surely it'll be noticed by the staff on Saturday?" Jake challenged.

"It's partly obscured by bushes, which is why it's been chosen," Mark said. "There's only a skeleton maintenance staff on Saturday. I doubt they'll do much searching."

"But the security guards will," Jake persisted.

"There's only one on a Saturday morning," Mark replied patiently. "I see your point. It's a matter of balancing risks. Speed is essential on the night for getting in and immobilising the guards before they can use their mobile phones. Cutting through the two layers of razor wire will take time and could be heard. And we want to know if the operation's feasible beforehand, not at the last minute on the night. I think, on balance, cutting ahead is the best option, especially as it won't be near the main entrance."

There were general murmurs of approval and consent for Mark's explanation. Jake still looked doubtful but raised no more objections. I wondered whether his observations had been more about point scoring, and getting at Mark, than genuine concern.

Mark described the timetable. The core group, which included Jake and himself, would go through the cut wire at fifteen minutes past midnight when the security lights went out after the guards' patrol. They would surprise the guards, tie them up in their hut and remove their mobile phones. Then Jake would lead his group to immobilise the security lights and CCTV, and open the main entrance gates for the vans.

"Kate will then let the rest of you in using the entry keypad for the main office. She'll take Martin and Pete to the main computer room first and then the rest of you to the sections housing the dogs and primates. Philippa, Steve, Jeremy and Sue will bring the vans through the main entrance to the back exit to collect the dogs and primates as you rescue them. It's essential you bring them out in cages if you possibly can. We don't want the distraction of fights in the vans, or any of them getting away before they've reached their new homes. If you can't find cages, there'll be a few for emergencies but no more than two or three in each van. It's a question of using common sense, doing what's possible in the time available and being adaptable.

"We can't predict the unexpected. Anything can happen, as we know from previous experience. We need to be alert, prepared and act fast. Someone's bound to pick up on the fact we're at DLS, however careful we are, and we may not have much time. It's essential in the time we do have we make an impact, show we mean business and that we're going to close this evil place down for good."

"You think we should use a bit more muscle this time?" a man called Mitch asked.

"Muscle in what way?" Mark asked.

"Smashing the computer, punching the guards if they resist."

"No," Mark shook his head emphatically. "There's absolutely no need to smash up the computer. Martin will be using a disk that'll wipe the hard drive clean. All their records for the animals and their business will be permanently deleted. It's only a pity we couldn't find a hacker who could do this long-distance. Something to think about next time. It's essential we use no violence either on the guards or police. Our action is against the whole creed of violence shown by the vivisectionists. We're not going to do our cause any good by sinking to their level."

"So you're not going to resist arrest even if it means a lengthy spell in the clink?" Jake spoke up again.

For the first time I noticed Mark hesitate. "It depends what you mean by resist."

"What do you mean?" Jake smiled. It was a smile of entrapment, not friendship. Mark could see that, I was sure, but felt impelled to respond.

"I think it's legitimate to try and get away, to wriggle free for example, but hitting out, punching and kicking, no. It's counterproductive and we could be charged with assault."

"Isn't that what you did in Paris?"

"I didn't, in fact, Jake. It's how it was interpreted."

"That's my point. There's no clear line, is there?"

"It's difficult, I agree, but it's not going to do our cause any good if we're seen attacking the police. Withdraw, yes, try to get away and take evasive action. We don't want to be arrested. That's for sure. But going on the offensive as regards the police, no. We won't win people over if they see punch-up attacks on TV. Our main aim is to close down DLS by making it dysfunctional. Not to attack the police."

"That sounds clear to me, and reasonable," Gemma

said, and the majority concurred, a couple whispering irritably to Jake, telling him to shut up.

Mark ended with a warning not to start any fires for fear of inflicting further suffering on the incarcerated animals and to leave behind animals that couldn't be handled or were too ill. He circulated talking to people individually then, reinforcing times and details and each person's particular role.

He had seen everyone by eleven and people started to leave. Steve had brought his old banger and offered me a lift but I had my bike, which I needed the next morning. It wouldn't fit into the car, so I told him I'd manage. It wasn't far.

I wanted to say goodbye to Mark but he was enclosed by a persistent remnant of the group. There was no telling when he'd be free. I was hungry and tired and decided I'd leave and ring the next day.

I was just cycling off, thinking I'd be alone, when Jake and Pete appeared, going in the same direction. I didn't like the idea of Jake following, but, as Pete was beside me, decided not to make an issue of it. We cycled quite happily for a while, Pete asking me how I'd felt about the meeting and saying what a great chap he thought Mark was. To my dismay, a mile before my house, abruptly he said goodbye and took a turning off the main road to the left. Jake then closed in where Pete had been, cycling alongside me.

"So you're not spending the night with lover boy then?" He turned towards me, clearly expecting an answer. But he had his own agenda. I could tell that from the meeting. He would never be satisfied whatever I said and I decided to ignore him.

"I take it that means no," he continued. "Quite a sensible move, considering. He won't stick with you, you know. He never does. He's been through every woman in the movement. Tells them all the same thing, that he can't be committed, that he's committed to his principles. Why? So he can screw them all in turn. He likes screwing, doesn't he? Gives him a perverse pleasure to have them all hankering after him. He's not biding his time, I can tell you, when he's not seeing you. He's seeing another of his groupies."

I tried to shut out what he was saying, telling myself, as we cycled, it wasn't true, that Jake just had it in for Mark for some reason. But some of it I knew was true. Mark had said for example that he couldn't be committed. It was also true he liked it. He liked the act of screwing, as Jake put it. Was the rest, though, true?—that I was just one of many?

As we cycled, I felt a growing nausea. Partly it was sheer hunger. I hadn't eaten all day, apart from a sandwich at lunch. But it was also the thought of Mark with other women. I knew in my heart, it was likely Mark might have other women. If I found him attractive, why should others not feel the same? Yet the thought was intolerable. I had no claim on him yet I couldn't bear even the idea of him in bed with someone else. I wanted to cycle back and challenge him, ask him if it were true but I was afraid deep down of making a fool of myself and losing his respect. No doubt some of the group would still be there. He wouldn't take kindly to a display of possessiveness. I didn't have the energy left anyway.

I felt completely drained by the time I reached the main road. Jake, to my irritation, was still cycling beside me. As I stopped and opened the wrought iron gate to my garden, he said, "Aren't you going to ask me inside?"

"I certainly am not."

"He's exhausted you, has he? How about tomorrow then?"

He was standing under the street lamp and his eyes were strained and intent, close to desperation. I felt afraid, yet at the same time had a confusing sense of pity for him. He obviously wanted, needed someone but it wasn't going to be me.

"Please go, Jake. I'm tired and not interested." I leaned my bike against the hedge and ran to the front door.

To my relief, he didn't follow but as I slammed the door shut, I heard him shouting, "You're not the first and you won't be the last. He'll ditch you in the end. You'll see. He always does!"

TEN

Life followed its usual inexorable routine of torture and destruction at DLS in the next two days. Twelve more beagles in our unit either died or were put to death. I tried but was unable to prevent Tess having her next allotted tablets and she resumed, to my dismay, her vomiting and general deterioration.

During my lunch hour on the Thursday, near the incinerator, I saw the mangled bodies of two monkeys, several beagles and a sack of dead guinea pigs. DLS wasn't just like Auschwitz; it replicated the horror and I couldn't wait for Saturday and the hope of changing things.

Joanna still watched me carefully, from the corner of her eye, whenever she had the chance. She and Tony were often oddly withdrawn. I overheard them, in the lunch hour, talking about the financial situation at DLS. They both seemed quite concerned that some key shareholders had pulled out. Mark's campaign giving shareholders information about DLS apparently was having an effect. On Friday afternoon I heard them mention security was to be increased at weekends and an extra guard employed. This was not good news and, as soon as I got home, I rang Mark to let him know. He was working late, according to his father who took a message.

It wasn't until Saturday afternoon he rang, saying he thought we'd cope; Steve had agreed to help with the transporting which would free Jason for the core group and dealing with an extra guard.

"Steve's mother's ill. Did you know?"

"No, but Steve must have taken that into account when he agreed to join in. It's his decision. He could have refused."

Mark sounded on edge and irritated I'd raised the matter. I put it down to the strain and tension of arranging the break-in. There was no doubt he was under enormous pressure, both from himself and the others, to deliver an effective outcome. But the implications were serious if anyone was caught, which was the reason I was worried about Steve. What would happen to his mother if Steve were arrested? He was taking a big risk and I wondered if Mark appreciated it.

There was no opportunity to pursue the matter. Mark said he'd got more calls to make and would see me at the lay-by with Steve, then rang off. As I put down the receiver, I felt I'd been talking to a stranger and was uneasy there might be more in what Jake said than I wanted to believe.

I tried to put Mark out of my mind as I prepared for the evening but almost everything I touched was associated with him in some way: my facemask, black T-shirt and jeans. Even the blankets I unearthed for Tess in the kitchen were there because Mark had made known her existence. I began to feel I'd known him all my life yet only recently become aware and I knew I couldn't

114

forget him, that he was a part of me now in a way no one else had ever been.

Whatever the risks involved, I needed to speak to him, I decided, and confront him direct about Jake's accusations.

The evening dragged despite my resolution and eventually I went to Steve's early to see his mother and check if he'd managed to find someone to sit with her.

His neighbour would come until midnight, he said. After, they would have to rely on the alarm system to the nurse.

"Can she contact you?" I asked.

"Well, no, not if I'm not here or at work."

"You'd better give her my mobile number," I suggested.

"It's all right, my dear," Steve's mother spoke quietly from the bed, "I'll be fine."

"Of course you will," Steve reassured her. "It's just a precaution." He rang the nurse and gave her my number, then made the bed and brought his mother some strawberry puree he'd prepared, with some cream. He was amazing with her, so caring and kind. I couldn't bear the thought of anything disrupting their last few months together.

As the time drew near for our departure, I felt increasingly nervous about the break-in and the role I had to play. Supposing the entry code had been changed without my knowing, or there were employees and extra guards actually in the building and with mobile phones. The police would be there within minutes before I could rescue Tess, let alone the other dogs and primates.

Steve was his usual calm self, trying to dissipate doubt and drama. He'd renovated his old transit van, which had managed miraculously to pass its MOT and could be used for the transportation of the freed animals.

There was a light drizzle as we set out with clouds covering a half-moon. It would be difficult to see once the security lights were destroyed, but the darkness had other benefits, Steve reminded me, and we both had torches.

The others were already in the lay-by waiting when we arrived; all dressed in black, according to Mark's instructions, their facemasks in place. It was difficult to recognise them as individuals. As Steve and I put on our masks, I had a strong sense of becoming part of a team, a group sharing a common task that mattered and demanded our allegiance.

There was an air of quiet anticipation as Mark confirmed positions and timing. No one talked above a whisper as we left the lay-by, then walked along the lane in the darkness to DLS and our allotted places.

We came to the razor wiring. Most of the group followed Mark to where he'd cut the wire in readiness on the northern side. Pete, Martin, Jenny, Gemma and myself waited, according to plan, behind the hawthorn near the razor wiring close to the guards' hut and main entrance.

For the first half an hour nothing happened. We could hear the guards inside the hut periodically laughing and what sounded like a quiz on TV.

Then abruptly at midnight the door of the hut was pushed wide open and the two guards I knew emerged with the Alsatian and started to patrol the compound. The security lights came on, throwing into relief the sharp razor wiring against a darkened sky.

The guards plodded painstakingly around but were more concerned, I noticed, with the area to the south near the main entrance, where we were, than the northern section. They failed, fortunately, to notice the cut wire nor did the Alsatian pick up our scent beyond the wiring. We were lucky with the wind direction. There was no sign of the third guard Tony Brown had mentioned.

As the lights went out again, following the return of the guards to the hut, we heard the clink of glasses and resumed laughter.

I became aware then of shadows, some creeping towards us outside the wiring, some inside close to the ground. Suddenly the compound was illuminated again and I could clearly see Mark, Jake and seven others in their masks, standing by to close in on the guards' hut. The laughter inside ceased as the guards noticed the lighting. There was a moment of eerie silence. My heart started thumping in my throat. I caught a whiff of sharp sweat from Pete and knew I wasn't the only one afraid. Then Mark, Jake and the others rushed forward, pushing open the hut door. I heard shouts, swearing, a crash of glass and wood splintering, then a heavy thud as someone fell to the floor. "We'll get you, you bastards!" I heard one of the guards shouting. Someone then, I think it was Jake, flung a mobile phone over the razor wiring, close to where we were hiding. "Gag him!" I heard Jake yell and he was away with two others, running to the main entrance.

Amazingly, in a matter of seconds, he'd opened the main gates. Three of those who'd come around the outside wire brought in a ladder and swiftly Jake was climbing up to each of the security lights and CCTVs, cutting off the power. He was incredibly agile, fast and competent too and soon had them all dismantled.

It was our cue. Leaving our hiding place behind the hawthorn, I ran with Martin, Pete, Jenny and Gemma through the main entrance to the reinforced glass door of the office block and pressed the numbers on the entrance pad I knew now by heart, 987467. To my relief, the door responded and I led the others through the second security check and on up the stairs to the computer room.

As I pushed open the door I saw then the computer room was not empty as we'd expected. In the far corner, one of the IT employees, whom I recognised from my previous exploration, was sitting in front of a lighted screen, typing on the keyboard. He wore earphones so hadn't heard our approach and sprang to his feet in alarm as he saw us.

"What are you doing here?"

There were dark rings under his eyes, a twitch in the muscles of his jaw, so I was almost sorry for him as we five advanced in our masks and black. Then I noticed him reaching out for his mobile beside the keyboard and already he was pressing numbers that alone, without speech, could be a warning.

"More to the point, what are you doing, mate," Pete demanded, "working for an outfit that tortures animals?" He seized the mobile, smashing it on the floor with the heel of his boot.

The man visibly began to shake. "You won't get away with it," he stuttered and made an effort to push between Pete and Martin to the door. Pete quickly gripped him and held him in an arm lock. Martin whipped out cord from his jeans and together they tied him up and gagged him, leaving him on the floor.

"We'll put him in a cage later with one of his CDs," Pete said mockingly. "Right, we'd better get cracking."

I left Pete and Martin to get on with disabling the computer and took Gemma and Jenny and the others to the animal units.

For a while it seemed we were flailing about in a building too big for us. Our dark, masked figures were trying to get a grip on a task too ambitious, too unpredictable in an abhorrent setting. Some were literally too upset by what they saw to act with any speed. There were problems Mark could not have foreseen like a shortage of cages and unfamiliar locks that could not be easily broken in time. And some of the dogs and monkeys were ready to bite, no longer willing to trust human contact.

Gradually I was aware of Mark alongside me, co-ordinating the rescue, directing and encouraging as he got his bearings. As the vans started to arrive at the back exit, taking the animals away, we all settled into our roles and I began to feel a new energy and purpose. We were at last achieving something and Mark's organisation was paying off.

I helped carry some of the dogs from sections 12 to 15, then decided to concentrate on section 18 to make sure Tess was rescued.

She was not in good shape. Her hair stood on end and her eyes were dull and bloodshot. There was blood on her back legs. She could only manage two short steps then collapsed on the concrete floor. I was sure she'd never cope with a rough ride and being jolted. I remembered a plastic box with a blanket in it Tony kept for emergencies in the lab. I ran up and fetched it, lay Tess on it, then carried her to the exit for the next van.

Steve was just about to drive off with a load but the cages, mainly of macaques, were tightly pack already and there was no room for Tess.

"I'll be back. Don't worry," Steve said. "Just give me twenty minutes and we'll have her away."

As he drove off, Mark told me he was going to check how things were going in the computer room.

"Right." I decided not to try and transport any more dogs for the time being but to stay with Tess in case she got confused and tried to get out of her makeshift bed. It was a relief to sit still with her a while, knowing she'd soon be away and free of her torment. Jenny and Gemma and the others meanwhile continued to bring out more beagles and macaques and as the cages piled up beside us I began to wonder if the vans could cope with so many.

It dawned on me gradually, as I waited, the vans were not coming as frequently as before; they were not, in fact, coming at all. Since Steve's departure, none, I realised, had returned, which was odd for there'd been a regular convoy. I looked at my watch. Thirty minutes, forty, fifty had passed already and Steve had promised to be back within twenty. I pressed open the exit door, leaving Tess for a moment and looked over the compound. It was dark still but strangely quiet, too quiet, I thought.

I ran to the computer room. Jake had joined Mark and together with Pete and Martin, they were bending over the main computer with its inner workings exposed as if about to undergo a brain operation.

"How's it going?" I asked.

120

"We're nearly there," Martin said quietly, "just ensuring the computer's memory will never regurgitate the data, even from the buried back-up." Sweat was pouring down from his freckled forehead as he scrutinised the guts of the computer. You could have cut the air with a knife, so intently were the others fixed on his concentration. Then with a modest air of triumph, he extracted a small piece of plastic, with nail-like pins.

"Right, that should do it. They'll have to start again and they won't be able to operate without rebuilding a new database."

He wrapped the piece he'd extracted in some tissue and put it in his pocket. It all looked so simple. Perhaps it was, but Martin's knowledge I guessed was far from being so.

"Does that mean the records are destroyed for good?" Mark asked.

"On this system, yes."

"Even with back-up disks?"

"Even with back-up disks."

Methodically Martin began to screw back the metal cover on the computer.

I felt I couldn't wait any longer.

"The vans have stopped coming, Mark."

I didn't need to elaborate. Mark was instantly on his mobile to Philippa. It was a terse call and he passed on his information without delay, the muscles of his face straining to retain their calm.

"The screws got a tip-off and they're waiting outside the main entrance for us to emerge. They've apparently arrested one of the van drivers. We can still get out, Philippa thinks, through the cut wire. We'll take as many animals as we can, but we'll obviously have to leave most behind without the vans."

"Thanks to this bastard who no doubt got through." Pete kicked at the feet of the IT employee still trussed up on the floor and seized the documents at his desk.

I looked at Martin who had been putting paper into a metal waste bin and watched him drop the computer piece onto it, then set light to it.

"What are you doing?" I asked.

"If I'm caught with this on me it can be taken to a techie who can put together most of what I've just wiped off with my disk. It'll take a while and be expensive, but easier than rebuilding their whole system again."

He waited about half a minute whilst the flames licked around the part then picked up the can of Coca Cola the computer operator had been drinking and poured it over the mess dousing the flames. Grabbing the piece again, he thrust it in his pocket to throw away outside and we ran to the back exit, crammed now with cages of bewildered and dejected beagles and macaques, all waiting for their exit from DLS.

It was like choosing in the death camps. Which animal to save? Which to leave behind? Though they were all deserving, I had to choose Tess. If I could but get her to Steve's van. As I stumbled in the dark, carrying her across the concrete compound, following Pete, I realised Steve might be the driver who had been arrested. The thought was too awful and I desperately hoped he would be at the lay-by where the animals were to be collected.

Then just as I was thinking of him, my mobile started to ring. It had to be the nurse, I thought, but didn't dare to stop and answer. It was impossible anyway to hold the phone with Tess as I ran. It was still ringing as we reached the wire. We could see lights flashing near the main entrance, a police car driving in, its headlights illuminating the compound and suddenly there were figures in fluorescent clothing running at us with torches and shouting at us to stop. Tess stirred with fear in her box and struggled to get up to escape from the noise. I put the box down, picked her up and pressed on to follow Pete through the wire. As I did so, I felt a hand grip my shoulder. I was wrenched around and a torch shone at my eyes.

"Put that dog down in its box. It's not your property and I'm arresting you for trespass and theft."

Pete had managed to get through the wire but three policemen, two of them holding truncheons, surrounded Mark, Jake, Martin and myself.

"She's ill," I pleaded with the nearest policeman. "She needs a vet."

"That's not your concern. She belongs here."

"No!" I felt suddenly an intense anger that Tess, a sentient being, should be condemned to this squalid place, a desperate determination that I was going to get her out. Now I'd got so far, she wasn't going to stay.

"She's dying!" I shouted. "And she's not going to die here."

Clutching Tess close, I turned and dived behind Mark and pushed through the wire. As I looked from the other side, I saw Mark blocking the way of a policeman about to follow. In the scuffle after my movement Martin, unnoticed, threw the computer piece over the wire and into the undergrowth.

"The dog's dying from torture," Mark shouted. "Don't you care?"

One of the policemen gripped his arm and pulled him away from the wire. There was a struggle as he tried to break free. He had not assaulted anyone. He had tried merely to enable Tess and myself to get away, but that's not how it was seen.

Suddenly all hell broke loose with whistles blowing and more policemen running.

It was Jake then who took the stage. As I moved with Pete away from the torchlight, I saw him, in a frenzy, hitting out at the three policemen who'd stopped us. Then he managed to get hold of one of the truncheons and lashed a policeman's shoulders with it.

I wanted to help Mark get out but Pete urged me to hurry: "They'll be round here in no time. There's no point in us all being caught."

"But Mark…"

"He'll manage. He'll find a way. Come on, or we won't get your dog away."

We stumbled across the field, Pete carrying the bundle of documents he'd grabbed from the computer room, with me clutching Tess. Holding her close, I could feel how thin she was, her ribs projecting beneath her skin. Every now and then I could feel blood oozing from her back passage onto my arm. I was desperate to get her home and to let her lie in comfort.

At the field's boundary we stopped and looked back. The DLS compound had quietened and police cars clustered together near the main entrance. Shifting torchlight and the glow of fluorescent clothing suggested a search was in operation but no one appeared to be following us.

We pressed on then to the lay-by where we'd all first met.

There was no sign, to my disappointment, of Steve's van at all. The whole area looked deserted. Then, as we hesitated thinking what to do, a dark figure rose from behind the gate to the field beyond.

"Thank God you've come," a weary voice said. It was Steve.

He told us he'd managed to deliver a last load of animals to the waiting cars at the lay-by but when he'd gone back and was about to drive in the main entrance again, he'd seen the police waiting. It was impossible to turn the vehicle around and drive away. He'd quickly removed the number plates and licence, abandoned the van then near the entrance, slipped away into the hedge with the number plates and come to the lay-by to wait.

I realised he'd come to wait for Tess and me because he'd promised. He could have gone home, got right out of it but hadn't despite his own problems and responsibility. I remembered the phone call then that I hadn't responded to and dialled the recall button.

The nurse immediately answered. She sounded very irritated. "Why didn't you answer?" she demanded.

"Sorry, I couldn't at the time. How is Mrs Hobbs?"

"She's not well at all. She's been asking for Steve. Is he there?"

"Just a minute." I handed the phone to Steve.

When he handed it back, he admitted with reluctance, "She seems to have taken a turn for the worse."

"We'll get there as soon as we can," I tried to reassure him.

It took us three hours to walk the eight miles into Horton. We tried to avoid the main roads where the police might be in case they saw us with Tess. Pete and Steve took it in turns helping to carry her but she seemed to want to be with me as someone familiar. We stopped by a stream to give her the chance to drink but she scarcely had the strength to lap.

It was just getting light as we reached Horton and said goodbye to Pete. There was no one out walking the streets but a few lights were on in second-floor windows and I began to be afraid someone, looking down by chance, would see Tess and report us. We could hardly have looked a reassuring sight, dressed all in black and spattered with mud.

We went first to Steve's. We found his mother, to our relief, asleep but a note from the nurse indicated she'd had a bad night and a relapse, and had needed sedation.

"I shouldn't have gone." Steve blamed himself.

"I doubt you could have altered things," I said and it was true. In the grey morning light, his mother looked even more pale and frail and I knew with dread in my heart it could only be a matter of weeks, not months before she left him.

I felt I should stay with him a while but he urged me to get Tess settled and hidden before any neighbours saw her. At my house, I took her into the back garden to an area sheltered by shrubs where she could not be seen and lay her on the grass. She'd probably never seen grass before or ever been in a garden. She looked bewildered briefly, then pressed her nose to the ground and staggered a couple of paces following a scent to a flowerbed. Her legs gave way then and she sank back onto the grass. I could sense her eyes were more trusting as she looked at me and, to my joy, she lapped some water and managed to eat a few teaspoons of an easily digested dog food I'd bought.

After all she'd suffered and was still suffering, rationally, I knew there wasn't much hope but as I carried her to the kitchen to a basket, more than anything I wanted her to live, to survive and triumph over all the torture she'd endured. I wanted all the unnecessary suffering of conscious creatures at the hands of money-driven, unfeeling women and men to end.

When Tess was settled in her basket, I rang Mark's mobile to see if he'd got away. There was no answer, no responding tone. I tried phoning his father. The phone went on ringing some time before his father answered.

"Is Mark there?" I asked.

"No, he's not home yet. Is that Kate?"

"Yes."

"Can you tell me what's happened? Where he is?"

"I'm not sure yet," I said. "I'm still waiting to hear."

"Please let me know—" there was a plea in Mr Stanton's voice now "—when you've some definite news."

"Of course. I'll let you know as soon as I can. Meanwhile, try and get some sleep, Mr Stanton." I sounded like a maiden aunt dispensing advice. It was a nerve considering Mr Stanton was twice my age. I knew he wouldn't take it anyway. He cared too much for Mark not to stay up.

Despite all that had happened, my concern about Mark and the fact we'd only half-achieved our purpose at DLS, I felt strangely elated, the sense of a purpose I hadn't acknowledged before.

Then the events of the night crept up on me. It was six in the morning. A car was already starting up in the street. I lay on my bed and fell instantly asleep.

ELEVEN

The persistent ringing of the phone awoke me around midday. It was Steve saying he'd heard from Karl that Mark and Jake had last been seen boarding a police van at the main entrance.

"I'd better let his father know," I said. "How's your mother?"

"Much the same, and Tess?"

"I've been asleep. I'm just going to see."

Tess was still in her basket where I'd left her. It looked at first as if she'd been there all night but there was a trace of blood leading to the mat by the kitchen door. I wondered whether to call a vet, but no doubt they would be informed soon about the missing dogs, which would mean Tess being taken away again. If the toxicity had really taken a hold, I reasoned, there was probably little a vet could do. If it hadn't, Tess would, in time, heal from her own resources.

I gave her instead an herbal preparation I'd got from a local shop and spread an old blanket for her on the floor of the kitchen. Now people were about, it might not be safe for her even in the sheltered part of the garden. Apart from Steve, there was no one in the road I could fully trust not to divulge she was here.

I rang Mark's father. He told me the break-in had been on the main news.

"What did they say?"

"Just some animal rights activists had broken into Draco Life Sciences, taken some animals and caused damage. They didn't say what to."

They didn't need to, I thought. It was the computer, for sure. What else? And wasn't it being headline news a tribute to Mark's organisation? But Mr Stanton was very concerned about Mark's arrest. It wasn't going to do his career any good, he predicted. But Mark, I realised even more now, was never going to be able to live on the basis of career prospects. He had to live and work for what he believed in.

"I'll ring again," I tried to reassure Mr Stanton, "if I hear anything more. You could probably speak to him if you ring the local police station." They were words I was to live to regret but at the time, from what we knew, they seemed the logical, natural thing to say. Mr Stanton agreed that was what he'd probably do.

As I put down the receiver I remembered, looking at the calendar, I was supposed to be going to Alan Masson's lunch party with Robert and Carol. It was already one and I wasn't even dressed. I didn't want to go. I didn't want to leave Tess until she was used to the place and I could see how she responded. I was about to ring up, saying I was ill, when Alan himself rang.

"I just thought I'd let you know," he said, "we're in the garden. Just come through the front door if you don't get a reply."

"Right," his voice was so welcoming I hadn't the heart to make an excuse. "I'll be a bit late though."

"Don't worry. Robert and Carol have only just arrived."

As we hung up, it occurred to me then Robert would know now about the break-in. How was he reacting? More importantly, how was I going to react and keep up the pretence of not knowing? I'd have to play really dumb to avoid giving anything away. I wanted even less to go to the lunch party.

As I settled Tess, dressed and reflected further, I realised it could be quite useful gauging Robert's reaction. It might even give me some inside knowledge of the real success, or otherwise, of our impact. Yes, I would adopt henceforth some of the ruthlessness of the other side and find out what I could. Mark was right. There was no point in being daunted by people prepared to torture.

I drew the curtains in the kitchen, in case Tess was seen, and, reluctantly leaving her, went along the road to Alan's.

"You look lovely," Alan said, greeting me in the garden and giving me a kiss. I'd put on the clothes he'd wanted, my long orange eastern skirt and loose black top—more, I must confess, because they were lying to hand than from any special preparation. "I must warn you," Alan lowered his voice to whisper, "Robert's not in the best of moods. Some maniacs apparently have broken into his firm and caused havoc."

"Really?" I raised my voice, feigning surprise. "What sort of maniacs?" If ever there was a misnomer for the people I knew in the movement, my friends now, it was this.

"You'd better ask him that yourself." Alan gave me a glass of wine and I sauntered as casually as I could to the teak wood table where Carol and Robert were already seated beneath a carefully slanted striped sunshade.

Robert was using his mobile. His back was to the house and he didn't notice me until I'd already sat next to Carol. Immediately, he stood and walked towards the house, speaking more quietly into the mobile, to avoid being overheard. I may have been imagining it but he seemed distinctly hostile as he looked back at me, as if he knew I'd been involved. Yet how? I felt unnerved, on edge, as Carol sought to explain his preoccupation.

"You'll have to excuse Robert," she said. "There's been a break-in at the firm and he's got a lot to sort out."

"I'm sorry to hear that," I ventured. I could hear my voice wavering like a piano out of tune and took a gulp of Alan's wine.

"It's those animal rights activists again," Carol snapped. "Honestly, Kate, I can't imagine how you could even think of joining them. The damage they do and for what? All the painstaking research over the past year, a lot of it's now been wasted because of the antics of these people."

Carol was good at contempt when she set her mind to it and she concentrated the full force of it now on "these people".

"They've even stolen animals involved in research. Whatever can be the point of that? What use will they be to anyone else?"

"Maybe it's not the use but the principle of it," I suggested. I began to feel irritated, a rising anger she could only see the use an animal might have for people, not a value in itself. "Animals aren't just commodities. They have a right to live as much as we do," I asserted.

131

"You don't support this kind of lawlessness though surely, breaking in, stealing and causing damage?"

I did support it, of course, because the torture inflicted at DLS was a greater evil but it wasn't the ideal moment to say so. Fortunately Alan arrived with some trays of food and Carol was distracted from repeating the question. As Robert returned from his wandering, pocketing his mobile, Alan pressed us to eat.

He had gone to a lot of trouble with the food. There was an elaborate salmon dish with mayonnaise, a cold chicken curry and numerous vegetarian salad dishes that I opted for. We all praised his efforts and for a while the conversation drifted over food but it inevitably returned to the break-in.

"What's the latest then?" Alan asked Robert.

"The latest," Robert replied, giving me a sideways glance of suspicion, "is the police have arrested three people but the two ringleaders have got away."

"You mean they were caught and got away or were never caught?" Carol demanded. She always liked to get her facts straight.

"The former," Robert said tersely, not looking at her. His lips were set in a thin line of discontent and I sensed anger seething up through his well-covered body, ready to blaze from his eyes.

For the first time I was afraid of him and what he might do. He was no longer the mild, genial Robert I'd known along the road but a man who felt threatened, his livelihood at stake. A man, I reminded myself, prepared for his livelihood to torture.

"A bit careless of the police, wasn't it?" Alan offered. "I mean I know there are shortages and all that but surely having arrested someone you don't let him go."

"Or her," Carol added.

"It isn't quite as simple as that," Robert stated acidly. "These people come armed with all kinds of weapons and they're prepared to use them. One of the policemen was knocked unconscious, another had his shoulder dislocated."

I wanted to shout out to Robert, "You're lying." I just didn't believe him. Such violence was against all Mark advocated. He had expressly enjoined the group not to use violence. Then I remembered Jake lashing out with the truncheon he'd snatched from the police just before Pete and I had escaped across the field. Had Jake finally got at Mark through his violence?

"Have they any idea who the two escapees were?" Carol asked.

"They didn't get round to taking names," Robert replied," and they were all in masks so no, they can't be sure but they've a good idea from the group's previous activities."

"I bet it's that Stanton fellow behind it again," Carol asserted.

"That's one of the names mentioned certainly," Robert confirmed.

"Well, let's hope the police track them down," Alan said mildly. I had the impression he wasn't that concerned, that he was speaking more from social sympathy and politeness.

"They'll get them in the end," Robert said, setting his jaw again, "and I'm going to do all I can to see they get a long sentence."

"Fair enough," Alan gave a conciliatory smile, "but you mustn't let it get to you, old chap, meanwhile."

"I don't think you understand," Robert rebuffed. "Some of the records they've destroyed are irreplaceable and could take years to rebuild."

No words, even of a supporter, could have been more of a tribute to Mark and his organisation. If only he could have heard them, but things didn't look too good for him, judging by Robert's news. I didn't, for a moment, believe he'd been the one to instigate the violence. I was sure it was Jake. That didn't mean Mark wouldn't get the blame and I felt increasingly anxious to know what had happened to him and where he was. Had he been arrested or was he one of the so-called ringleaders who'd got away?

I wanted to go home to call Steve and Mark's father to see if they had any news and see Tess. Restless, I took some of the empty dishes to Alan's kitchen, calculating how soon I could excuse myself and leave. To my surprise, Robert followed. He wasn't carrying anything. I thought he was probably just coming to get some wine for Alan, but as I stacked the dishes out on the draining board, ready to go in Alan's dishwasher, Robert came up behind me, carefully closing the door behind him.

"You can drop the pretence, Kate. You've had a hand in all this, haven't you?" There was a knife in his voice, one ready to stab me in the back.

"I don't know what you're talking about," I said.

"Haven't you been working at Draco these past two weeks?"

It was obvious he knew, so how could I deny it? How did he know though? I was sure he hadn't seen me on the stairs.

"What if I have?"

"So you don't deny it? But why should someone like

you want to work at a level that's no more than a kennel maid?"

"I need the money," I said, trying to sound convincing.

"Kennel maid's money when you could get a professional salary?"

"That's just the point," I said, gaining more confidence, "I haven't been able to get a professional job as Carol will tell you. I had to get something. It's not a job I want or enjoy but it's a job for the time being."

"How come you've kept quiet about it then and not told Carol? You don't sound very convincing, you know. It's my belief you were persuaded there to help the Animal Rights' Movement gain entry. As such you're partly responsible for what happened and I'm going to see you are investigated unless you agree to pass on certain information."

"What information?"

"If you'll tell the police all you know about the Animal Rights Movement and the people responsible for the break-in, particularly about this Stanton fellow, his methods and plans, we'll drop our investigation of you. Otherwise, I'll see it goes ahead."

As Robert stood there, confident he had the upper hand, I said, "I shouldn't do that if I were you, Robert," and turned to face him. "If you do, I'll tell Carol about seeing you with your blond flossy in the lay-by near Youlton. Let's see now, it was last Wednesday, wasn't it, about six-fifteen in your BMW?"

Robert stared at me a moment in disbelief. Then the anger that had been seething in him erupted. He gripped my shoulders, shaking me.

"Why, you prying little bitch!" He pushed me against the fridge adjacent to the washing-up machine, gritting his teeth in an effort to control himself. If he could have strangled me without being caught, he'd have done it.

Then abruptly he let go and strode to the window. His eyes shifted between me and Carol and Alan still seated together in the garden. I could feel him trying to work a way out of his dilemma. The muscles of his face were taut like a pulley beneath the skin.

"I'll say nothing to Carol if you'll drop the investigation," I prompted. I was uncomfortably aware I was betraying Carol, who'd been a good friend to me and should be told, but the suffering of the animals at Draco was more important and I resolved I wasn't going to be distracted.

"I'll drop the investigation of you but not the animal rights people," Robert said then, trying to retain control over the situation. But he knew as well as I did the police would carry out an investigation anyway and he had no extra knowledge now to give them. There was no point in not agreeing.

How much I could trust him was another matter. He'd lost too much face to act the gentleman, but now I had my own retaliatory card to play.

As we stood in silence, assessing each other, Alan came in from the garden to make some coffee. "You must be having a very interesting conversation after all this time," he smiled congenially, unaware of the icy vibes. "What's it all about?"

"You'd better ask Kate that," Robert threw at him, promptly making his exit.

"What's the matter? Have I said something?" Alan

watched with a bewildered frown as Robert went to join Carol.

"He's probably still upset about the break-in," I said.

"Yes, I suppose that must be it."

"You've gone to a lot of trouble, Alan. I'm sorry but I'm going to have to go soon."

"Really? I'd hoped you'd be able to stay a while. I mean on your own." His eyes had a wistful look and I felt I'd hurt him, wanting to go. But I knew I'd got to stick to my guns, both for Tess and Mark. I didn't want to get involved with Alan anyway. He was a nice enough guy but he wasn't Mark.

"It's kind of you, Alan." I tried to think of an excuse other than the truth. I plumbed finally for Steve's mother, saying I'd promised to help out. I felt a blatant hypocrite playing the selfless neighbour when I had totally other intentions, but Alan, to my relief, seemed to accept my excuse.

"At least let me walk you home," he said.

"Really there's no need."

"I insist." He put his arm around my shoulder and kissed me lightly on the cheek. "Thanks for coming," he said quietly. "It hasn't worked out quite as I'd hoped with this break-in business. Perhaps you'd like to come to a concert or play sometime—just the two of us?"

"Thank you."

"I'll give you a ring when something interesting turns up, hopefully soon." He took my hand and we walked into the garden so I could say goodbye to Robert and Carol. Carol beamed with the satisfaction of thinking she'd brought us together but Robert refused to look at me.

"You don't seem to like Robert," Alan said as we walked up the road.

"Don't I?" I didn't want to think about Robert any more. I wanted to find out what had happened to Mark and see Tess. "Perhaps it's more he doesn't like me," I batted back flippantly.

"I can't think why." Alan said. It was an invitation but if I told him one thing, it could lead to another, then it would all come out with unpredictable consequences for Mark and the movement. How much could I trust him anyway? How much could I trust anyone outside the movement? Very little, I suspected.

I was conscious, as I thought this, of having separated myself from people outside the movement. There was a widening river now unable to be bridged with the same assumptions and communication. I felt saddened yet simultaneously conscious I belonged, at last, to something I believed in.

"There aren't answers to some things, are there?" I said.

"There may be to your window frames, though," Alan smiled as we stopped outside my house.

"What do you mean?"

"I mean I think you need new ones," he said. "Do you mind if I have a look?" He went up to the bay window of my sitting room, then felt the wood of the sill and frame. I knew it was bad but not as much as he was suggesting. As he pressed one section, the wood literally crumbled. "I think you should have the whole thing replaced, don't you?" It was a rhetorical question.

"I'm not sure if I can afford to just now."

"I know a builder who's reasonable. I could get a quote for you, if you like." He was feeling the frame at the side when, suddenly looking in the window, he said, "I didn't know you had a dog."

"I don't." I was quick at once to deny. Then, following his gaze, my heart missed a beat, for there lying on my father's Bokhara carpet, looking up at us, was Tess. I couldn't believe she'd made it from the kitchen, and how stupid I'd been to leave the door open. I'd drawn the curtain at the back yet failed to ensure she wasn't seen from the front. As Alan looked at me quizzically, I blundered on, "What I mean is I don't own her. I'm looking after her for someone on holiday."

"She doesn't look very lively," Alan observed. "Is she old?"

"She hasn't been too well," I said. "Look, I'd rather you didn't say anything to anyone about her." I lowered my voice. "It's my neighbours, you see. They don't like dogs and I could have a problem with them."

"Don't worry. I won't say anything." He gave a conspiratorial smile: "Even to Carol and Robert."

Had he guessed already about Tess's origins? I could have kicked myself for agreeing to his coming with me. Now there was no knowing whom he would tell. Alan seemed decent enough but how much could I trust him when the search for the beagles began in earnest?

When he'd gone, I carried Tess to the kitchen. She'd made a mess on the blanket I'd put down and there was another thin trail of blood to the back door but she'd taken more food and drunk a whole bowl of water. I began to feel there might be some hope if I could get the toxins out of her body. I gave her another of the preparations I'd got from the herbalist and rang Steve.

As soon as he heard my voice, Steve told me Mark and Jake were no longer held by the police.

"What's happened then?"

"Jake seized one of the police truncheons and lashed out with it as you saw. The police got it away from him and took Mark and Jake to the police van near the entrance. There was a scuffle and some of the others who'd been waiting outside joined in and Jake and Mark got away."

"Do you know where they are?"

"Jake's gone to Pete's and is hiding in his cellar but Mark, I don't know."

"Does his father know?"

"I haven't rung him."

"I'd better get onto him straightaway."

Suddenly I realised the awful blunder I'd made in suggesting to Mr Stanton he rang the local police station for contact with Mark. It would confirm he'd been involved with the break-in when the police might not even have his name at all. What a fool I'd been. Quickly I rang Mark's father, hoping he'd taken no action. The phone kept ringing but there was no answer.

I tried again an hour later but still no answer. Perhaps Mr Stanton was still in his garden, I thought, or had fallen asleep after being up all night. The evening seemed an unlikely time for him to be sleeping and he would surely have kept the phone near him even in the garden, since he was anxious for news of Mark.

At eight o'clock after trying in vain for the seventh time, I rang the operator, who informed me there was a fault. I decided then to cycle to Youlton to deliver the news of Mark in person.

En route, I tried to think where Mark could have gone. If he wasn't at Pete's with Jake, where was he?

TWELVE

There was nothing at first to suggest anything unusual had happened at the cottage. Bathed in the last of the evening light, it presented a picture of charm and calm, with its leaded windows, its climbing roses over whitewashed walls and an abundance of flowers in the front garden. Coming closer, I noticed then all the windows were closed and the curtains drawn as if Mr Stanton had gone away, or died.

Propping my bicycle against the hedge, I pushed open the wrought iron gate, went to the front door and rapped on the brass doorknocker. As I'd half expected, there was no reply. I walked around the cottage to the back garden but there was no sign of Mr Stanton either in the greenhouse or the vegetable plot beyond.

Coming back to the front door, I looked up at the window of the bedroom where Mark had made love to me. I felt a sudden overwhelming longing for him, a need deeper at that moment than hunger or thirst, a premonition I wasn't going to be able to manage without him and everything else was somehow irrelevant, on the edge.

I could feel my heart racing as if it was trying to leave

my body and reach out to him, a dizziness in my head. I thought I was going to faint. Geraniums, begonias, hollyhocks, sweet williams and sweet peas started to cartwheel across the sky.

I sat on the lawn close to some purple, white and pink sweet peas, trying to steady myself. Perhaps it was the pervasive scent of the flowers but after a while the dizziness passed and my senses sharpened again, alert.

Glancing up at the second window over the porch, I saw then that the telephone wiring was broken and hanging loose. It looked as if it had been cut. By whom, though and why? And where was Mr Stanton? Was he still there in the cottage behind the closed curtains and windows?

I pushed open the brass letter flap set in the door. The flagged stone floor was lit by evening shafts of sunlight penetrating from a window facing the back garden. It was a light that threw up shadows and I was sure, as I looked towards the small room Mark used as an office, I saw a shadow move and merge with that of the walnut cabinet dominating the hall.

I called through the letterbox. "It's Kate, Mr Stanton. I've news for you."

There was no reply. I stepped back and looked up at the window again. I could have sworn I saw the edge of the curtain in the downstairs dining room move. Someone was observing me? Who?

I stood back on the lawn for a good five minutes, feeling increasingly uneasy, about what might have happened, when I heard a key turn in the lock. The front door opened and a thin-faced woman with grey hair, wielding a long broom, confronted me.

"What do you want?" she demanded. Her lips were pursed, her eyes hostile.

"I came to see Mr Stanton," I replied. "I've been trying to phone but the phone's out of order."

"And a lot more besides. Who are you?"

"I'm a friend of Mr Stanton's son. I came to bring him some news."

"It had better be more cheering than the usual then. Mr Stanton's in hospital. He was set upon by two men who came looking for his son this afternoon."

"Two men, you say?" My heart sank.

"Two men in broad daylight attacked him when he tried to stop them getting into his own home."

"You mean they deliberately injured him?" The thought was appalling.

"When he tried to shut the door and told them to go, they punched and pushed him. He fell and broke his leg. And all for that son of his who should have been here protecting him."

"I'm sure he would have been if he'd known."

"That's as maybe but he wasn't, was he? And they're not the only ones who've been. The police have been too. All this animal rights stuff. He hasn't stopped to think of all he's done over the years to his father. Caused him no end of grief he has, and now this. A man shouldn't have to defend his own home and suffer because his son's wanted by the police and other ruffians."

I wanted to defend Mark and put the record straight, tell her of all the good he'd done, the sacrifices he'd made but I guessed she wouldn't listen and I'd waste precious time.

"Did they take anything away?" I asked.

"They took some things from the office."

"Can I see? I had some tapes there."

She hesitated a moment, looking at me with suspicion again, then waved me inside and locked the door. "You'll have to be quick. I've got my husband's dinner to prepare."

It didn't take me long to see they'd taken mainly admin tapes and CDs. The old computer was still intact and realistically they'd have made no money from it. But taking the tapes and CDs meant they had access to Mark's address list and plans. It wasn't good news.

Worst of all was the fact the two men now knew where Mark's base was, which reduced considerably his chances of evading the police.

"Have you known Mr Stanton long?" I asked, going towards the front door.

"I've known him since before you were born, young lady, and I've cleaned for him twice a week since his wife died."

"You live quite near then?"

"Two doors down. You can't live much nearer than that, can you?" She told me her name was Doris and she'd be looking after the house and garden until Mr Stanton returned. She was obviously genuinely concerned for him and was becoming more friendly and forthcoming but it was already getting dark and I wanted to go. I didn't want to be out at night if the two men were still at large in their Land Rover nearby.

"Which hospital is Mr Stanton in?" I asked.

"Stowton General. You can visit between two and four, and seven and nine."

"Right, I'll try and go tomorrow then."

"It's already been reported to the police." Doris threw me a parting smile of satisfaction, "I took down the number of the Land Rover when I saw it hanging around."

"Well done." She'd been a lot quicker than I had, I thought. I only hoped the police would act on it and get Mark's enemies before Mark himself. I was even more desperate to find Mark and tell him what had happened since the break-in. Yet still I had no clue as to where he had gone.

I arrived home to find Tess in the sitting room and lying quite at home on my father's Bokhara carpet. She even wagged her tail at me. She hadn't taken much food but had drunk all her water, which gave me hope the poisons would be washed out in time and against the odds she might recover.

There was a message from Alan on the answerphone inviting me to a concert the following Wednesday and a message, more ominous, from Steve asking me to ring as soon as I got home. He came round then straightaway to say the police had been to his house searching for both Jake and Mark. It was increasingly obvious, as he listed the other raids, that the two hunters had wasted no time in passing on the information they'd gained to the police. But so far, Steve said, neither Mark nor Jake had been found.

"Where are they? Do you know?"

"Jake's gone to ground in some outhouse Pete found. Mark I don't know, but he's bound to surface by Tuesday."

"Why Tuesday?" It seemed too precise a time for someone on the run and I felt on edge again, not knowing, not meant to know. But I wanted to know now.

I wanted, above all, to see Mark, to warn him about the raid and his father, to know he was safe.

"Didn't Mark tell you? There's going to be a raid on the suppliers of cats to DLS at Greenacres Farm."

"Greenacres, that's near Oxford, isn't it?" It was a name that had struck me as a classic misnomer when I'd been in Mark's office. A leaflet with photos taken by an undercover worker had shown rows of cats, far from green acre fields, in narrow, cramped cages like those at DLS. I felt at once a knot of anger as I remembered. How could they do it, take sentient creatures from their natural families, their territory and confine them so they could barely move, then hand them over to torture?

Money was at the root, yes, but there was also callousness, a lack of imagination and self-deception that didn't want to see the cruelty involved. Greenacres—so innocent a name, yet in essence a prison, a hell.

I wanted at once to join the raid, to help cut one artery at least supplying DLS.

Steve told me then there'd be an organised raid and if I wanted to join it, the mini bus, with rescue cages, would be leaving at four in the morning from the Sports Centre bus stop on the outskirts of Horton. He gave me Pete's telephone number and address but warned me not to discuss arrangements on the phone. I was to say I was going to his party and mention a different date. He himself was working that day and couldn't go.

"Do you think Mark will be on the minibus?"

"I can't say, but he'll be at Greenacres, I'm sure. He planned the raid and he's going to see some shareholders afterwards."

"Isn't that rather a risk with the police stepping up the

search? He can hardly hide his face, talking to a shareholder."

"You don't know Mark," Steve said, in the trusting way he had. "He'll do what's needed, what's decided. The risks don't count with him."

Foolhardiness or bravery? I wasn't sure. I was disappointed Mark hadn't confided in me about the coming raid. Did it mean he didn't trust me or merely he'd forgotten, having other things on his mind? It seemed petty to worry about it when there was so much suffering, not only at DLS but so obviously reaching out beyond. But it was important to me that I was trusted by Mark. I was part of the movement now. The means could be debated but I believed in its objectives. Mark had opened my eyes and I didn't want to close them again. I couldn't now. There was too much to do, too much cruelty, too much wrong in our relationships with other species and the natural world, too little time. And Mark was vital with his leadership and tactical skills. We had to make sure, all of us, that he wasn't caught.

I didn't tell Steve all I was thinking. I had noticed him looking a little strained sometimes when I spoke of Mark, as though he was apprehensive or wary of our relationship. So I merely said I would be visiting Mr Stanton in hospital the next day and would ask him if he knew where Mark was. But, first, in the morning I had to put in an appearance at DLS.

"You mean you're going back?" Steve looked alarmed.

"They'll be more suspicious if I don't."

"Maybe, but take care. Their profits are at stake. They won't have taken this lightly."

Steve was right. I arrived at DLS the next morning to

find the compound and entrance hall swarming with police, solemn administration types in grey suits and two extra guards at the entrance gates. One of the policemen checked my name against his list and asked to search my handbag and pockets. Fortunately, I was carrying only a purse and cosmetic bag, nothing incriminating, but was warned I'd be interviewed before leaving.

It was a problem acting as if I were surprised and knew nothing of the break-in. It had been headline news and I should have known, of course, but having decided on the innocent, ignorant approach I had to go through with it.

The receptionist emerged from her usual quiet restraint with an indignant, angry tirade against the whole Animal Rights Movement. "They should all be locked up. They're terrorists, nothing more!"

"Do you know any?" I asked. She looked at me suspiciously then and I had to change tack. "What did they do?"

"Do! What didn't they do? They destroyed the records for a start and stole all the best dogs."

"There must be contingency plans for something like this, surely?"

"Yes, but one doesn't expect the whole security system to be breached, unless it's an inside job."

She gave me a measured look. It was my cue to go.

"I'm sure the police will sort it out," I said, trying to sound confident.

At Section 18 I found Tony Brown stamping around the office with barely suppressed rage. He hadn't been able to use the computer as planned and all the results of the past few weeks had been erased. A fantastic tribute to

Mark's organisation and Martin's expertise but Tony Brown, of course, was never going to see it that way.

His lips were set in a thin line as he challenged me, "What do you know about all this then?"

"About what?" I feigned an innocent, wide-eyed surprise. "I'm sorry, I've been away. I realise something's happened…"

"Happened! It's a bit more than happened! It's criminal entry and destruction." He muttered a series of expletives under his breath, then reached out for a mug of coffee on the table. As his fingers closed over the handle, like the legs of a spider over its prey, I knew he'd do anything he could to ensure his survival.

How much did he suspect me, I wondered? How much was he taken in? More importantly, what influence and contact did Robert have? I hadn't seen him since our encounter at Alan's but any moment he could appear and point an accusing finger. Would he though, if it meant losing Carol's trust and the children?

I needed to get out before I was exposed but had a compulsion to find out more about the next security move and the true extent of the damage we'd inflicted.

My heart raced with excitement and fear. If Tony Brown knew the true extent of my involvement, he'd throttle me, I was sure.

I stared at him for a few moments, uncertain what to say and how to get through the next few hours. To my relief, his mobile rang and I slipped away to the kennels to see the remaining animals we'd been unable to rescue.

They were all older dogs that had been subjected to the extremes of the toxicity tests and were in worse shape even than Tess at her weakest. Two were lying listless, close to death. The other five huddled at the end of their bleak concrete cages, trembling and shivering from the effects of poisons and fear. Blood stained the concrete, the meagre straw and remains of food.

As I thought of Tess lying on the Bokhara carpet, I felt nagging guilt we hadn't managed to rescue them and give them a few hours at least of kindness and relief from their suffering.

Fortunately, Joanna was still on holiday, unaware, I hoped, of what had happened. She would have been one of the first to suspect my involvement and I was only too thankful she wasn't around. Tony, I could hear, from time to time, talking on the phone in tones of crisis and emergency. I was tempted to have a prowl around while he was preoccupied and see if I could discover what the next security arrangements would be. But a low profile seemed wiser with all the extra police and grey suits in evidence and I decided to stay sitting with the dogs, unobserved.

About two hours later Tony appeared at the top of the steps and shouted down to me, "We're packing up for the day. New arrangements are being made."

"You mean I can go now?"

"Yes, but you've got to see the police first. They're interviewing at reception. You have to report there."

"What about the dogs?"

"They're going to be put down. There's no point in keeping them without the tests and they're invalid now."

"But surely they could be found homes?"

"We're a business, not a charity. No one would want them now anyway in their state."

I wanted to shout at him it was all his doing and pump

the poison he'd forced into the dogs into his own fat fingers, so he would know how it felt. But it would be pointless, I knew, to give the game away now, just to vent my feelings. Forcing a smile, I asked him what the work arrangements would be for the next day.

"Report at nine. We'll tell you then."

"Right." I made my way back to reception.

I didn't need to report. One of the policemen was already waiting for me, clearly knowing I was coming.

He had a broad, florid face with a moustache and a deep, peremptory voice I recognised instantly as the voice that had challenged me as I'd tried to leave DLS with Tess on Saturday. I'd had my mask on at the time but how much had I given away in the confrontation? My heart raced as he led me into a small reception room, simply furnished with a table and two chairs, and motioned me to sit down.

"You're well aware, Miss Wilson, I'm sure, of what happened at the weekend. I won't go into details. Suffice it to say that a large number of animals, important for the research here, were stolen and the computer system put out of action. We're interviewing staff to see if they have any helpful information. If you can think of anything you have observed or heard that may be significant in leading us to those responsible, then please let us know."

"Of course." I got up to go but he motioned me to sit down again.

"Regarding your own situation, Miss Wilson, I understand you've only been working here for two weeks."

"That is correct."

"And previous to that?"

"I was working at some kennels in Wales."

"Even though you have a professional teaching qualification?" His eyes were fixed on me now, sceptical, probing. He hadn't wasted his time, I thought. Or had Robert told him? Robert, I realised then, was too angry not to have had a hand in it.

"I haven't been able to get a teaching job."

"So you decided to come to DLS. For what reason, Miss Wilson?"

"The same as any job, to earn a living."

"This isn't any job though, is it, Miss Wilson? This is experimenting on animals. I suggest you are opposed to this and you came here as a spy to help the Animal Rights Movement."

"That's nonsense and you've got absolutely no evidence for it." Or had he?

He proceeded to fire a series of questions about my whereabouts on the night of the break-in and the previous Saturday when Mark and I had reconnoitred the grounds. I hadn't time to invent a good story and automatically fell back on Steve and his mother as an alibi. I knew they'd support me, but had Steve himself been identified?

The sceptical eyes gave nothing away and I couldn't tell if he believed me. I thought probably not. His questions were too pertinent and suddenly he surprised me by producing a photo of Mark. It was an enlargement, obviously selected from a group photograph, grey without clear definition, suggesting nothing of the light in Mark's eyes or his character. But it was Mark all the same and as the eyes looked out at me, I wanted to cry with longing.

"Do you know him?"

I should have answered immediately, but couldn't. I

wanted him too much. And suddenly I knew it was much more serious for Mark than I'd realised. The police were as intent on capturing him as the hunters were and they were going to trap me if they could and use me, blame us both for the break-in.

"Do you know this man, Miss Wilson?" the peremptory voice repeated with an edge now of impatience.

I feigned a return from a daydream.

"I'm sorry," I said. "My mind was elsewhere. No, I don't know him."

It was the only answer to give but I felt oddly guilty as if I was denying Mark's existence and his rightful place in the Animal Rights Movement. Why should he have to go into hiding when he was fighting a just cause? It was Robert and Tony Brown and all the other torturers at DLS who should be the ones in the dock.

"You've never set eyes on him then?"

"Never." And I hadn't in a way, not the false Mark being presented.

"Right." He promptly put the photo back in his file. "When, if, you do see him, you'd be well advised to let us know. Any association with him could be interpreted as aiding him in his criminal activities. Mark Stanton, I need to inform you, Miss Wilson, is wanted not only for the break-in here at DLS but for a number of other incidents relating to the Animal Rights Movement."

He paused, looking at me intently; trying to intimidate me, I guessed. When I didn't respond, he went on, "I suggest you have a think about your situation and its implications, Miss Wilson. A more lenient view may be taken of any involvement proved against you, if you help to catch the main perpetrator. Remember we're here to talk to. If you find you have anything to tell us, you can contact us on this number."

He handed me a card with a telephone number and his name, Det Insp J Rowlinson. The interview was over, if it could be called that. An attempt to trap would be more appropriate terminology. He obviously knew I'd been involved but wanted the greater prize of Mark. Mark who was still elusive and hidden but whom I was more than ever determined to find.

THIRTEEN

I cycled back home, thankful to be out of the suspicious and charged atmosphere at DLS and gave Tess some more of the herbal powder and let her out in the garden. She really seemed to enjoy sniffing at the borders where a fox had visited a couple of nights before. It was a joy to see her taking more interest although she was still very thin, lacking energy and there were still ominous stains of blood on her blanket. It was going to be a long haul and I didn't like leaving her. She tried to follow me each time I went to the front door. But I knew I couldn't keep calling on Steve who had increasing problems with his mother's health. Reluctantly, after some lunch, I settled Tess in her basket and cycled to see Mr Stanton in hospital.

I wasn't sure what I expected to find or what I could achieve. I hardly knew Mr Stanton. He was clearly concerned about Mark but how much did he really know of Mark's activities with the movement? Did he know where Mark was?

It took me a while to find him. The hospital was large and rambling with overworked staff that had little time to deal with enquiries. By a process of elimination, I tracked him down eventually to a ward with three other beds, all occupied by frail elderly men, asleep or dozing.

Mr Stanton, by contrast, was sitting with his left leg stretched out in plaster cast above the bedclothes. He had a pile of forms in front of him and was frowning. I hesitated, wary of disturbing him. Then he looked up and saw me and, to my relief, he smiled.

"I'm glad you came. I had a feeling you would."

"Really?" I felt touched, accepted. There was none of the ice to break I'd feared.

I asked him how he was but he brushed his health aside, saying he'd be home in two days and would soon recover. It was clear his focus was more on Mark than his own disadvantage. He lowered his voice, "Have you heard anything?"

I looked around, following his cue, at the frail, elderly men opposite. I could have almost laughed at their lack of interest, but I whispered my answer, "No, except the police have searched a number of his friends' homes."

"But they haven't found him?"

"Not yet, no." I hesitated. Now that I was close to him, he looked more tired, paler than I remembered and strained. He'd obviously suffered some shock from the fall but I had to know. "What do you think, Mr Stanton? Have you any idea where he might be?"

He looked out of the window and I could see, in his eyes, his mind travelling around the cottage and its surrounding woods and fields. Suddenly I knew, without his speaking, that Mark was in the woods across the stream, on the sheltered bank where we'd first made love. It was the obvious place, the place he knew, could trust from

156

his childhood, sheltered, hidden from prying eyes. Why hadn't I thought of it before?

"It's where you've been," Mr Stanton said at length, turning back to me.

"I know. I've just realised."

"So you'll go and see him?"

"I'll go this evening if I can. If not, tomorrow."

"Be certain no one follows, no one sees. The two men who came to my home are nasty, vicious. Mark needs to be warned."

"I know."

"And tell him I'm sorry."

"Sorry?"

"I shouldn't have opened the door to them. None of this would have happened and he wouldn't have lost his tapes if I'd done as he said and kept it shut."

"I'm sure Mark won't blame you," I tried to reassure him. "These two men are very determined and you can't keep your door barred all the time."

"I know, but tell Mark what I said and ask him please not to take any more risks. He's done all anyone could expect from him and more. Let someone else take over."

"I'll tell him if I can, if I find him."

A few moments later a nurse arrived to prepare Mr Stanton for his consultant's visit. I promised him I'd go and see him again when he was back at the cottage and left.

It was an overcast day but there were still six hours of daylight left and as I cycled to Horton I decided to search for Mark that afternoon.

I phoned Steve and asked him to check on Tess some time in the evening in case I was late back, then I got together some cheese, bread, satsumas and biscuits for Mark and set out for Youlton. I hid my bike just inside the hedge of Mr Stanton's garden, then crossed the fields to the woods as Mark and I had done on our first evening together.

There was no sign of anyone following, no Land Rover on my trail but I was conscious of Mr Stanton's warning about leading the hunters to Mark. I looked back every few minutes, feeling every breeze, every movement in the hedge as a threat. I hid once in a gap in the hedge to see if anyone walked by. I stopped a second time, climbing high on a stile to look in every direction but saw only a few tame pheasants waiting to be shot.

As I entered the wood, I paused and from behind an oak tree looked back along my path. It was then that I saw them, a black retriever and two men following in my track. They had hunters' caps pulled down over their faces. I couldn't see them clearly but I knew who they were and what they wanted, knew I couldn't go on now farther into the wood to find Mark.

I froze for a moment, puzzled how I'd missed them earlier. Where had they come from? I didn't want to turn back and risk a confrontation. It came to me then, with Mr Stanton's plea, that my best course was to divert them, let them think I was leading them to Mark but lead them away.

I turned back towards the edge of the wood, following an easterly direction, instead of south as before, making sure they'd seen me.

So began a long diversion that lasted the rest of the afternoon. The two men followed. I could see them from time to time, could hear the retriever close on my heels.

I knew, like the police, they were interested in Mark, not me. I was afraid all the same of what they might do if they caught up, recognised me from the demo and realised the ruse. I walked as fast as I could but each time I looked back they were nearer.

It seemed an eternity before I completed the detour and reached the main road near Youlton. I felt dizzy, a terrible longing for Mark, just to be near him, to be able to talk to him and feel his arm around me. I couldn't walk any further.

A bus was coming down the road. As I saw the two men emerging from the field over a stile, I signalled the bus down and climbed aboard. One of the men, as I looked back, was shaking his fist at me, in a pretend wave.

At home, I found Steve in the kitchen feeding Tess.

"You look exhausted," he said. "Let me make you some tea."

He insisted I sat down and Tess came and sniffed me, wagging her tail. It was one of those moments when all the strain of the break-in seemed worth it.

"Thanks, Steve, for coming."

"No problem." He handed me a cup of tea. "Did you find Mark?"

"No." I explained about the two hunters and the police. "They're all after him, Steve."

"And you're worried because you haven't found him?"

"I think I know where he is. It's more the fact they're closing in."

"He's been in this situation before, you know."

"But perhaps not as deep. The hunters and police, they're both intent on finding him. The police are saying he's a criminal and the break-in was a criminal activity."

"Which it is, in their eyes."

"In their eyes, yes, but it's not really, is it? How can it be a crime to free animals from torture? It's just a way of viewing which is totally outdated now. We know it's unnecessary now to experiment on animals. We know, when it happens, the results are often dubious."

"We know, yes, if we're interested but we have to persuade and it takes a long time. There's bound to be injustice in the meantime."

"But Mark shouldn't be a victim of injustice, should he? He's one of the people who move things forward, necessary like the suffragettes were, necessary for our future, not only for animals but people as well. We can't let him be caught, Steve."

"He won't be caught if he doesn't want to be."

"But I don't think he knows the danger he's in."

"What do you suggest then?"

"I don't know. He'd probably be safer in another area. Alternatively, he could come here."

"Here?" Steve's voice sharpened with alarm. "Wherever could he hide here?"

"There's a cupboard in my bedroom which Dad built as part of the wall. He could hide in there if they come searching. They'd never find him."

"If he wasn't taken by surprise, which is usually the case. No, it's too much of a risk for you. You could be charged for aiding and abetting. You shouldn't even think about it." It was the most emphatic statement I'd heard Steve make and I was taken by surprise.

"But I thought you admired Mark and wanted to help."

"I do, but not if it means damaging you."

"I wouldn't be damaged by him, Steve." I wanted to

tell Steve how much I loved Mark and needed to be with him, no matter what happened, but Steve's eyes had darkened into an expression that didn't want to know. We sat in silence for a while and I was aware of a distance between us that hadn't been there before.

Steve said at length," I'll have to get back to Mother soon. If you need a lift first, I'll take you back to Youlton."

"If it's not too much trouble, thanks."

"You won't know what to do, will you, until you've found him?"

Steve ran his hand over Tess's head and down her spine as if pouring into her some vital feeling of his own and I sensed Tess responding, looking up at him with more trusting eyes as if she'd turned a corner with him.

We spoke only of Tess as we drove out to Youlton. It was already seven and I hadn't much time if I was to search in daylight. As I climbed out of the car, Steve took my arm,

"You must do what you think best. I don't want to see you hurt. That's all."

"I know."

"I'll be around if you want me."

"Thanks, and thanks for bringing me."

I could still hear Steve's words as I retraced my steps to the wood. I knew I'd alienated and hurt him and there was a wedge now in the openness we'd had between us. Although we'd never committed ourselves to more than friendship, I felt in a strange way I'd betrayed him. But I knew I could never feel for him as I felt for Mark. It was Mark I loved, Mark I had to find.

The light was fading as I entered the wood for a second time that day. I waited a good fifteen minutes to ensure

161

the hunters were not on my trail again. A fox came sniffing the path with sharp eyes and nostrils, then ran as it caught wind of me. Nothing else stirred and I pressed on while I could still see.

After another half an hour and a couple of wrong turnings I reached the stream. I waited, straining my ears for the tell-tale snap of twigs, the crunch of leaves, but all I could hear was the surging and gurgling water of the stream at my feet. Then I jumped as Mark had shown me, onto the opposite bank, and climbed up onto the open patch of moss and grass between the trees.

I stood looking around, but there was no sign of Mark. Then, in the gathering darkness I noticed the ridge of a small green tent enclosed within a circular clump of bushes. Cautiously, I crept forward and quietly called Mark's name but there was no reply from within the tent or outside. The opening flap, carefully concealed by a branch, had been pegged down and I concluded Mark had already left for another hideout or destination. It occurred to me then he might have left a message. I extracted the peg, pulled back the flap, and shone the torch inside. To my amazement, he lay enclosed in a sleeping bag, fast asleep, his face darkened with unshaven growth.

"Mark."

He didn't answer and I had a terrible fear for a moment he had already been found by the hunters.

"Mark."

I touched his forehead. It was hot and bathed in sweat. As he opened his eyes and looked dazed into the torchlight, I could see he was feverish.

"It's all right. It's only me, Kate," I tried to reassure him as he started to struggle out of his sleeping bag.

"What time is it?" He felt with his left arm over the ground sheet to a patch of grass and grasped a water bottle. He drank as if he hadn't drunk for weeks, draining the bottle dry.

"Can you get me some more?" He held out the bottle.

"From the stream you mean?"

"Where else?"

"Are you sure it's safe?"

"Safe or not, that's all there is."

"I've got some orange here." I undid the parcel of food I'd carried and offered him some bread and cheese but all he wanted was the drink.

He started to shiver as I poured the orange into a cup I'd brought. I wanted to tell him we'd go to my place and I'd look after him, but he clearly wasn't up to such a journey nor would it be safe, or wise, with the police still searching. The only solution was to bring some medicine here to reduce the fever.

"What day is it?" he asked.

"It's Monday, Monday evening."

"I'll have to get moving tomorrow."

"Moving where?"

"Oxford. We've got our crucial raid there early on Wednesday and shareholders to see."

"You can't go, Mark. You've got a fever. Besides..." I hesitated, not wanting to alarm him.

"Besides what?" He shivered again, spilling some orange juice on his sleeping bag. I took it from him and urged him to go deeper into his bag to keep warm; irritated with myself I hadn't thought to bring any paracetamol or aspirin.

He lay back at last, his face gaunt and pale in the

torchlight, and I wondered when he'd last eaten. I didn't want to tell him about the burglary and his father, but I knew he'd want to know, that the truth and facts mattered to him.

"The police are out looking for you, Mark, as you know. They've been to Pete and Steve's and your father. The two hunters have been too. Your father's now in hospital. They broke in to take some of your tapes. In trying to stop them, your father fell and broke his leg."

"You've seen my father?"

"Yes and he's on the mend. He'll be all right but he's asked me to tell you not to take any more risks."

"What? After what those bastards have done?"

"He's more concerned about you, Mark. He thinks you should lie low and wait till things have quietened down a bit."

"And get some conventional safe job, I suppose."

"He didn't say that."

"No, but it's what he thinks."

"He's got a point though about lying low. You won't be able to do anything if they catch you. I doubt they'll let you out on bail."

"True but I can't leave things now. It's vital we act while DLS is down. We have to close the suppliers as well as DLS itself. We have to get the last few shareholders on board. The real push is now. If we don't push now, DLS will revive and all the torture with it."

"Does it have to involve you though? Apart from the danger, you're ill."

"I'll sleep it off. It'll be gone tomorrow."

"Why are you taking the blame anyway?" I persisted. "It was Jake, wasn't it, who assaulted the police?"

"He was responding to police assault when he rescued a tortured dog. I don't call that assault. We're all in it anyway together. Jake can't be made the only one responsible. Without Jake we wouldn't have got to where we are. His knowledge has been vital for every raid."

"He's a bit extreme though, isn't he?" I wondered if Mark realised how jealous Jake was or was he trying not to realise? He looked so drained and tired, I wanted to take him in my arms and carry him home, an impossible feat, I knew. I switched off the torch, leaned over and kissed him.

"I love you," I said.

His hand reached up to me, touching my cheek. "I love you too," he said.

"There isn't someone else?"

"Not now." His hand flopped down again and he was quiet. Switching the torch on, I saw he'd closed his eyes and was drifting off to sleep again.

I waited beside him for an hour then walked back through the woods to Youlton. I decided I would go back the next day as soon as possible with the appropriate medicine to help him get well again.

It was very dark under the trees and I stumbled into the stream, despite the torchlight, and tore my jeans on thorns. Twice I lost my way back to the field path to Youlton. I was afraid the hunters were still lurking, waiting. I was concerned about Mark's fever. Yet his words of love had given me hope and I felt renewed, strengthened by his determination to finish, for good, the torture at DLS. However ill he felt, he wasn't going to give up his objective. Would he succeed though or were the forces established against him, stronger, more wily?

FOURTEEN

I awoke next morning wondering whether to show my face again at DLS. Both Robert and the police were clearly suspicious. It wouldn't be long before Tony B joined the band. Yet to stay away would be admitting to fear and guilt, and I wanted to investigate any new security arrangements and find, if possible, another entrance for Mark. It could well be my final chance. I decided to risk Robert exposing me.

I arrived at the main gate to find two security guards checking all entrants by car, foot and bike. The code to enter the offices and kennels had been changed and I had to wait until I was checked in. None of us were given a new entry code. We were handed, instead, a list of various meetings. The first one, for all staff, was at nine-thirty to hear an announcement by Robert in the main lecture hall.

At Section 18, Tony Brown was even more disgruntled than the day before, flapping about like a helpless penguin because he could no longer use his computer. There were only six dogs left to attend to. The others, he informed me, had been put down. Just before nine-thirty he locked the office door and ordered me to Robert's meeting.

The hall was crowded; I hadn't realised so many people worked at DLS. There must have been at least six hundred people, from suited admin types and white-coated technicians like Tony to cleaners in blue overalls, crammed together; all smoked from their recesses by fear and concern for their jobs.

As I sat at the back of the hall, ready to make a quick exit, I could hear expressions of anger against the Animal Rights Movement mixed with worry about the future of DLS. No one looked happy, or at ease.

Robert was already ensconced on the stage, flanked by two security men and the assistant director of research. He looked pale, tired and nervous even from my distance. I bent my head, hoping he hadn't seen me but as he rose to speak, I was sure he was focussing in my direction, seeking me out.

"All of you will know," he began, "about what happened last weekend. I won't go into all the details. Suffice it to say that two-thirds of our animals have been stolen. These can be replaced, but not so easily our records. Records, vitally important and necessary for our research, were destroyed last weekend by interference with our main frame computer.

"I don't need to tell you how important our research is into cancer, heart disease and more recently Alzheimer's. We have built up a deservedly excellent name for ourselves in these spheres. Many lives have been saved by our efforts. All of you will have friends and relations whose lives have benefited from our work.

"The onslaught here by the Animal Rights Movement on Saturday night was, and still is, a deliberate attack against society itself. As a society, we cannot allow ourselves to be bullied in this way. As a firm, we cannot let ourselves be damaged and destroyed. We are necessary, vitally necessary for the nation's health, and advances in medical knowledge.

"If we just sit back without retaliating, we will be giving in to mob rule and terrorism, for this is what the members of the Animal Rights Movement are, a band of terrorists, which could set back our knowledge for years.

"We are determined, therefore, not to give in to them, nor let ourselves be intimidated. With the help of the police, we are going to do everything possible to track down those responsible for this recent outrage, so they can be put where they can no longer do harm.

"The police are conducting an investigation. It is hoped there will soon be arrests and charges brought."

Robert was looking directly at me now, warning, it seemed, telling me the search for Mark would be relentless. What a lot of rubbish he talked, I thought. The toxicity tests on poor Tess and the other beagles had nothing to do with the nation's health but a washing powder for commercial gain. Tests on animals anyway had been proved repeatedly to be grossly misleading for human health. I wanted to stand up and shout "bullshit", expose the falsity of his claims.

"What's the matter?" Tony muttered in my ear.

"Matter?"

"You look wound up."

"Do I? Well, it makes one angry, doesn't it, stopping the research?"

"We cannot let vital research be terminated by mob rule"—Robert was bringing his homily to an end— "Whatever these terrorists and ignorant activists do, we will not be defeated. I ask all of you to resist this menace and co-operate with all your strength and resilience to keep DLS going.

"Our security arrangements, both for entry and exit, are currently being reassessed, redesigned and reinforced to prevent a recurrence. Your section managers will be holding meetings to explain the new arrangements and decide the best arrangements for each department. Meanwhile, thank you all for coming."

The rallying call to the faithful and they rallied, smiling, determined, as they streamed from the hall, no longer downcast.

"So what did you think of it?" Tony asked, unlocking the office at Section 18.

"He said what needed to be said, I suppose," I answered cautiously.

"But you're not convinced?"

"I didn't say that."

"No, but you think it, don't you? You think this place will crumble because a few nutcases with nothing better to do have broken in and made an impact." His eyes slithered, trying to find vulnerable flesh for his fangs.

"I don't know enough about it," I hedged.

"Don't you? I think you do," he sneered and I began to feel trapped, afraid. How much did he know? How much had Robert told him?

I considered bluffing my way out with a show of anger to challenge his accusation but it could all too easily backfire. His position was stronger than mine and he knew it. I didn't anyway want a showdown until I'd found an alternative entry to rescue the remaining animals. Clearly the main exit was now impossible.

I knew there was an emergency exit in the kennels where the storage section and dustbins were, but it had always been blocked by sacks of food and I'd never properly investigated. There'd never been the need but clearly there was now. Would I be able to though?

Tony was watching me, not letting me out of his sight all the morning, even when he was on his mobile, as I tended to the last six dogs. I had the sense of his waiting for some signal and felt apprehensive, on edge.

At noon, to my relief, a message arrived asking him to go to a meeting of technicians. I waited five minutes, in case he came back on some pretext, then crept into the storage section.

It was a small, dark, rectangular section, relying on neon lighting from the kennels. To the right were large, black plastic containers where we deposited sweepings and soiled sawdust. To the left were sacks of dried food and sawdust stacked nearly to the ceiling. One of the sacks of food at the bottom had split open and mice droppings trailed over the scatter on the floor.

I couldn't see if there was a door behind the sacks but it seemed the only likely place and I set about pulling the sacks down and moving them. There were at least forty. The sawdust was easy, but the food sacks were heavy and at least two more split open, releasing yet more dried food onto the floor. It was a good fifteen minutes before I'd removed the sacks to see there was indeed a door, a small metal door, half the height of the other doors in the building, with a bracket hinge allowing it to swing both ways. It was secured with two bolts.

The problem was how to leave the bolts open for Mark whilst stopping the door from swinging outwards and acting as a beacon to attract any wandering security guards. Improvising, I pulled back the bolts and wedged some newspaper in the jamb. I then stacked a layer of sacks a few inches from the door so Mark, pushing on the door and dislodging the paper, would just be able to squeeze inside. It might not work, I realised, with the weight of the other sacks on top but I could think of no other way, nor had the time to be more inventive. Any minute Tony would return and I couldn't afford to be exposed and let Mark down. As fast as possible, I re-stacked the rest of the sacks on top of the first layer. Sweat streamed down my forehead, my back and thighs from fear and effort before I'd finished. I felt nauseous, drained but didn't care. I'd made it.

I was just sweeping up the scatter of food when I heard movement on the steps leading to the kennels. The next moment Tony was striding the concrete corridor, between the kennels, towards me.

"What are you doing?" he demanded.

"I noticed some of the bags were split," I said. "I thought I'd sweep up in case we attracted mice."

"A few mice won't hurt us. They're not dangerous, not like moles which worm their way into an organisation."

"Meaning?"

"Meaning, you're sacked! I've just had a meeting with Robert Sykes and he wants you out. There's no more work for you so you're redundant."

"I see." It was pointless I knew to challenge or ask the real reason. I could well get more than I bargained for. It was obvious anyway there wasn't going to be work for some time and if we had our way, never. "Well, I'll be off then."

I handed Tony the broom and looked at the six dogs cowering at the back of their cages, wishing I could take them with me. I doubted they'd last until Mark's rescue.

"Your P45 will be sent to you and whatever, if anything, is owing."

"Good." I climbed the steps, afraid of what I'd say if I stayed longer. I spoke to no one on the way out and no one spoke to me, or said goodbye. It was a soulless end to a soulless place and I was only too glad to be out of it.

Cycling home, I began to reflect on Robert's action. I suppose I'd known all along he was too angry not to retaliate. Had he proof, though, of my involvement and what was he planning next? What were the police up to and how much did they keep Robert informed? Why had Robert defied my threat to tell Carol about his mistress if he wasn't confident of some kind of coup?

Well, we could both play the game of betrayal. I was free now, I reckoned, to pass on my information to Carol.

But as I stopped outside Carol's house, seeing her car, I suddenly thought of what her reaction might be, of the problem of actually telling her, raising the matter abruptly out of the blue, and I realised I couldn't. I was ill-prepared and in a sense had no right, despite Robert's behaviour. I would leave it, I decided, until I'd thought things through.

Back at home, I fed Tess and let her out into the garden. Then I collected together paracetamol, cheese and rolls for Mark. I was just packing them ready to take to the woods when the doorbell rang and I found, to my surprise, Carol on the doorstep.

"Have you got a few minutes?" She was agitated, her eyes reddened by crying.

"Of course, come in." Forgetting Tess, I led her through

to the kitchen. As I put on the kettle, Tess came in from the garden. I waited with dread for Carol to ask the crucial question but, to my amazement, she didn't even seem to notice her. Her eyes were fixed on the kettle, as if she was trying to find some meaning in its shape. She had dark pouches of tiredness, like bruising, beneath her eyes and, uncharacteristically for Carol, was wearing no makeup.

"You don't look too well," I said. I made her coffee and urged her into the sitting room, shutting the door on Tess.

"I'm all right." Tense and upright, she sat on the edge of the settee. "I'm sorry coming like this. I can't stay long. I've got to pick the children up early today."

"Would you like me to?" I wondered if she was sickening for the fever Mark had.

"No, it's all right. I'll manage. I…" Suddenly she started to cry, a deep gasping kind of crying as if she was trying to get her breath, grasp a meaning.

I'd never seen Carol cry before and was taken aback, uncertain how to react. She'd always been so in control, the one who knew what direction to take, what to do.

"I'm sorry, I've had a bit of a shock."

I knew then she knew about Robert and I went and sat beside her, waiting. It came out in stabs, like the prick of a needle, each time penetrating further. A series of hints, she'd noticed, with the secretary next door, absences growing longer, times unaccounted for. Then the previous day she'd arrived home unexpectedly and found them together in her bed, their own bedroom.

"Yesterday? But I thought Robert was involved in the crisis at DLS." I stared at her, unable to believe Robert had found the time.

"So he was or supposed to be." A hint of bitterness crept into her voice. "But he still managed his bit on the side or rather she managed him."

"It may be only fleeting," I said. I couldn't think of anything else to say. Robert was a bastard on all counts, as far as I was concerned but I wasn't sure it would help Carol to hammer this view.

"Fleeting for whom?" she asked. "He's betrayed his family, the children and me. I could never look at him with trust again."

"That's understandable."

"Is it? I'm not sure. I'm not sure of anything, any more. And I feel bad. I'm supposed to be working on this holiday course. I just couldn't face it. I said I had flu. I've never lied like that before."

"Because you've never had time off before. You've always put the college first, Carol. But you need it now, deserve it after all you've done."

"Do you really think so?"

"Yes, I do." I put my arm round her, less hesitant now.

"It's not clear though what I should do."

"Don't do anything then, for the moment. Robert will in any case have to provide, for the children, I mean."

"If he can." Carol looked sceptically at her mug of coffee. "DLS is heading for trouble by all accounts."

"You have your own job though," I reminded her. "You're not entirely dependent." I didn't want to be drawn into a discussion on DLS. I didn't doubt what Mark was doing was right but I could hardly justify it to Carol in her present state. There were always effects more complicated than one wanted.

"No, there is that," Carol conceded. She stood up to

go. "How about you? Have you had any luck on the job front yet?"

"Not yet, no." DLS was behind me now so I could truthfully say I hadn't any employment.

"You should take up with Alan, you know," Carol said, calmer now as she moved to the door. "He likes you and he's a really nice guy. He'd look after you."

I felt like suggesting she should take up with him, she was the one needing a shoulder but it wasn't the right moment.

When she'd gone, I waited until Steve arrived home, and then told him about Mark. His mother had a friend visiting in the evening so he said he'd come with me to the wood in case I needed help.

He unearthed an old stretcher he had in his garage and together with medicine and food, we set off in the early evening. I checked carefully no one was following and we reached the bank where Mark had been camping within half an hour whilst it was still light. But there was no sign, to my concern, of the tent between the bushes. No sign of Mark himself, no message.

I stared at the flattened, discoloured grass where the tent had been, numb and bewildered that Mark could have moved and uprooted himself so soon in the state he was in the previous night. Or had he been driven? Had the hunters at last found him and flushed him out? There was no sign though of a scuffle, no tins, bits of paper, cartons left behind in haste.

"I can't understand it," I said.

"He must have decided to leave early for Oxford," Steve stated matter-of-factly.

"But he was ill, Steve."

"That hasn't stopped him before."

"But to go without leaving a message even…"

"You don't get it, do you? Mark doesn't conform in this way. One can't tie him down with expectation. He acts in the way he feels best for the cause. You have to accept that."

""Do I?"

I felt suddenly shaky, a nausea creeping up again. Then the bushes where the tent had been were spinning and Mark was a fox fleeing from the hunters.

"We've got to help him, Steve."

"We will." Taking my arm, Steve made me sit on the riverbank and gave me some of the orange and paracetamol and the bread and cheese we'd brought for Mark. "We will," he repeated, "but we won't do it by staying here. Come on. Let's go. The minibus leaves at four in the morning and you need to get some sleep if you're going to be on it."

FIFTEEN

I was woken the next morning by Tess licking my hand. She had come all the way upstairs, a remarkable achievement considering her state, and I couldn't resist making a fuss of her.

It was only then, looking at my bedside clock, I remembered the minibus and realised I'd slept through the alarm. In a frantic rush, I dressed and ran all the way to the pick up point to see the rear lights of the minibus receding up the hill out of Horton. It hadn't gone early. It had waited ten minutes. I had only myself to blame. I waved my arms in the hope of catching attention, and then feebly burst into tears.

As if the elements were in sympathy, it started to rain. Fortunately the bus stop still had a few panes of glass unvandalised and I sat on its multi-scratched and carved wooden bench wondering whether to hitch a lift or go home. There was no way I'd ever get to Greenacres in time by public transport.

I'd had no breakfast, or even a drink and feeling nauseous and dizzy again, I decided to go home. I was just leaving the bus stop when I saw car headlights coming towards me.

As it neared, the vehicle slowed. It was still dark and I couldn't see the make or who was inside and was immediately wary. I backed further onto the pavement, as the car stopped. A window wound down and a voice called, "Want a lift?"

The voice sounded familiar, but I didn't recognise in the shade of the car's dashboard the broad-faced man with short fair hair leaning forward.

"You've missed the minibus, haven't you?"

Something in the disgruntled intonation clicked then. It was Jake's voice but Jake with a new outer persona.

"It seems like it." I couldn't see anyone else in the car and hesitated on the pavement, remembering the night of the meeting at Mark's father's cottage.

"Well, do you want a lift or not?"

"I was thinking of going home."

"Why? Are you afraid I'm going to rape you or something?" His voice had taken on the challenging sneer he used when things weren't going his way.

"It's got nothing to do with you. I'm hungry!"

"Well, if that's the only problem, feel free." He bent down, then dangled a packet of rolls for me to see. "Eat while you ride. You want to be in on the action, don't you?"

"Of course."

"Well, you won't help by standing there."

And he was right. I wouldn't and I wouldn't see Mark and be able to help him if he needed it, or know what happened.

"You're going straight to Greenacres?"

"I'm hardly likely to be driving all over the country with the pigs after me, am I? For Christ's sake, get in or we'll never get there."

As I climbed into the passenger seat, he revved up the engine and we were away up the hill. It was still dark and I couldn't see the condition of the car but it felt and smelled old, damp and decayed. There was also, I suspected, a lingering odour of the mangled beagle's body Jake had theatrically exposed at the demo.

We ate the rolls in silence. They were stale, without fillings, but they calmed my nausea and I began to feel better.

I noticed Jake glancing at his wing mirror every few minutes whilst he leaned tensely forward over the steering wheel. I needn't have worried about any designs on me; he clearly had other things on his mind.

"Have you seen Mark?" I asked.

"Not since Saturday."

"Do you know where he is?"

"No idea. Why? Afraid he won't turn up, are you?" The familiar sneer had crept in again and my earlier unease returned.

"Not afraid, just concerned." I tried to keep my voice steady. I was more than concerned. I kept thinking of Mark staggering across country, sleeping in hedges. He should have stayed on the bank. Why hadn't he? Why? My head spun with tiredness and questions needing answers.

A car overtook us at speed, followed by a police car flashing it to stop. They disappeared in the distance and I heard Jake mutter with relief.

I started nodding as Jake turned into a country lane before the outskirts of Oxford. I had an impression of a maze of high hedges like old men frowning, sheltering their past. Then the warmth of the car beguiled me and I fell asleep.

I awoke with a start some twenty minutes later to feel a cool breeze on my face. The car had stopped. Jake was no longer in the seat beside me but moving something in the boot. The sky had lightened and we were in a glade or wood. Ferns brushed my legs as I opened the car door. I noticed Jake carefully putting a box in a sports bag. Then seeing me, he hurriedly closed the boot.

"What's happening? Where are we?" I asked. He looked preoccupied but I was still wary.

"We're leaving the car here." Without further explanation, he locked the car and positioning his bag cautiously over his shoulder, started walking along a track to the lane. If I'd known what was in the bag then, I'd have kept my distance. As it was, I was only too relieved he'd kept his and made no advances.

We walked for about twenty minutes along the lane then across some fields. In the grey early light then I saw a black and white thatched farmhouse with a white gate and well tended garden.

"Is this Greenacres?"

"The innocent face. The dirty work's behind. Come on, or we'll be late!"

Jake led the way across two more fields and around to the back of the farmhouse. I could see what he meant then; a range of four bleak concrete sheds stretched to a copse beyond. As we reached the trees, a lean figure in black emerged signalling us to keep quiet and come further. It was Pete.

"The others have started on the first shed," he said. "I'll show you where the cages are."

He led us through the copse to a field on the other side and out through a gate to the lane beyond. Here, hidden by a high hedge, two lorries were waiting, together with the minibus I'd missed.

An assortment of cages was stacked in the back of both lorries with some cats already in two of them. Pete reached up to the first lorry and handed us empty cages.

"Try to keep the cats in families," he warned, "and don't let any escape. They'll have problems feeding themselves and we've homes lined up."

As he spoke, Jason, whom I'd seen briefly at the meeting at Mark's father's house, jumped down from the driver's seat.

"Has Mark come yet?" he asked.

"Not yet," Pete said.

"You mean Mark's not here?" I stared at Pete.

"He's had problems," Pete said matter-of-factly," with transport."

"I see." My heart sank. I'd never visualised Mark not being here and had to force myself to follow Pete to the copse. Figures in black, with black balaclavas, passed us running with cages. I recognised the voices of Martin, Karl and Gemma greeting us but the only voice I wanted to hear was Mark's. Where was he? What had happened to him?

"We'll start on the second shed," Pete said. "Dawn's already unlocked the padlocks."

"How did she do it?"

"Copies of duplicate keys from undercover." Pete handed me a balaclava and put one on himself.

Like the kennels at DLS, the sheds at Greenacres had no windows, no external lighting. As we pushed open the metal door of the second shed and switched on the neon lighting, we saw the same dismal scene familiar from DLS.

Iron cages, with concrete floors, lining a concrete pathway through the shed. Cages without stimuli, comfort, hiding place, only minimum straw. There was a strong smell of urine.

The cats, not yet tortured, were more alert and trusting than the dogs at DLS. Curious to see us at such an hour, bright-eyed they padded to the front bars of the cages. Most were tabbies with number tabs on their ears.

Then I noticed four cages at the end of the passage, where some older cats were stretched out, suckled by kittens some three or four days old. They looked exhausted and barely lifted their heads. One with tortoiseshell markings had the same numbed inertia I'd seen with Tess and I decided to take her first. She scarcely responded as I lifted and lay her on some sacking in the cage I carried. Then, one by one, I picked up her seven kittens and put them inside with her. One was so bony and small I was afraid he would slip through the bars so I carried him in my hand.

I hurried to the two lorries where Jason loaded each cage and handed us an empty one.

Backwards and forwards we went for the next hour, fleeting figures in black, loading the vehicles from the first three sheds. Unlike the dogs at DLS, the cats were fortunately quiet in response and we managed to get to the lorries each time without incident, unnoticed.

Then at five-thirty the dog in the farmhouse started barking. Almost immediately a light went on in an upstairs window. It was the signal to leave.

But there were still twenty cages at least from the fourth, the last shed, to be rescued. Martin was all for leaving them and pressing on with what we had but Pete wanted to take more and I agreed with him. There were some beautiful cats still of only three to four months and I couldn't bear the thought of them being left to the mercy of DLS for the sake of some pointless product we could all do without.

It was agreed Martin would drive away the first lorry load and take the cats straight to Philippa for distribution to the allotted homes. Jason would wait with the second lorry for the cats from Pete and myself. Pete would then drive the minibus bus back to Horton.

For ten minutes Pete and I kept at it while the dog continued to bark in the farmhouse.

Then, as I was in the shed lifting out one of the two month old kittens for my final load to follow Pete, the metal door of the shed was thrust open. An elderly, burly man, with a grey moustache, stood in the doorway pointing a shotgun at me. Beside him stood an equally stout woman with fuzzy blonde hair, in a housecoat, with a camera in her hand. As I looked back startled with the kitten in my hand, I heard the camera click. Then the woman shouted to someone called George, urging him to come and help.

The elderly man, meanwhile, continued to point the gun at me, as I stood mesmerised with the kitten still in my hand. I felt in some obscure way our fates were intertwined, that if I held onto her, I would get out of the situation unscathed. It was illogical, of course. The elderly man, the farmer, I presumed, had the upper hand and property rights to back him. More ominously with the gun, he was looking angry, very angry, as if about to explode.

I heard running footsteps then, a clang as the door

jerked open and a younger man of the same build entered the shed. He had no moustache, no gun but muscles in lieu and steel grey eyes.

"What do you want me to do with her?" he demanded.

"Take her to the house and lock her in the dairy. Go and see who else is about then. I'm going over to Jim to phone the police. They've cut the line."

As the elderly man and the woman withdrew, the younger strode to where I was crouching with the kitten. Quickly I slipped the kitten in my jacket pocket and pulled up the zip. He didn't seem to notice nor did the other cats concern him. His objective was to get me out of there and into the dairy, which he proceeded to do unceremoniously with force, bending back my arms so that I felt any minute they'd be wrenched from their sockets. The pain was excruciating and I cried out as he kicked me from behind while pushing me out into the yard.

Outside, he pulled off my balaclava and eyed me a moment as if he couldn't quite make up his mind. Then he spat with contempt.

"So they send bitches now to do their dirty work, do they? Well you'd better not be on heat, my lovely, or you'll get more than you bargained for. Thought you'd come and wreck our livelihood, did you? Well, we'll soon see about that. You'll not be wanting to do this again by the time we've finished with you."

He gripped my shoulders, spun me round and kneed me in the back, pushing me towards the house. I felt waves of pain and nausea again and knew I'd got to get away. I twisted as he momentarily relaxed his hold, then bent my head and bit into his hairy hand. Then raising my right leg, I kneed him hard in the groin. He gave a shout, which alarmed me, but it worked. He let go and I started running as fast as I could back past the bleak ugly sheds to the copse.

But he clearly knew the lie of the land better than I did and was upon me before I reached the last shed. He brought me down on the concrete, fastened himself astride and started banging my head. I thought I was going to pass out. I could feel his weight crushing my hips, blood seeping down my neck. Then suddenly the weight was gone, the banging stopped and he was lying on his side groaning. A figure in black, with a black balaclava was bending over me, lifting me up.

"He's out for the count now. Don't worry. We're going. You're safe."

I didn't need to look at the eyes looking down at me. I knew the voice too well. It was Mark.

So great was my relief I can't remember fully the sequence of what happened next. I recall Mark carrying me to the minibus, then Pete and Jason applying pressure to stop the bleeding. I remember unzipping my pocket and drawing out the little kitten, to my surprise unharmed, and handing it to Jason for the lorry. Then Jake, whom I'd hardly seen during the rescue, arrived telling us he was going to delete the records from the farm office. By delete, we assumed he meant an operation similar to the one we'd effected at DLS by incapacitating the computer. I remember thinking it was a good idea and seeing Jake plod rather pedantically through the copse and past the dismal sheds to the farmhouse.

There was a long silence in which we lost sight of him. Then we saw him running, zigzagging like a hare across two fields to the west of the copse, towards the wood where he'd left his car. He was still running, when three minutes later, there was a great explosion, which shook even the minibus and a whole wing of the farmhouse collapsed and went up in flames.

"My God! That's done it. The fool!" Mark stared in dismay at the farmhouse.

We all did. It was as if our very plans had gone up in flames, an outcome never intended, one we knew at once would bring horror and condemnation, not the support we wanted.

"Come on. We've got to get out of here and fast," Pete urged. We ran, for all we were worth, across the field to the lane. Jason leapt into the lorry cab and Pete took over the minibus as Mark and I clambered inside.

Pete drove like a maniac then, weaving in and out of country lanes, twisting and turning every time we heard what sounded remotely like a police siren. Eventually he stopped by a farm gate in a country lane some twelve miles away.

"Now what?" Pete swung around from the driver's seat, focusing on Mark. His eyes were bright set, hard with anger.

Mark had taken off his balaclava. The muscles of his face were corded, tense, as if he was determined to deal with the situation but he still looked ill, pale and strained. His forehead was beaded with sweat.

"I think we should go and see the shareholders as planned, then lie low for a while," he said.

"I don't mean our physical direction," Pete said. "I mean mentally, our general direction, where we go from here. He's blown it for us this time, this protégéð of yours."

"He's not my protégé, Pete. He's just a member, like

the rest of us, concerned to put an end to this beastly trade."

"And he's just about put an end to us now by his actions. We're all going to be branded with his brush now, a terrorist willing to bomb, to kill."

"He's gone too far, using explosives, I agree."

"Why didn't you stop him? Surely you knew what was in his mind?"

"I didn't, in fact. If I had, I'd have tried to stop him."

"Someone must have known," Pete asserted.

It dawned on me then that the someone was me. I should have been far more suspicious about the way Jake was acting with his bag and the boot of the car. I felt angry then like Pete that Jake had persuaded me into a car that could at any minute explode.

"He should have been booted out weeks ago," Pete continued. "The way he behaved at the demo was for his own aggrandisement not the cause. He's always been in it for himself, not from genuine concern. He's a terrorist basically, looking for a cause."

"That's not quite fair, Pete," Mark said. "He's been very useful to us at times."

"But he's not any longer. He's got to be thrown out and disowned. He's done huge damage now. People will focus on the bomb, not our real objectives and all the cruelty involved. We've got to get it into the press this was an isolated person with an agenda of this own, not a genuine member of the Animal Rights Movement."

"All right, I'll have a go but there're more essential things to do first."

"Which are?" Pete demanded. He was like a terrier now, not willing to let go.

"The last three shareholders with a significant amount of shares in DLS. I need to see them before they hear about Greenacres."

"You really think," Pete persisted, "they'll give up their precious money now with little more to lose?"

"We have to try," Mark said. His voice was becoming increasingly strained. He needed bed not a grilling.

"What about the final raid?" Pete asked.

"I was coming to that. We need a venue to sort out the plans."

"Well, it can't be my place this time," Pete said. "The pigs have already been around twice, looking for you and Jake. The same goes for Martin and Gemma and presumably your father's."

"Yes," Mark agreed. "We need somewhere new."

"You could come to my house," I offered. I spoke without thinking of the implications, the problems involved. It was Mark, of course, I wanted, not the meeting. The meeting was merely a means to be with him, to have him near.

"Are you sure?" Mark said. "There'll be ten at least. Coming into a terrace house, they'll be seen."

"They can come over the back wall," I said.

"Okay, if you're sure. What do you think, Pete?"

"Fine, if she wants us."

It was agreed we'd all meet at my house on the following Friday to plan the final raid on DLS the following week. Pete, meanwhile, was still angry about Jake. He declined to go with Mark to see any shareholders but said he'd drive him into Oxford and collect him later. Wary of the minibus being detected, he spattered the number plate with mud and drove to the Park and Ride.

"Would you like to come?" Mark turned to me then.

"Yes, yes, I would." I'd no idea what to say to the shareholders. I doubted I'd be much use at all, but I wanted to be with Mark and share what mattered to him.

At the Park and Ride, we went into some toilets to spruce ourselves up, Mark emerging, surprisingly, in a conventional shirt and trousers with his hair swept back.

"Corporate man, I see," I teased.

"Not at heart but it works." He smiled but his eyes were alert, uneasy as we walked down the hill into Oxford and across to the Banbury Road.

In retrospect, it was incredibly brazen of us seeking out shareholders and exposing ourselves after being on the site of an explosion. Who would believe that we hadn't intended it that way? Who would care about the cats when violence was an issue? I kept thinking about the kittens and hoping they would be safe in their new homes. I kept worrying about Mark. It was an enormous risk he was taking and he knew it but he was an idealist at heart and the cause, as I was to learn to my cost, mattered to him more than comfort and the confines of a safe personal life.

"I want to see DLS consigned to dust before I'm caught," he said.

SIXTEEN

R ight! Here goes."
We were standing outside a late Victorian house in the Banbury Road that had seen better days. There was moss along the damp course; the windowsills were peeling and the curtains hanging at the castle turret styled windows had a tired, limp appearance.

Mark pressed the bell next to the name of a shareholder, Gilda Summers, on the ground floor and then stepped backwards onto the gravel path, expectantly watching the door. Unlike the windowsills, it had been newly painted a dark forest green. But, as if the paint had sealed it, it remained firmly shut with no sound of movement coming from inside. It was the usual story, I suspected, of everyone out working. Mark pressed the bell a second time.

We were about to give up when we heard a chain rattling behind the door, which opened a few inches to reveal the face of an elderly lady peering at us. She had silvery white hair drawn back into a bun, olive-coloured skin and deep wrinkles carved like knife marks down her cheeks and across her forehead. She was old, very old, in her late eighties I guessed but her eyes were young, open, alert, not myopic as they often are at her age.

"What do you want?" she asked. Her voice was deep like a man's. "I'm afraid I can't buy anything from you."

"We're not selling anything," Mark said hastily. "We've just come to ask you to reassess your shares in DLS."

"They're not doing very well, are they? I certainly don't want to buy any more."

"We're not asking you to, Mrs Summers. We're asking you to sell them."

"Sell them?" She frowned, looking at Mark more sharply.

"Yes. You may not be aware that DLS does a lot of experiments on animals, many of them extremely painful. Dogs, cats, rabbits, rodents, monkeys, they all suffer at DLS."

"Dogs and cats, is that true?" She looked surprised and concerned.

"It certainly is. I've photos here I can show you, taken secretly."

Mark pulled out a bundle of photos of mangled cats and dogs' bodies and showed them through the narrow opening of the door.

"I never realised. It's disgusting but it must presumably all help for diagnosis for humans and the drugs involved or they wouldn't do it, would they?"

"They would, I'm afraid," Mark replied, "for money. The big companies pay well in order to cover themselves if drugs go wrong but in fact animals respond in many cases quite differently from humans to drugs and other chemicals. Animals share only 1.16 per cent of known human diseases. Experiments, such as those carried out at DLS, are totally useless owing to this difference." Mark proceeded to cite examples then as he had done at his meeting.

"What do you want me to do?" Gilda Summers asked when he finished.

"Sell your shares now. You've presumably got a stockbroker?"

"I've a financial advisor."

"Ask him to help you sell them and then send us confirmation and we won't bother you again."

"You still haven't told me who you are."

"We're from EDAC, End Draco Animal Cruelty and here's our address, email address and web site." Mark handed her his card through the chained door, which she took with a long, slender, bony hand. How beautiful she must have been once, I thought, looking at her eyes, her hands. A dancer perhaps? She still was beautiful and sympathetic and open, not like most old people I knew.

"Please," Mark pleaded, "sell them today. You could lose everything otherwise."

"What do you mean, lose everything?" a harsh woman's voice suddenly demanded from behind Mark. "Who are you and what do you want? You've no right to come here bullying and threatening an old lady."

We turned around to see a short, dumpy woman with frizzy, black dyed hair and suspicious eyes, standing with two shopping bags behind us.

"They're all right, Doris," the old lady said. "They haven't been threatening me. They've come about my shares in DLS and I agree with them."

Doris pouted, clearly put out by this support, and said, "You have to see your financial advisor before you take any decision. I've told you before not to listen to people from off the street."

"We agree," Mark said, smiling, trying to win the dumpy woman over. "She should first see her financial advisor. We're not pressuring her at all."

"You better hadn't or you'll have me to deal with." So saying, Doris stomped to a side door with her shopping. A few moments later we heard her on the other side of the front door.

"Come on now, Mrs Summers." Determined, firm, she drew Gilda Summers back with her into the shadows of the hall and slammed the door in Mark's face.

I really felt for Mark then. He'd been so near to winning Gilda Summers over, one of the principal shareholders with 60,000 shares. Now the door was closed, thanks to an interfering ignoramus over whom we had no control. It was frustrating, but Mark tried to take a positive view.

"I'll come again when we know that silly bitch isn't here," he said.

"Or I can," I offered. He didn't reply, but took my hand and we walked on, cautiously observing the road, to the next address.

It was in the Woodstock Road and the home of an elderly man by the name of Chris Hammond who lived in a modern block of flats. Tall and thin, he swayed, bending over us like a willow, smiling tentatively as Mark put his case. Yes, he had thought of giving up DLS. Yes, he was concerned. It was all a question of timing he said. He didn't want to lose everything.

"But you will if you wait," Mark said.

He nodded sagely then agreed he would sell and send us confirmation. It was all too easy this time; we couldn't believe it. Encouraged, we proceeded to the third and final address in a side road between the Banbury and Woodstock Roads.

I had an intimation as soon as I stepped through the white gates of "Cranston Lodge", there would be resistance. It may have been the brand new Mercedes in the drive or the regimented garden. The hard eyes of the well fed, well-heeled, broad-faced woman who opened the door supported my first impression.

Initially, to my surprise, she smiled: "Come in. The jumble's all ready in the hall."

"Jumble?" Mark queried.

"You're from the church, aren't you, from St Bartholomew's? I understood two people were coming."

"I'm afraid it's not us," Mark said. "We're here about another matter."

"What matter?" She frowned now with suspicion. "If you're selling something, the answer's no."

"We're not selling anything. We've come," Mark reassured, "to ask if you'd consider selling your shares in DLS."

"Selling my shares in Draco?" She made a swift transition now to indignation. "Why should I want to sell my shares in Draco?"

"Partly because they're not going to be worth much if you leave them. Mainly, and you may not be aware of this, Draco uses animals for its experiments. There's an enormous amount of cruelty involved which is quite unnecessary."

"Unnecessary in your view maybe, but not in the shareholders'. If they help the drug companies to establish standards, that's a good thing in my view."

"Doesn't it trouble you thousands of dogs, cats and

monkeys suffer for this and often do not produce safe results?"

Mark took out his bundle of undercover photos and showed her a picture of the mangled body of a beagle. She gave it merely a cursory glance.

"Do you expect me to accept that as proof? It could have been taken anywhere."

"It was taken secretly in Draco."

"It doesn't matter where it was taken. It's still selective and it won't change my view. Now please go. I'm busy."

"If you're not concerned about the cruelty, surely," Mark persisted," you're concerned about the price of Draco shares falling."

"I never sell when shares are falling," she answered promptly. "I buy when they're rock bottom. Now please go."

But Mark did not intend to give up so easily. The Huntley-Jones, as I learned later was their name, were major shareholders with 100,000 shares in Draco, a prize to be won in Mark's view, whatever the problems of persuasion.

"I'm asking you to consider possible effects on your own status too, Mrs Huntley-Jones. You wouldn't want other people in the neighbourhood to know you were investing in animal abuse, would you?"

"Are you threatening to blackmail me, young man?" She raised her voice and I realised someone else was near and she wanted him to hear. A moment later, a man, with fair, wispy hair and a stomach overlapping his belt, appeared in the hall behind her.

"These people are threatening us, George, trying to get us to sell our shares in Draco."

"Are they now? Well, we'll soon see about that."

He disappeared into a room off the hall. I didn't like his sneering voice and had a feeling he wasn't just disappearing off the scene.

"Please, Mrs Huntley-Jones, reconsider," Mark persisted. "We aren't threatening you. We are simply trying to tell you the facts so you know what goes on there."

"I'm not bothered by what they do. That's the management's business, not the concern of outsiders like you."

"In that case, we'll have no alternative but to name and shame you, if you persist in investing in animal abuse."

"And I'll have no alternative but to call the police if you don't leave our property." So saying, she slammed the door in Mark's face. Mark had just turned away, disappointed, when suddenly a spurt of water hit him in the face then sprayed over his body, drenching his trousers and shirt. Mr Huntley-Jones appeared from the side of the house with a hose in his hand, which he proceeded to turn on me too, soaking us to the skin.

Strangely, it was all done silently without his uttering a word, but I could hear Mrs Huntley-Jones through an open window calling the police. She may have been pretending but we couldn't afford to take the chance of being caught.

We ran out of the drive and left into the Banbury Road to the University Park by the museum and labs. We were just about to enter the park, when, looking back, we saw the Mercedes, that had been in the drive, had followed us and the wispy haired Huntley-Jones, in the driver's seat, was talking on his mobile as he stopped near the park entrance.

196

We ran as fast as we could into the park, not stopping until we reached some bushes where Mark changed out of his wet, conventional clothes back into jeans. It was good to see him looking normal again. I didn't like him in formal dress. It wasn't his style or in character.

As he bundled his wet clothes into his haversack, he leaned forward and kissed me, "Thanks for coming," he said.

"I wasn't much help, I'm afraid."

"Yes, you were, by being here. You were calm when most would panic. I feel I can trust you. In fact," he hesitated then added, "I'd like you to take on certain aspects of this work, if I'm caught."

I couldn't think for a moment what to say. I felt touched and honoured but uncertain what he meant, what was involved.

"Let's hope you won't be caught," I said.

"It's bound to happen sooner or later."

"Not if you hide well, surely?"

"You can't be effective in this business if you're hiding all the time."

"Where are you planning to go?"

"Back to the wood for the time being."

"Why not come to my place?" I stroked the back of his neck, his hair. His hair was beautiful, jet-black and thick, with a wave. God, how I wanted to make love to him.

Then I saw the doubt in his eyes, "I'm not sure it would be wise," he said. "Harbouring me could cause you a lot of trouble later. It'll be a criminal offence."

"I'm not bothered," I said rashly. "You won't be caught anyway. I'll see to that."

He smiled, stroking my hand. Then he glanced momentarily around the bushes, back at the park gate we'd entered and frowned. "We'd better get moving."

Looking at the gates, I saw a police car and Huntley-Jones pointing in the direction we'd taken.

"Yes, you're right."

We followed a back route then, half-running, half-walking back across the river and up through Headington to the Park and Ride.

Pete, to our relief, was waiting in the minibus.

"The explosion's been on the news," he said.

"Any witnesses?" Mark asked.

"None mentioned so far but they're blaming us, of course."

"We'd better get moving. Our last shareholder has also called the police."

"Right." Pete was soon onto the M40, as anxious as we were to leave the area.

Mark was at once on his mobile, calling Gemma to see if the lorries had arrived. The news was good. They had both arrived safely at Gemma's and most of the cats had already been distributed to their new homes. Mark tried ringing Jake but there was no reply.

"Probably blown himself up," Pete commented caustically. He was still very angry about Jake's intervention and with justification, I felt. Jake was becoming more and more of a loose cannon that could harm the movement and bring it down. How though control him and if Mark couldn't, who could? What sort of leverage worked with someone like Jake? Expulsion, or tolerance and reason, hoping for the best? There were no simple answers and it made me realise how well Mark managed to get things done and people to work together despite the individual egos involved.

Mark wasn't happy though about the visits to the shareholders. True, Chris Hammond had promised to sell his shares but the Huntley-Jones, who owned the most, had been a real disaster area.

It made me feel more than ever I wanted him to come back home with me. I was wondering whether to try and persuade him again when I saw Mark looking warily behind him. I turned to see a police car following us. It seemed at first to be a routine motorway police car but, after a while, we realised it was keeping the same steady distance behind us, as if it had no other purpose.

"They're following us, I'm sure," Mark said. "Take the next exit."

"And then?"

"There's a roundabout. Take the first left, then left again. There's a beech wood just beyond. If they follow, drop me at the first lay-by."

"If you're sure."

"I'm sure." Mark picked up his haversack from the seat behind us as Pete swerved without signalling into the next exit. I thought briefly the police car was going to pass the slip road but suddenly it too swerved, following us.

Pete pressed hard on the accelerator, barely pausing at the roundabout, narrowly missing another minibus, white like our own. For a moment it confused the police and gave us extra time. Left and left again, Pete followed Mark's instructions. At the lay-by as Pete paused, Mark pressed my hand. "I'll see you."

Then he was gone, plunging down from the minibus into the beech wood below.

It all happened so quickly. One minute Mark was cruising with us on the motorway; the next he was gone into an unknown wood, an uncertain time. Pete took it all in his stride, pressing on resignedly until the police caught up with us, flashing their lights to flag us down. Pete stopped at another lay-by and wound down his window.

"Is something wrong?" he asked before the officer emerging from his car had time to speak.

"Yes, we'd like to speak to Mark Stanton. We believe he is with you."

"Mark Stanton?" Pete shook his head, feigning bewildered surprise. "We've no one of that name aboard."

"We'd like to look inside."

"By all means." With a gesture of compliance, Pete opened the minibus door.

As he did, I noticed Mark's balaclava on the seat where the haversack had been. I was going to put it in my bag but the officer had already seen it. He walked between the seats of the minibus, looking under each of them in turn, then picked up the balaclava.

"Whose is this?" he asked.

"It's mine," I said.

"Bit big for you, isn't it?" He held it up to the light, looking inside. I didn't know what he expected to find there. A trace of hair maybe? There was fortunately no name label on it.

"Where are you going?" he asked Pete.

"Home," Pete answered," if that's allowed."

The officer, a robust looking man with a sceptical voice and cautious eyes, ignored the sneer.

"Been to Oxford, have you?"

"Yeah."

"Which part?"

"The centre mainly," I said. "We were shopping."

"You haven't by any chance been to Greenacres Farm?"

"Greenacres Farm?" Pete put on another of his expressions of surprise. "Never heard of it."

"Perhaps I'd better remind you then." There was a siren quality in the officer's voice. "It's a cat farm near Clayton, supplies cats to Draco Life Science. I'm sure you've heard of that." He looked at Pete sternly and inquisitively. "A bomb was detonated there this morning during or after an early morning raid when more than a hundred cats were taken."

"That may be, but why should it concern us?" Pete challenged.

"Because a minibus like yours was seen in the area."

"Like ours?"

The officer made no riposte, knowing there were thousands of white minibuses in the country. He proceeded to ask for our names and addresses, the hire company of the minibus and Pete's licence. I didn't think quickly enough to give a false address. Pete gave the address on his licence though he was no longer there.

After writing down the details of the minibus, the officer warned Pete about his failure to give a signal at the exit and his driving at the roundabout. He clearly wasn't convinced, despite Pete's acting skills and when we drove on to Horton, I sensed things had taken a turn for the worse. I could be visited any time now by the police, having given my address, which was not what I wanted at all if Mark came. True the police would need a warrant for a search and were hardly likely to intrude without questioning me further, which would give Mark time to escape. But their coming at all could have unforeseen results. The only relief was that Mark had got away for the time being, unseen, but for how long?

"Do you think anyone saw us long enough to get the registration number near Greenacres?" I asked Pete.

"Not a chance. I changed the plates before we drove there, then back while you were in Oxford. Didn't you notice?"

"What did you do with the other plates?" I could have kicked myself being so unobservant.

"I buried them."

"So these are the originals?"

"Yep, and not seen within ten miles of Greenacres. They won't get to us through the minibus."

"You sound very confident."

"I am on that score. It was a perfect operation, except for Jake."

"Maybe, but I don't think you can blame Mark for Jake."

"I'm not blaming him. I just think he should exercise more control and boot Jake out."

"But if Jake's been useful?"

"He hasn't, not in any vital sense. Any of us could have done the electronics and lighting with a bit of practice. No, Mark's a great guy but he's too weak when it comes to Jake."

"He didn't know about the bomb, I'm sure."

"No, but he should have done, shouldn't he? That's my point. He's great, the best we've got. He inspires people, keeps them together. He'd give his life if need be but there are times, as a leader, when you need to be tough."

"Do you think Jake could harm him?" I asked.

"It's possible, yes. He's frustrated, unpredictable, like a bomb himself, waiting to blow up."

"Where is he now? Do you know?"

"I've no idea, but he may try to come to your place for the meeting. Whatever you do, don't let him in. Tell him to bugger off."

"If he comes," I said. Desperately I hoped he wouldn't. I was sure Pete was right. Jake was trouble but wouldn't it be easier to control him if he was with us, rather than acting as a maverick? What did Mark know about him that we didn't?

We drove on in silence for the rest of the journey. I felt we'd exhausted the subject of Jake and was too tired to raise another. Pete was anxious to deliver the minibus to the hire firm before extra charges were imposed and dropped me at the end of my road.

As I got out of the minibus, I saw Robert emerging from his front door with two suitcases. As he noticed me, he glared, his eyes narrowing. If looks could kill, I'd have been flat on my face on the pavement and I was frightened of him again, of what he could do.

The effect of this confrontation, combined with tiredness from the events of the day, made me feel nauseous again and weak. It wasn't far to my house but the walk seemed endless. I struggled to the front door from the garden gate, my head spinning as I put the key in the latch. I had a glimpse of an envelope addressed to me in Alan's handwriting on the doormat. I was bending over to pick it up when I heard a movement behind me. I turned to see a tall, thickset man silhouetted in the doorway. I knew who it was, but before I could scream, he'd lunged forward, clamped his hand over my mouth and kicked the door shut behind him.

SEVENTEEN

K eep quiet or you'll get more than you bargained
for."

He pushed me into the sitting room and onto
the settee. I was aware of a stained, thick-bladed knife
with a sharpened tip close to my face. Behind the knife,
the ice-blue eyes, the lined, discontented face of Craig,
the hunter, who'd thrown the stones at the demo and
tracked me through the woods. I was terrified. It was more
his eyes than the knife. They were cold, hard eyes, without
light, determined to get what he wanted and this, he soon
made clear, was Mark.

"Where is he then?"

"Where's who?" I played dumb.

"You know who I mean. Your boss, lover boy Stanton.
Where did he go after he'd frisked the shareholders on
the Banbury Road?"

I couldn't believe it. How did he know? Had he
personally followed us or someone else informed? Who
and how? I tried to sound calm while my brain whirled.

"Shareholders? I don't know what you're talking about
and I've no idea where Mark Stanton is."

"I think you have."

Craig moved the knife closer to my cheek. His breath was stale and smelled of beer and smoke. There were tufts of grey hair like wire in his nose. I felt dizzy again and sick.

I lost all sense of time as he sat, pressed against my thighs, holding the knife. It seemed an eternity, the smell of him, the coldness, the point of his knife which had ripped, I didn't doubt, many a non-human carcass.

As the light faded, I was increasingly desperate for a drink. Several times I thought of asking if I could get some water or make tea. Then I remembered Tess in the kitchen. He'd know at once where she came from and could well injure or kill her if he got frustrated. I couldn't take the risk of his going in there and seeing her.

Every few minutes he would ask the same question, "Where is he?" And I would answer still, "I don't know." And I was glad in a way I didn't know for after a while, though he wouldn't admit it, I think he believed me. I was afraid all the same Mark would suddenly appear at the door. How then would I warn him for hadn't I persuaded him to come?

At nine, as the street lights came on, to my relief, Craig went to the window, still watching me with the knife ready in his hand. I took the opportunity to swing my legs back onto the carpet into a sitting position. I felt better then, more in control and able to act. I told him there was no point in his staying, no prospect of seeing Mark.

I couldn't see clearly the expression on his face, only the blade of the knife, caught in the reflected light of the street lamp outside. I was aware of a hesitation in his movements, as if he might go, when suddenly, in the quiet of the darkened room, I heard footsteps coming up the path to the front door.

Immediately, he grabbed my arm and pulled me to where he was standing facing the closed door. He head locked me then with his left arm and with his right held the knife in front of me, pointing it up at an angle against my heart. Even if I'd wanted to, I couldn't shout, so firm was the upward thrust of his arm on my neck.

All I could do was to listen as the key turned in the lock and footsteps padded along the passage to the kitchen. I heard Steve's voice calling Tess. Two minutes later, Tess pushed open the sitting room door.

She came immediately up to me, wagging her tail. Then the hair on her back bristled and in the light of the street lamp I saw her eyes roll with the fear she'd shown during the experiments at DLS and she drew back, uncertain.

"Come on, old girl. You've got to eat."

Unaware behind her, Steve turned on the light.

"What the hell!"

Steve stared uncomprehending a moment. Then, to my surprise, he said calmly, "Put down that knife or I'll call the police." He reached into his trouser pocket and took out his mobile. "Thirty seconds or I ring."

Suddenly Craig released his head lock, pushed me down on the floor and sprang at Steve with the knife. I saw Steve get a grip on his arm, struggling to keep the knife away from his face. But Craig was stronger and with his left hand seized the mobile and, punching Steve, sent him sprawling onto the settee.

Blood was flowing from Steve's nose as Tess suddenly went for Craig's leg. He wore thick leather trousers but her teeth penetrated to his calf and he let out a great howl, dropping the mobile and knife. He was about to pick the knife up but Steve this time was faster and, seizing the knife, flung it over the settee so it clattered beyond reach behind my father's old oak bookcase set against the wall.

"Now get out!"

Steve's face and shirt were covered in blood but he was the one in charge now. Like most hunters, Craig was nothing but a wimp without his weapon. Kicking out at Tess, he limped to the door and out into the street. Quickly, I locked the door behind him, and turning off the light, we watched him get into a Land Rover further along the street. It wasn't the last we'd seen of him. I was sure of that. But for the moment, the immediate danger to Mark had passed.

I drew the curtains, wondering if anyone had seen the incident from outside. There was no sign of movement on the street but I couldn't be sure. I urged Steve to sit and lean forward, pressing his nose to stop the bleeding but, although he did as suggested, he was more concerned about me.

"It's not safe for you to stay here at night alone, not with maniacs like that about. We need to report him to the police. He could have killed you with that knife and he might come back."

"Only if he thinks he'll get Mark."

"We could get him locked up after this, with two of us as witnesses."

"Yes, but if the police come now, there's more danger for Mark."

"You mean Mark's coming here?"

"He may do. I don't know. I said he could."

"I don't think that's wise."

"He's got to go somewhere, Steve."

"Yes, but not where it implicates you. You could be imprisoned for a long time harbouring him, you know."

"I thought you admired him, wanted to help."

"I do."

"What's the problem then? He wouldn't get caught here. You know that, not with Dad's secret cupboard."

"I wouldn't be too sure of that. Once they get searching, the police are very determined. It's up to you, though, of course." Steve paused, looking at me more intently. "Are you all right?" he asked.

"Yes, why?"

His nosebleed had stopped. He looked a mess with blood all over his clothes but, thanks to Tess, our intruder hadn't done him real harm. I stroked Tess's head as she sat at my feet. Her eyes had lost their fear but she was still trembling and there was a trail of blood from her on the floor. Like most animals she knew who her enemies were. The hunter, indistinguishable from the vivisectionists, had set her two steps back again.

"I know it's none of my business but you don't look too well," Steve continued.

"It's just the events of the day."

"No, you haven't looked right for a couple of weeks now. You've been sick, haven't you? Why not go and get a check up?"

"I could I suppose." I had been feeling under the weather; it was true. I'd put it down to the way I felt mentally about DLS and working there, something that would pass now I'd left.

"I'm going to collect a prescription for Mother in the morning. I could drive you to the surgery if you like."

"Let's see how things are in the morning, shall we?"

"Sure." He cleaned up his face in the kitchen and left his shirt for me to wash so his mother wouldn't know what had happened. A few minutes later, after making a fuss of Tess, he left.

I slept badly again that night. I kept thinking I ought to warn Mark not to come, but I desperately wanted him with me, despite the danger. I tried convincing myself Craig wouldn't come again but I knew in my heart, he was too determined not to try. He'd never give up until Mark was either imprisoned, injured or dead.

I felt Steve was right, that we should report the intrusion but feared it would backfire and the police would be on to Mark rather than Craig. They would assume it was too much of a coincidence I had worked at DLS and was in the vicinity of Greenacres when it exploded and certainly wouldn't believe I didn't know Mark. Doubtless the Huntley-Jones would have given my description to the police too. I was too tired to think clearly and make decisions but the questions themselves wouldn't go away and I began to feel nervous about noises outside. Footsteps and the clatter of bins, noises I'd always taken for granted before, now seemed ominous, foretelling Craig and his mate again.

At six o'clock, after sleeping intermittently for three to four hours, I was sick again and decided to act on Steve's suggestion about going to a doctor.

Before he came, I went to the corner shop and bought a newspaper to see if there was anything about our raid on Greenacres and Jake's bomb.

Some minor government scandal had seized the headlines but on page three was a photograph of the burnt-out wing of Greenacres Farmhouse with the caption

"ANIMAL RIGHTS TERRORISTS STRIKE AT COUNTRY FARM".

'Animal rights terrorists,' the article beneath began, 'have sunk to new levels of violence in their campaign to drive Draco Life Sciences into the ground. They have targeted now the suppliers, Greenacres Farm, where cats are reared for vital life-saving experiments to test important drugs for the nation's health. Masked raiders stole over a hundred cats in the early morning, leaving William Black, the owner, deprived of his livelihood. Mr Black himself interrupted the raid, but his son, in trying to arrest an intruder, was knocked to the ground unconscious. 'These people will stop at nothing,' Mr Black said, 'to get their way.'"

It was a typically biased report. There was no mention of the suffering the animals endured or the fact most of the testing was for inessential products, not life-saving drugs at all and often inaccurate at that.

The editorial was no better. It raged against the Animal Rights Movement, urging business to stand up to the pressure and government to bring in tougher legislation to curb demonstrations and intrusive activities. "The leaders should be given longer prison sentences to teach them a lesson. These people are mostly unemployed layabouts, trying to find a media role for themselves." Nothing was printed about the financial motivation, the huge profits, research facilities and drug companies made, or the possibilities of using other means than animals for testing results.

It was depressing reading and as I turned the page, I saw another article with passport-sized photographs of Jake and Mark with the headlines: WANTED STILL FOR

THE RAID ON DRACO. The photographs were not that well defined but Mark was recognisable and I was instantly concerned he'd not escape arrest before the final onslaught.

Steve, when he came, reiterated Mark had eluded arrest countless times before and would no doubt do so again. As usual, he tried to cheer me up but had troubles of his own.

His mother, despite her amazing resilience, was steadily deteriorating and he needed to take more and more time off work to be with her.

"I just wish I could do more. It's no life for her. I sometimes think she's had enough but I don't want her to go."

"Of course, you don't." I knew how he felt from experience with my own father. My father had always been there and I couldn't bear the thought of his not being but the suffering, the dependence, had been too debilitating, reducing what he was, his essence. It was the same, I sensed, for Steve's mother.

"Perhaps you could ask for compassionate leave," I suggested.

"Yes, I might do that. I don't want her to feel she's been neglected in her last days."

We'd arrived at the surgery. Steve collected his prescription and said he'd wait in the car park. I was lucky and managed to get a slot from a cancellation with a woman doctor.

She wasn't much older than I was, a woman with tightly curled, shoulder-length auburn hair and steady brown eyes, which put me at ease. She asked at once what my problem was.

"I'm not sure. I'm tending to be sick quite often."

"When are you sick usually? Is it after meals?"

"No, it's usually early in the day, in the early morning."

"Is there any chance you might be pregnant?"

"Pregnant? I don't think so. I mean I could be, but I've been pregnant before and didn't feel sick like this."

"You have a child already then?"

"No, I had a miscarriage." Suddenly it all flooded back and I was close to tears, swayed by hormones beyond control.

"Pregnancy doesn't always follow the same pattern. I think we'll do a blood test on you for a start," she said matter-of-factly.

She checked my pulse and blood pressure, took a blood sample and told me to check between five and six that evening for the result.

I drifted to the car park in a daze. Steve was waiting, patient as always and concerned.

"How did it go? Good news I hope."

"I don't know. I had a blood test, that's all."

To my relief, Steve asked no more questions and once home left to see his mother.

I lay on the bed, trying to take in the possibilities of what the results of the blood test might be. There was no point, I told myself, in facing up to things if I wasn't sure. For a while I managed quite an effective state of denial, as if I was suspended, hovering like a glider over unknown territory, not wanting to come down, enjoying the spectacle and space of not knowing.

But as the day wore on, I knew in my heart I was just deceiving myself; there could be no other explanation except that I was pregnant. It all made sense, the timing, the fact I'd taken no precautions, the way I felt about Mark. The signs had all been there in my sickness at DLS and the feeling of nausea since. How could I have been so naïve as not to have realised before? I didn't need the results on the phone. I could feel my breasts filling, my moods shifting as I'd done with my previous pregnancy.

I rang the surgery all the same when five o'clock came. The doctor I'd seen that morning, to my surprise, herself answered.

"The result is positive," she confirmed. "Presumably you want to keep the baby?"

"Yes, yes, of course."

"Right. You'll need to make an appointment at the prenatal clinic. Make one if you can for next week. I'll see you there. Meanwhile, take care."

"Thanks."

As I put down the receiver, the practical aspects hit me. I felt as if I'd been thrown off an express train into a ditch and had to find my bearings again. How was I going to manage? I had no job nor an immediate prospect of one. I was still, ironically, living off my two weeks' earnings from DLS and I'd spent all but a few pounds. I started flicking through the job adverts in the newspaper containing the anti-animal rights article but was too agitated to focus properly on what might be suitable. My head spun and I couldn't take in the print.

I tried to calm myself with a meditation technique I had learned as a student. I closed my eyes focusing on a mantra, a word I'd used. It wasn't a real word, just a sound, imm, deliberately meaningless. After a while by repeating it and letting it come to me in waves, I managed to blank out the external world and its associations. I think I may have fallen asleep for when I came to, aware again, I felt refreshed, calmer. What struck me then was not the practicalities but the momentous nature of what had happened, that Mark's son or daughter was growing inside me.

A miracle it seemed then and I was overwhelmed with a sense of joy. I wanted to thank Mark, to share it with him, share my joy.

It was only later I remembered what he'd said on that walk to DLS our first evening together about having children; he didn't want the commitment.

I began to be afraid then of what he'd say, afraid he already knew, had sensed it in some way and was deliberately staying away. Why else had he not come? He'd said he would come. If he'd been caught, surely he would have phoned, let someone know. But there'd been no phone call, nothing at all.

As the evening wore on, I became more and more anxious that something had happened to him, that he'd been taken ill again in some bleak, inhospitable part of the country. I tried ringing Pete but there was no reply. I tried Martin but he'd heard nothing. Philippa, Karl, Jason and Jenny, none of them knew where Mark was or had heard from him.

I had just got into bed shortly after midnight when my mobile rang.

EIGHTEEN

K ate." The voice was muffled with a strange background gurgling sound as if coming from a drain.

The room spun as I sat up, trying to focus.

"It's Mark."

"Where are you?" My heart started racing in fear.

"Not far. I'm on my way, but I need someone to get a message through to Dad. There's a police van parked outside the cottage all the time."

"You want me to go, you mean?"

"I want you to tell him I'm okay."

"Are you? You don't sound it."

"I've had one of those hunting bastards on my trail. I've only just lost him."

"Do you want me to get Steve to come with the car?"

"No, it's too risky. Just go and see Dad, will you, and tell him I'm sorry about his leg and everything."

"I'll go in the morning."

"Thanks. Are you okay?"

I hesitated, wondering whether to tell him about the baby but a deeper instinct and fear told me it wasn't the right time.

"Yes, I'm fine. When will you be here?"

"Sometime tomorrow, if I can make it."

"Come the back way, won't you," I warned, "over the wall."

I hoped he'd heard me as the phone gurgled again and faded.

It took me some time to get to sleep. I woke then late to the sun streaming through the window. I decided to cycle out to see Mr Stanton, instead of relying on Steve's help, but just as I was leaving, he appeared and insisted on driving me, saying he was collecting the home help for his mother.

As we drove into Youlton and along the lane to Mr Stanton's cottage, we passed a police van, as Mark had indicated, parked outside. I couldn't see anyone in the passenger or driver's seat but they could well have been at the back of the van, observing unseen. The fact the van was there at all made me feel edgy. They had reckoned accurately Mark would want to return to his home base.

Dropping me at the gate, Steve said he would return in two hours when he took back the home help.

I found Mr Stanton already, to my surprise, walking on crutches in the garden. His right leg was in plaster to his thigh; his left, thin and white in the grey shorts he was wearing, looked strangely inadequate for the task of compensation and he was straining as he walked, his deep-lined forehead furrowed even more with the effort.

"Now, that's enough, Mr Stanton." I heard the voice of Doris coming from the kitchen.

I don't think she was altogether pleased to see me. Her lips were pursed in the possessive way some people have about their spouses but she offered coffee as she tutted, helping him to sit on the wooden chaise longue on the verandah. He looked more relaxed and smiled as Doris went back to the kitchen.

"How are you feeling?" I asked.

"I'd like to get about more but I'm on the mend, let's say." He lowered his voice. "Have you heard anything?"

I looked around. There was no sign of anyone listening or watching, but how could I be sure? There were too many people chasing Mark to take risks of any kind. I pulled my chair nearer to Mr Stanton and whispered, "Mark wants you to know he's all right," I said. "It's the reason I came. He'll get in touch with you when the police van has gone as soon as he can. He wants you to know he's very sorry about your leg."

"Where is he? Do you know?" Mr Stanton looked at me intently; his eyes focused with a concern far beyond his own pain.

"I don't know exactly," I said, for Mark could have been anywhere, caught, even ill again. He'd told me nothing when he phoned. I knew no more than Mr Stanton did but I felt I owed his father some reassurance. He'd had more than his fair share of pain, even if indirectly, from the cause. "He's planning to come to my house later today. I've a place where he can hide."

"You think he'll be safe there?"

"As safe as anywhere else, yes." How much should I tell Mr Stanton? How much conceal? What would Mark do? Keep quiet I imagined, not wanting to cause his father concern. But hadn't his father a right to know and wasn't knowing better for those concerned? Knowing you could adjust, rationalise, compensate, make plans. Not knowing left you in limbo, unable to act and move on.

Sitting close to Mr Stanton, I could feel his fear alongside my own. I told him what had happened the day before, about the raid, our visit to the shareholders, the police car following and Mark slipping into the woods.

"What are his plans now?" Mr Stanton asked.

"To finish off DLS."

"With a last raid, you mean?"

"That's the idea, yes. It's not finalised yet."

Mr Stanton was silent for a while, and then looked thoughtfully at his greenhouse.

"I hope that will be the end of it. I hope you'll tell him. If DLS falls, he'll have achieved a great deal. He should be content with that and let others take up the cause. It's never ending otherwise and he'll have lost the chance of a normal life."

"Do you think he wants one?" I asked. Normal conveyed a semi-detached existence, reining one in and I couldn't see Mark conforming.

"Not immediately perhaps, no. But I think he will. A satisfying job, a family, children. There's nothing to beat it. You realise that as you get older. Children especially, they're our purpose, our genes. And Mark's very good with children. Did you know that?"

He was looking at me with a quizzical smile, probing, and I wondered briefly if he'd guessed I was already pregnant with Mark's child, if I'd somehow given the game away. Yet how could he have? I'd told no one. I was still the same shape and size.

"No, I've never seen Mark with children."

I felt a sudden overwhelming desire to tell him about the baby, that his wish was already fulfilled and Mark would have a child. But how could I? I hadn't even told Mark himself.

I was turning away to hide my agitation, when my mobile rang. I immediately answered, thinking it must be Steve with a change of plan for collecting me.

To my surprise, it was Jake. Jake whom I'd have thought would have gone to ground for some weeks at least. He demanded to know when the meeting was to discuss the final raid on DLS.

"Nothing's been arranged yet," I said.

"Come off it! You were there with them, weren't you, when they took away the cats? Where's Mark anyway? I can't get him on his mobile."

I got up and walked down the garden.

"I don't know where he is."

"Shit! I bet you do. The same with the meeting. You don't want me to be in on it, do you?" His voice rose, arrogant yet pleading.

"It's not for me to decide," I said. "But it would hardly be surprising, would it after what you've done?" The thought of the bombing set me off again on a spurt of anger.

"What I did," Jake retaliated, "was vital. No one listens otherwise. We need publicity to expose the shit and we have to get it."

"Not if it turns people against us, people who sympathised."

"It's a power struggle, don't you see? We have to up the stakes in a way the opposition understand, to beat them at their own game. All they want is power, a power we have to match or we go under, a power we have to take away by force, if need be."

He was beginning to rant and I was afraid his voice could be heard beyond my mobile and he'd give something away.

"We'll talk another time," I said and switched off the phone and returned to Mr Stanton.

"Have another coffee," he said. "Someone's upset you, haven't they?"

"It was a friend of Mark, Jake. Do you know him?"

"Jake, yes. He's been here a number of times."

"What do you think of him?"

"I don't know him that well, but from what Mark has told me he's had a lot of problems to overcome, which may account for his attitude."

"What sort of problems?"

"He was abandoned, I gather, by both parents then raised by an uncle who abused him. There was a lot of violence in the home and the street. No proper schooling at first. He had a bad start."

"But he's had chances since?"

"I heard a teacher took him under his wing and he's made his way since. He's quite clever, I believe. Mark seems to think he's useful at any rate."

"In his way," I agreed, "but…"

"But what?"

"He acts on his own. He doesn't consult. He was the one who set off the bomb at Greenacres, entirely without the group's consent."

"Then he should go. You can't have someone wrecking the group's name, no matter what their childhood traumas have been."

"That's what I think." Would Mark, though? There was something ominously personal in Jake's antagonism that

Mark couldn't seem to see. Was it jealousy or a power struggle, an echo of the power struggle Jake had delineated on a wider scale? Whatever it was, Jake seemed more than ever a loose cannon that could wreck Mark's final plans for DLS. He had to be controlled before and during the last raid, but how? How could one control someone in a structure without a real system of control, that relied on its flexibility and individual action to succeed?

I was about to ask Mr Stanton what more he knew about Jake when Steve arrived, needing to get back home. As we left, Mr Stanton said quietly, "Look after yourself and Mark for me, won't you?" He pressed my hand and I had a strange feeling again he already knew about the baby.

❄

Mark came eventually at nine that evening. I was feeding Tess in the kitchen. She'd been reluctant to go into the sitting room since Craig's visit and I was stroking her as she fed, when I looked up and there he was at the back door, quietly closing it behind him.

He was dressed in exactly the same clothes as when he'd slipped away into the wood, a black T-shirt and jeans, only they were caked now in mud, more brown than black and there were scratch marks on his face, debris in his hair and dark rings round his eyes. Yet his eyes themselves, intensely focused still in their blueness, betrayed no weakness, no tiredness. He must have felt shattered from his days on the run but he didn't show it, as he bent down, joining me and stroking Tess.

"Are you alone?"

"Yes."

"Not expecting anyone?"

"No."

"And no one's been?"

"Only Steve. No police."

"Sorry!" He stroked my arm. "I need to be sure. There's too much to do to be cornered now."

"I know."

"Show me this hiding place you've got, just in case."

He took off his boots and I hid them in the breadbin in the pantry beneath the bread.

Upstairs, I drew the curtains in my bedroom and pressed the exact part of the panelling by the fireplace that enabled me to push it to the side. A small opening just large enough for a person to climb inside revealed a dark, oddly shaped cupboard space, broad at the front, then tapering around to the back of the fireplace. It would have been very hot and claustrophobic, I suspected, in my father's time but there would be no fire burning for Mark. He climbed inside, trying it out. He couldn't sit but could lie comfortably enough by stretching his legs behind the fireplace.

"It's great as long as I make it in time and there are no sniffer dogs around."

I hadn't thought of dogs and tried not to. I couldn't bear the thought of Mark being caught now.

"You think it'll do then?" I asked as he emerged. "You feel safer now?"

"As safe as I'm ever likely to feel."

"You'll stay then?"

"Yes, and thanks, thanks for all your help the other day."

He kissed me. He smelled of mud, sweat, the staleness

of three days but I didn't care. He'd made it. He'd come and I loved him in that moment more than ever. I'd have gone to bed with him then and there, filthy as he was, but he insisted on having a bath and said he was starving.

I gave him a towel and a dressing gown Simon left behind and, putting his muddy clothes in the washing machine, set about cooking a meal. I cooked him a huge plate of mushrooms, eggs, tomatoes and peas and a dish of rice to fill it out. He ate every scrap, every grain of three helpings.

"What have you eaten in the last three days?" I asked.

"Blackberries and a couple of bars of chocolate I had."

"Nothing more?"

"I had plenty to drink, plenty of streams. It hasn't done me any harm. Keeping in touch was the problem. My mobile went kaput after I spoke to you. Have you heard anything? Has anyone rung?"

"Yes, Jake."

"What did he want?"

"He wants to know when the meeting is for the final raid."

"So what did you tell him?"

"I told him the truth, I didn't know."

"Did he say anything else?"

"He seemed quite agitated. He's convinced bombing is the only way to make people sit up and take notice."

"And he's right in a way. Most people don't listen without headlines. You can reason till you're blue in the face with MPs and the like and they don't take a blind bit of notice if there are no votes in it for them. That doesn't mean to say bombing is right. It isn't. But sometimes drastic measures have to be used to end an evil situation."

"You think that's what we've got now with DLS?"

"I think we have, yes."

"But surely you're not going to agree with Jake going ahead with another bomb?"

"I've got to discuss the whole strategy with Pete, Martin and the others to decide what's best. DLS is tottering with shareholders pulling out but the Probate Bank has extended its loan which is counteracting this and I think DLS is trying to raise more capital in America. The influx of money could rebuild the company very quickly if we don't take drastic action."

"But the risk of alienating people is surely not worth it?"

"People have short memories, Kate. DLS has to go. It's not a decision to be taken lightly but Jake's contribution has to be considered."

"He's dangerous, Mark. Dangerous to you, I mean."

"I think you're being a bit over-dramatic now. It's not a personal matter."

"Isn't it? I think it could be."

But Mark shook his head, disbelieving. The machine stopped running and I took out his clothes.

"There you are. Perfect laundry service. Clean and dry and new."

"Except they've shrunk," he teased.

I made him put them on to prove they hadn't and he asked me about his father.

"How was he? How's his leg?"

"He feels he's on the mend," I said.

"But?"

I hesitated. I didn't want to worry Mark. At the same time I felt he needed to know. It came out then, perhaps for deeper reasons, more my own.

"He's worried about you," I said.

"In what way?"

"He wants you to hand over to someone else when DLS falls. He wants you…"

"I know. He wants me to have a normal life, a family and children. He's been saying this for years."

"He says you like children."

"I do, but that's not the same as saying it's a good idea to keep breeding and having one's own, is it?"

"Does that mean you never want children?"

"I wouldn't say that, no, but certainly not now."

"I see."

"I'm not ready. There's too much to do."

"Supposing you knew you were a father, though?" I posed. I hadn't meant it to come out this way. It just came.

"Well, I'm not, am I? So there no point in constructing a case on theory." He laughed, turning away, then suddenly turned back, looking at me sharply, "What are you saying?"

It wasn't so much the sharpness. It was more the fear in his eyes that alarmed me as if it was a death he was confronting, not life, a birth. But I knew I had to tell him and now.

"I'm pregnant," I said.

He stared at me then for a long time in silence. At last with an effort he said, "Are you sure?"

"Yes, very sure. I had a test two days ago. There's no doubt."

"And you think it's me?"

"I know it's you, Mark. It couldn't be anyone else. There is no one else," I added, "I'd want it to be."

He got up and started pacing round the room like someone caged.

"What are you going to do about it then?" he said at length.

"Do? What do you mean?"

"About getting rid of it."

"You mean you think I should get an abortion?"

I couldn't believe what he was saying. I could understand his alarm, yes. But wanting an abortion, no. Something of my revulsion must have conveyed itself, for he hesitated then.

"I don't know. I need to think."

"It's yours, Mark, in case you're doubting."

"I'm not doubting that."

"What then?"

"Myself, I'm not ready for the responsibility of marriage and a child."

"I'm not asking you to marry me," I said.

"Aren't you? I thought that's what most women want when they have babies and it's fairer, isn't it, on the baby I mean?"

"I don't want to tie you, Mark, against your will. I just, I just want to share things, share him, between us." I had an intuition even then it would be a he.

"I need to think," he repeated. He picked up his haversack from the floor, got his boots from the bread bin and opened the door.

"Where are you going?" I had a terrible fear that if he walked out now, I'd never see him again.

"I don't know. I'm going to walk for a while."

"But where? You've only just got here. The police—they're still out looking for you."

"I doubt it. Not in the middle of the night on some obscure road."

I wanted to say that was exactly where they would be looking but he wasn't listening. Impelled by some new momentum, he opened the back door, went out into the garden and over the wall.

For more than an hour I sat dazed by what had happened. I couldn't believe it had all gone so wrong, that he'd reacted so badly. I could understand his fear of being trapped but not wanting his own baby aborted and leaving as he did. Why couldn't he have stayed and talked it through? It was crazy taking such a risk when he was wanted.

As the hours passed from nine to midnight, I became increasingly depressed, convinced he'd gone for good or been caught. I wasn't sure which was worse.

Eventually, feeling too tired to think, I dragged myself to bed. I woke at two with Tess licking my face. She'd pulled herself all the way upstairs but now seemed anxious to go down again.

I got up and followed her, thinking she wanted to go into the garden. I switched on the light in the kitchen and there he was, standing by the back door, taking off his boots again.

"You should lock the door, you know," he said. "There are bad people around. Like me."

"Are there?" The relief of seeing him was so great, I immediately burst into tears.

He looked across the kitchen at me, hesitating a moment, unsure, then kicking aside his boots, he put his arms around me, kissing my forehead, my hair.

"I'm sorry. I didn't mean to be away so long."

"Where did you go?"

"I went back to the bank in the wood again."

"Did anyone see you?"

"Only a fox and a badger. It was very quiet. Sitting on the bank, it made me realise."

"Realise?"

"How much I love you. What I said, how I acted, I'm sorry. It was the suddenness, a shock. I wasn't prepared. I had too much else in my head."

"I should have chosen a better time."

"No," Mark insisted then. "It was right to tell me, and I will help you. We'll get together and do something about it when DLS is finished. I've got to give everything I can to it at the moment. You know that, don't you? But after, I'll try and get some regular work."

Mark said more than I ever dreamt he would in my kitchen, in the small hours that night, and I believed him, trusted him that he would help rear our child. Whether we were married or not didn't seem to matter, only that we were together.

"What shall we call him while we're waiting?" I asked.

"Dmitri," Mark said. It was a name that came straight into his mind without thinking. And so Dmitri it was.

Upstairs we made love again. It was like the sealing of a contract and as Mark entered me, I felt our love for each other reaching out, growing, adding to our love for Dmitri already there, our love for Tess and all the other animals we knew to have suffered and be suffering.

NINETEEN

I woke late the next morning to feel the sun on my face. The curtains were drawn and Mark was already up, sitting alert by the window, looking down through the net curtains onto the street.

The sun illuminated the scratch marks on his face, the darkness of his stubble but he looked like a god to me sitting there, naked, with his dark tousled hair and the rippling muscles of his back. More than ever I wanted him.

I was about to get up and draw him back into bed, when he frowned, following some movement in the street. He turned and started to put on his clothes.

"What's the matter?"

"Pigs! Two of them just got out of their van coming this way. I'd better get in the cupboard."

"And your boots."

I went downstairs, retrieving the boots, checking all the windows and doors were closed and Tess shut in the kitchen.

Mark was already in the cupboard when I went upstairs. I closed the panel, making sure none of his clothing was around and then went to the window to watch.

The two policemen came slowly up the road as if they'd no particular objective in mind. I recognised one of them as the officer who'd questioned Pete and myself in the minibus. The other I thought I'd seen at the demo. He had a weathered face and large hands. I could feel my heart thumping as they came nearer. What would I say exactly if they asked about Mark? How would I hide my nerves with assurance? It seemed an eternity before they reached the gate.

They paused then, looking up at the roof and that of the terrace house adjoining, as if assessing a means of access from the sky. To my surprise, they then moved on up the road, looking at the roofs of the other terraced houses. They pushed open no gate, rang no bell. It seemed an odd exercise knowing how stretched the police were for manpower and resources. It struck me they might be planning a police operation, knowing already Mark was here. Yet how could they know? Mark had climbed over the wall late at night. He was sure he hadn't been seen and I believed him. He had too much experience of being on the run not to know. The police had my address, of course, from the questioning with Pete but nothing as yet, I thought, to fix on me. Yet I felt nervous that they'd passed by so casually in this way and almost wished they'd come and ask direct questions and get it over with.

I watched them saunter back along the road without looking up this time at either roof or window. Outside Carol's they got into the police van but it was another ten minutes before they drove away and I could safely tell Mark to come out of the cupboard.

He was concerned when I told him about the two

policemen surveying the roofs and considered returning to the woods.

"You'll be just as vulnerable there from Craig," I said.

"Possibly, but free to move."

"You can be free here if we can devise a disguise." I couldn't bear the thought of his going now and within the hour I was rummaging in Oxfam and the wig centre in Horton.

I came back with the latest fashion for men in the form of a short fair wig together with a blue suit that had just come in at Oxfam. The wig cost a fortune. Ironically it took half of my earnings left from DLS but I reckoned it was worth every penny if it kept us together, and Mark free.

We laughed as he tried it on together with the suit. He looked quite the salesman, not at all in character but it gave him the confidence to launch forth in the day.

He didn't feel it was safe now for the others to meet at my place. It was too much of a risk, he thought. Everyone could be cornered and arrested, thus jeopardising the raid itself. He would go and see everyone individually, he decided, to finalise plans.

I could see the logic but in the days that followed found it a slow torture waiting every time he went out for the hours to pass until he returned. Each time he was late, I feared the worst, that he'd been followed or caught.

The police were more in evidence and likely to wreck his plans but it was Craig and his mate I feared the most. They'd have no compunction about harming Mark, even killing him. They were solely bent on revenge.

Sometimes I thought of following him when he went to see Pete or Martin to reassure myself he was safe, but often didn't feel well enough. I was still sick most mornings and it was as much as I could do to drag myself to the bathroom. I also had to look for another job and started on the usual grind of ringing agencies and filling in forms, which consumed some of the time when Mark was out.

One evening when he was out in his disguise, sorting arrangements for the final raid, Alan appeared to ask what I'd decided about the concert. Truth to tell, I'd forgotten all about it and, feeling guilty, made the mistake of asking him in.

"I take it you have other things on your mind." He wiped his shoes carefully on the doormat, although they were already immaculately polished and clean, unlike Mark's. I hoped he wouldn't stay.

"I have been a bit busy," I said curtly.

"Work or pleasure?" He sat on the settee, looking at me with a curious smile.

"Not exactly pleasure. I'm trying to get another job."

He raised his eyebrows in surprise. "I thought you had one. I'm sure Robert told me you had."

"Robert?" I looked at him sharply. How much did he know? Or had he been sent to probe?

"Yes, Robert. He works at DLS, doesn't he? I got the impression you work there too."

"Really? Well I don't."

"Oh well." He shrugged indifferently, too much so, I thought. "I obviously misunderstood him. All this business has been pretty hard on Robert, hasn't it? I mean, if the share price for DLS goes on falling and these raids go on, he could lose his job."

"I'm sure he'll soon find another. Whereas the animals

killed and tortured at DLS can't find another life, can they?"

"Of course, I'd forgotten." He gave a patronising smile. "You're into all this anti-establishment, animal rights stuff, aren't you?"

"So you agree with torturing sentient creatures, for the sake of another washing powder on the market, just for profit?"

"Surely it's more," Alan countered, "for vital medicines, isn't it, to control disease?"

"That's the impression places like DLS want to create, but it's false. A lot of the experiments are for useless products we don't need. And as far as medicines go, animals don't react like we do which is why so many mistakes are made."

"How do you know all this, if you don't or didn't work there?" Alan challenged.

"Because I've made it my business to know." He had come to probe I was sure. "Other methods could be used like tissue culture and computer modelling. We have to move right away from using animals to test products."

"And meanwhile what happens to people like Robert? Poor Robert. He's already been ousted, as it is, from his home."

"Ousted? He chose to go, Alan. He's the one who had the affair."

"Well, perhaps you're more in the know than I am. I expect you girls have got together and talked it over. But I can't help feeling sorry for Robert with all this other business as well. It is his home."

"If it meant so much to him, why did he have an affair then?" I was feeling more and more irritated with Alan's condescending attitude and wished he would go. I was worried that at any minute Mark would return, unaware, and be seen.

"A change of scene, who knows? I doubt it meant that much to him anyway," Alan said.

"It obviously did to Carol."

"I sometimes think," Alan said ponderously, "it's better to turn a blind eye when there are children involved."

"And live dishonestly, you mean?" My irritation was getting the better of me and suddenly I felt sick again. "Excuse me."

I went to the kitchen, hoping to get away from him, but he followed. I wasn't sick but still felt sick and strangely hungry with it, a gnawing hunger making me shaky and weak. I had a craving suddenly for bananas and macaroons or something else with an almond taste but there was nothing in the kitchen at all in either category.

"Are you all right?" As I sat at the kitchen table, Alan put his arm around my shoulder, looking at me with concern.

"Yes, I'm fine."

"You don't look it, if I may say so. Why not come back to my place? I'll give you a meal and set you up again. I was going to ask you anyway." He kissed me lightly on the cheek.

"It's kind of you," I said, I thought firmly, "but I can't."

"Why not?"

"Do I have to give a reason? I don't feel up to it. That's all."

"You mean you don't want to or you don't feel well?"

"Both."

"I see." His eyes darkened with disappointed anger and

I knew I'd offended his pride. Perhaps I should have told him I was pregnant since he'd expressed concern but didn't want the news broadcast until it was obvious. Besides, it wasn't his business.

"I'm sorry," I said. "I think you'd better ask someone else to the concert."

"I'll certainly do that. You know what I think…" He paused and then with a chauvinist look of contempt, as if I were soiled goods now, to be rejected, said, "Robert's right. You're not quite all you seem."

He turned towards the front door and would have made, no doubt, a satisfyingly theatrical exit but at that moment it opened and Mark appeared, with an equally thespian gesture, taking off his wig.

The two men stood staring at each other in the hallway. Alan narrowed his eyes. Frowning, he studied Mark as if trying to identify him. Then he strode out through the front door, not looking back.

"Who was that?" Mark asked.

"It's just a chap who's moved in along the road. He came to see if I would go to a concert with him."

"He looked as if he recognised me."

"I don't see how. Your photo in the paper isn't that clear and he hasn't seen you before face to face."

"But he has now. How reliable is he, do you think? What views does he take?"

"Not ours but not entirely the opposite either."

"Do you think he'll tell the police?"

"I shouldn't think so. He was annoyed because I wouldn't go to his place but I wouldn't think he'd be vindictive. No, I think Alan's basically okay," I said.

✳

How wrong can you be about people?

The police came the next morning at five.

Hearing the bell, I got up and looked out of the window. A police van was parked directly outside my gate and the officer with the weathered face and large hands I'd seen the week before stood just inside my front garden. Another officer was in the porch but I couldn't see him clearly in the subdued light at this angle.

As the bell rang again, quickly I woke Mark and persuaded him into the cupboard with his boots and clothing. I straightened his side of the bed then went downstairs to open the door as the bell rang a third time.

"Kate Wilson?"

I nodded, looking irritably up at the uniformed figure standing in the porch. I'd not seen him before. He was a tall, military-looking man with a neatly clipped moustache and sharp blue eyes that were already looking past me into the hall leading to the kitchen.

Briefly he introduced himself as Inspector James. In a quietly confidential yet warning tone he stated, "We have reason to believe, Miss Wilson, Mark Stanton, the animal rights activist, is staying here. We want to speak with him."

"Mark Stanton?" I screwed up my face in the most dozy, puzzled way I could muster.

"We had a report he was seen here yesterday evening."

"From whom?" I asked.

"I'm not at liberty to divulge our sources, Miss Wilson. Suffice it to say, it came from a reliable one."

"I don't think so, Inspector, because there's no one of that name here. There's only me and I strongly object to being woken at this hour due to a malicious rumour. What is Mark Stanton wanted for anyway?"

"Breaking and entering at Draco Life Science, resisting arrest and setting off an explosion at Greenacres Farm."

Which he didn't do, I wanted to assert. Jake's actions were already, to my concern, being hung like a noose round Mark's neck. But to assert Mark's innocence now could well increase the suspicions I was close to him, prolong the encounter and put Mark further at risk.

"Since Mark Stanton isn't here, Miss Wilson, perhaps you could tell me when you last saw him?"

"I can't remember offhand." I reverted to my earlier dazed expression. "It was probably at a demo a few weeks ago."

"So you have been involved in demonstrations at Draco Life Science?"

"There's nothing wrong in attending a demo, is there?"

"Not as long as the law is kept." He gave a quick glance back at the officer waiting at the gate. "We'd like to look around."

"Feel free." I turned on the lady bountiful, waving them both with a casual gesture inside. I guessed they hadn't a search warrant but, if I refused, they'd be back with one within hours. I watched tensely as they poked and prodded around. They started in the sitting room, opening up my father's walnut cupboard and the teak chest he'd brought back from India in his younger days. Then they went to the attic, pulling down the folding rickety ladder for access. There was nothing there, of course, no place in fact to hide. Irritated they'd collected dust on their uniforms, they climbed down to look at the two bedrooms. The smaller bedroom had only one cupboard and a bed which were soon dealt with. In my own, the larger room, they searched more painstakingly in the two wardrobes and under the bed, opening even the large bottom drawer of my father's old mahogany chest of drawers. How they thought Mark would fit in there without suffocating, I don't know. I couldn't help smiling at this stage.

It wasn't so funny when Inspector James stood within an inch of the panelling that Mark lay behind. I could feel my heart thumping so loudly I was sure he could hear and he was standing, as if listening, as he looked out of the window, as if he knew Mark was somewhere near. The two minutes he stood there were the longest I'd known.

When eventually, to my relief, they went downstairs I remembered Tess. Whatever else happened, I had to make sure she didn't come sniffing upstairs. Inspector James had other ideas about Tess. As we opened the kitchen door, she cowered away from the two men in her basket.

"Where did you get her?" he asked suspiciously.

"A friend. I'm looking after her while my friend's abroad," I quickly improvised.

Inspector James wasn't convinced, but time was pressing. He looked at his watch with other commitments in mind and the prodding continued through the kitchen cupboards and into the garden. Eventually, seemingly satisfied, he straightened himself and put on an ancient mariner act with his eyes.

"You do realise, don't you, Miss Wilson, it's a crime to shelter wanted criminals and escapees. If Mark Stanton comes here, it's your duty to let us know. I don't think you'd want to go to prison yourself, would you? It's easy to be persuaded otherwise but I'd strongly advise you not to be, if he comes. The courts don't take kindly to people who harbour criminals evading the due process of law."

I felt I wanted to shout at him that Mark was not a criminal, that he'd done what he had because it was morally right, despite the outcome and danger. But it would not have been any use, I knew. It would have made him doubt me even more and class me likewise as a terrorist or nutter.

I waited a good half an hour after they'd gone before letting Mark know it was safe to emerge.

It was clear they were sceptical about my story for I noticed them parked further along the road later the same day. Even disguised, it was going to be difficult for Mark to venture out during daylight. At night there was still the risk of scaling the garden wall, for one couldn't be sure until virtually over it, there might be police the other side. All of which was a problem for Mark organising the final stages of the raid. I managed to get his phone mended so he could contact Martin and Pete and the others who had mobiles.

Mark didn't take kindly to being confined. We were very happy together in bed at night and in the evening but he was used to action and exercise in the day and needed them. He would prowl around the kitchen in the afternoon like a tiger exiled from its territory. Tess, though, benefited. His enforced confinement gave him time to give to her and she grew daily more confident beneath his touch and reassurance. Together we also started to write the script for the film on DLS Mark intended submitting to ITV. His friend had completed the editing and the film was virtually ready for a thirty-minute slot. But Mark was anxious to get some footage included on the primates in the final raid if he could, footage on the organ transplants he'd heard were being carried out between pigs and baboons. This, he hoped, would finally convince people and win them over.

The only person who called was Steve, but he had problems of his own with his mother's deteriorating health and could only leave her for a few minutes at a time when the two carers were away. He managed though to get messages to the group members, without mobiles, which was a great help to Mark.

The newspapers continued their diatribe versus the Animal Rights Movement and Mark's photo appeared again in two of the tabloids. At the same time came the welcome news the share price of DLS was continuing to fall. Mark was keen to revisit Gilda Summers, but it was still too risky during the day and she was unlikely to open her door to strangers at night. We finally decided I'd go but Mark would ring first to remind and prepare her for my visit. And it worked.

She was a lovely old lady with her open mind, alert eyes, olive skin and silvery hair. Her interfering helper was fortunately out shopping and she asked me in for tea, saying she had already instructed her stockbroker to sell all sixty thousand shares and invest them in gilts for the time being, as Mark suggested.

"Keep up the good work," she said as I departed and I was almost tempted, in a final coup de grace, to call on the hose-wielding Huntley-Joneses but decided it was probably pushing our luck. I was already worried leaving Mark alone in the house in case of an unexpected police raid. It wasn't so easy closing the panel of the fireplace cupboard from inside.

I arrived home to find him dressed all in black and ready to go out.

"What's happened?" I was immediately disturbed. He hadn't been out since the police raid and I was by no means certain the police weren't around, keeping a watchful eye.

"Nothing's happened. Jake's rung, that's all."

"What did he want?"

"To be in on the raid."

"The others won't want him surely."

"That depends on what he's got to offer, which is what I need to find out."

"It'll be more of the same. He's obsessed, Mark, dangerous."

"He still does a good job with the lighting. On anything else, we'll have to stand firm."

"Can you? He's a loner. He won't listen. He acts on his own."

"We're none of us fixed entities, Kate, even Jake."

"I'm worried you'll be caught." I put my arms around him, kissing him. "Please don't go."

But Mark stood his ground.

"Jake's more dangerous outside than in," he said. "I'm sure you'll agree when you've reflected. And I won't be caught. I've managed before and I'll manage now."

He kissed my lips, ran his hands over my breasts. "I love you. Remember that and I'll be back to hear how you fared in Oxford."

He moved to the back door and I knew I couldn't stop him.

"Don't wait up for me," he said. And he was gone, climbing over the wall in his black attire into the darkness of the night beyond.

TWENTY

I tried to be rational that night and convince myself Mark knew from experience what he was doing, that it would all work out and he'd achieve his objective of closing DLS down.

But I couldn't get Jake and his private agenda out of my mind. His motive in wanting to destroy DLS and the power of such organisations was clear enough but not his motive with regard to Mark. Why, if he resented Mark, did he want to entice him into his own plans? What was he really up to? Did he himself really know? It was this, the unpredictable, I sensed in Jake that made me feel most afraid, particularly in the way it could affect Mark.

I woke the next morning at eight with a headache and the lingering threads of a nightmare where Jake had set off another bomb. Mark had not returned and there was no message on my mobile.

More to divert myself, than from necessity, I went to the corner shop to get eggs and a newspaper. On the second page there was a brief article on DLS, reporting their share prices were continuing to fall as increasing numbers of shareholders sold. A worrying footnote suggested financial support was coming from the States, a transfer of funds from a similar company to keep DLS going. The struggle to close DLS was far from over.

On my way home, I saw Carol hovering in her front garden, as if she'd been waiting for me. She didn't look her usual smart self. She had no make-up on and her hair was straggly and uncared for, with dark roots showing through the blond.

"Can I ask a favour?" she said.

"Sure."

"Can you spare a moment to come inside?" Her voice was strangely deferential, unrelated to the confident Carol I was used to. She didn't wait for an answer but led me straight into her lounge.

Carol was proud of her lounge. She'd spent a fortune on its cream carpet, its cream curtains and cream settee and chairs. She'd spent hours keeping it spotless and childproof. But the pristine cream was shadowed now with piles of files and books and clothing, Robert's I guessed, and there were even crumbs on the carpet, a dirty plate and a scatter of children's toys.

"Sorry about the mess. I told you, didn't I, that Robert had moved out?"

"Yes, I'm sorry."

"He says he wants a divorce as soon as possible, a clean break."

"So soon?"

"He's been put up to it, of course, by that floozy next door. She's moved out now, thank God, but she's pregnant."

"You think you'll agree then to a divorce?" The word pregnant hit me as a reminder of my present state.

"I thought not at first. But now, I've decided, yes.

There's no point in hanging on when something's finished. I wouldn't have him back now anyway. It's a problem though with the children in the afternoons when I'm working. Robert used to come home early two of the days to pick them up."

"How will you manage?"

"I've fixed up someone to have them after school from October but I'm stuck for Thursdays in September. I wondered if you could help me out for three weeks."

"Of course, no problem." It seemed the least I could do. I was going to be at home after all. I found it a bit unnerving though that they were not just Carol's but Robert's children. Robert who directed an institution that had reduced Tess and thousands like her to such a terrible state. It struck me then as odd that Carol didn't appear to know I'd even worked at DLS. Why hadn't Robert told her? Was it just secrecy, the fact that he didn't want anyone outside to know what went on inside DLS? Or was it that he and Carol hadn't really been communicating at all? Either way, I don't think she knew the extent of the suffering of the animals at DLS. If she had, she would surely not have supported it. Or was I just deceiving myself? I felt confused talking to her, as if I had a foot in each camp and was betraying both, torn between sympathy for her predicament and antagonism towards the institution that had clearly in part provided for her. And suddenly everything seemed grey rather than black and white, complicated.

"Thanks, Kate. Thanks. It's a great relief to know the children will be safe. By the way are you still looking for a job?"

"Well, yes, yes, I am."

"You might like to know Betty Simpson who got that job you wanted has had to up sticks suddenly and go to France. It's available again."

"Do you think I'd get it?"

"Yes, I do. You were second choice, I know. It's only part-time though."

"Part-time would suit me better anyway."

"Why, are you planning something else?" Carol looked at me curiously. "Don't tell me you're pregnant," she said.

How she guessed I don't know. Perhaps I just looked pregnant. Perhaps she wanted me to be or thought I should be, aware of my biological clock ticking away. Whatever the reason, she seemed genuinely pleased.

"What does Steve feel about it?" she asked.

"Steve?"

"He is the father, isn't he?"

"Steve and I have only ever been good friends, Carol."

"Then who?"

"It's not someone you know."

"Not Alan then?"

"No, definitely not!"

"A pity, he's a nice guy. He'd suit you, look after you."

Carol had an uncanny knack of extracting names and sources once she'd set her mind to it. I knew I had to divert her from guessing Mark.

"Perhaps you should cultivate Alan then," I suggested.

"I haven't time to even consider new men at the moment, nor the inclination frankly. But if I had," for the first time since I entered the house she smiled, "Alan would certainly be the one I'd choose."

At home, I completed another application form and letter for the part-time post at the college. Carol said she would put in a word for me and I began to feel hope, at last, I would be able to support myself adequately. But the day, once I'd sent it off, seemed endless. I bathed Tess and played with her, cleaned the house from top to bottom and cooked an elaborate vegetarian meal ready for Mark but still the hours dragged waiting for his return.

At last close to midnight I heard the key turn in the back door. I ran downstairs to find Mark standing by the kitchen sink with a black eye and a bruise across his cheekbone.

"It's all right. It's nothing much," he smiled tiredly as I fell into his arms.

"What happened?"

"I tried to see Dad. The police van wasn't there, but Davies and Craig were waiting in the garden."

"How did they know you'd be there?"

"They didn't. They obviously guessed sooner or later I'd turn up. It just shows how bloody determined they are."

"So you didn't see your father?"

"No, I had to run for it. Fortunately they don't know the place as well as I do and I got away."

"You don't think they followed you here?"

"No, no one followed. God, I'm tired. I didn't sleep last night at all."

"You managed to see Jake then?"

"Yes, I saw Jake."

I was longing to know what the outcome was but Mark said he'd tell me the next day. He was too tired even to eat. Upstairs, he undressed and fell into bed. Within seconds he was asleep.

In the morning, when I woke, he was sitting at the desk

by the window writing. It appeared to be a letter. Every few minutes, frowning, he looked out of the window, pondering, as if he was writing something important to him.

"Who are you writing to?" I asked as he turned, noticing I was awake. His bruise looked raw and swollen in the morning light.

"It's a letter to Dad to explain things just in case."

"In case of what?"

"Thing don't work out the way we want."

"What do you mean?" My throat began constricting from fear. Mark had never expressed himself in such pessimistic terms before.

"I mean—" he hesitated then "—I could get caught. I probably will get caught. I need to know there's some provision, I mean, for the baby."

"Oh Mark." I got out of bed and went over to him and hugged him. "You don't need to worry your father. I'm halfway to getting a job now."

"Really?"

"Something's come up at the college. I think it may work this time."

"Dad would be able to help all the same, would want to help. He needs to know."

"But you can always tell him even if you are arrested."

"Maybe, but it's safer this way. I want you to promise me, Kate, you'll give him the letter if I'm not around." Mark folded the pages and put them into an envelope, writing his father's name, Mr Richard Stanton, on the outside. "Will you promise?"

"If you insist, as long as you promise me something."

"Which is?"

"That you'll tell me everything you decided with Jake."

"Very well, but you're not going to like it. We've decided to let Jake in on the raid."

"But surely Pete could manage the electronics, the lighting?"

"Manage, but not so well. It isn't just that though."

"What is it then?" I guessed with dread what was coming.

"We have to do something more than rescuing the animals. DLS's share value is going down. People like Gilda Summers are selling but Robert Sykes has got a loan from some US Company that can keep them solvent and active. No matter how many animals we rescue, they can build up again from this base unless…"

"Unless what?"

"Unless we destroy everything, the main building particularly, so it costs just too much."

"So you're going to let Jake loose with his bombs again?"

"When we've rescued the baboons, the monkeys and dogs, yes, he's going to plant three devices in the main building."

"Ones he's made himself?"

"Virtually, yes."

"So you're not involved?"

"Not in the planting, no."

"Don't let yourself be, will you, Mark."

"Why?" Mark smiled. "Do you think he's going to blow himself up then?"

"He's not an expert."

"He's not far off, I'd say."

"What do Pete and Martin think?"

"They both agree we have to up the stakes now."

"Even Philippa and Jenny?" Surely I wasn't the only one afraid and doubting.

"Everyone now or it's all over. Don't you see, with the loan they'll be up and running in no time and we'll have to start all over again. But the loan won't cover a new building and they'll be finished. It's not what I wanted but it's necessary now. For the sake of the animals, for the sake of the ultimate objective, we'll have to risk losing some support. I know how you feel but sometimes one just has to change one's mind and we can't afford to fail, not now. No one will be hurt I can assure you. We'll make absolutely sure no one's in the building."

What could I say? Mark had worked things out in the way he saw fit and best for the cause. It sounded logical, reasonable with the change in circumstances and the loan. And Mark was reasonable. The most reasonable person I knew and with admirably consistent principles for action. It was one of the reasons I loved him. But relying on Jake, knowing Jake's jealousy of him, filled me with concern.

Mark's mind though was obviously made up, with the backing of the others, and I didn't want to spoil our time together. As he detailed the plans, I went along with them. It was now Thursday morning and the raid was set for the next day, Friday, in the small hours beginning at two. There would only be twelve people involved this time, not twenty.

"The fewer who know, the better," Mark said.

Philippa and Jenny were to be in charge again of the animal rescue. Philippa had already found a couple of sanctuaries to take the baboons and monkeys and Jenny had found homes for the dogs, such as remained alive.

There were not so many animals to rescue and they would be taken out of the end door of Section 18 I had opened behind the sacks of food before leaving DLS.

I only hoped it was still open. There was no saying what the suspicious and sceptical Tony might have done since I'd left but I doubted he'd have bothered to move all the sacks of grain and I offered to show them where to push the door open from the outside. My main job was to keep watch outside and warn of any police arriving.

Mark told me the damaged wire from the previous raid had fortunately not been replaced, which suggested Draco was not expecting an immediate repeat raid.

"I wouldn't be so sure," I warned. "There may be extra security guards. Robert won't give up without a fight."

"Nor will we," Mark said simply.

"No." I couldn't resist him as he turned to me, the sunlight on his face, his bruise, his black eye. I loved him so much then I knew, whatever he decided, whatever the outcome.

We made love all morning and afternoon that day, only getting up to see to Tess and when hungry. As the evening drew in then, Mark had several calls on his mobile from Pete, Martin, Philippa and Jenny.

Jake did not ring and I kept hoping he'd pull out but it was not to be.

At ten o'clock Mark dressed in his black outfit and scaled the wall to make his way to the site of DLS across the fields alone.

Two hours later Steve called and drove me to the meeting place, as before, a half a mile from DLS. It was a clear night with a quarter moon. I heard Tess whimper as I closed the front door.

TWENTY-ONE

The others were all ready waiting when we reached the lay-by: Pete, Martin, Jason, Karl, Gemma, Philippa and Jenny, but not Mark or Jake.

"Has Mark come yet?" I asked Pete. I was afraid even then something could have happened to him en route across the fields.

"He's gone to recheck the wire and the number of guards." Pete tried to sound calm but his voice was tense as if he was afraid, as I was, that things were not going to go to plan.

"And Jake?"

"He's gone to check the main gate."

"We may not get the vans in, you mean?" I knew the entry code had been changed but Jake, Mark told me, had broken into a car and stolen a plastic card that he hoped would do the trick. If not, it was going to be a problem getting through the narrow confines of the wire with cages of sick animals, almost impossible unless the wire was cut further back.

There was also the problem of the security lights and CCTV. The new installations were too high now for Jake to reach even with the ladder he'd lost in the last skirmish.

Perhaps not surprisingly, there was none of the banter there'd been on the last raid. Even Jason and Karl who usually joked were talking in subdued tones and Jenny and Philippa were sitting silently in the vans they'd acquired for moving the animals.

It was make or break time for DLS and everyone knew it. From the next day DLS would either fold or flourish. The idea of it flourishing and going on for yet more years didn't bear thinking of and I longed for Mark to be with us to reassure and confirm the wisdom of Jake's plans.

Though it was barely twenty minutes, it seemed hours waiting for him. Then, as I strained my eyes in the darkness, I saw him coming along the lane towards us. He had taken off his balaclava and his face looked strangely pale and vulnerable against the backcloth of dark trees and hedging and black clothing. I had a strong impression for a moment of the night closing in on him, like a warning not to go back down the lane again.

Then he was in the midst of us, his eyes and voice, as ever, resolute.

"There are three guards now," he warned, "which means six of us instead of four will be needed to tackle and hold them. I suggest Pete, Martin, Jason, Karl, Steve and myself, working in pairs. We rush the hut as before, just after they return from their rounds. We'll take their mobiles first, then tie them, keeping them confined in the hut.

"Jake reckons he can open the gate now so Phil and Jen you'll be able to go in with the vans but wait till we've got full control of the guards. Kate's going to check the main entry point at Section 18 and, Gemma, could you start then loading the dogs from Section 18 and the two sections beyond? There won't be anything like as many this time but they'll be in worse condition."

"Sure," Gemma smiled, ready as always to co-operate as a team.

"Martin, Pete and I will come and join you to move the cages," Mark continued, "as soon as we've dealt with the guards. Karl, Jason and Steve, could you please stay with the guards keeping watch until the operation's over."

The men nodded their assent. No one mentioned Jake. Our roles decided, we all put on our balaclavas and deposited unwanted items in the car. Mark came over to me then.

"How are you feeling?" he asked.

"Fine, as long as the door to Section 18 hasn't been re-bolted."

"You think it may have?"

"I don't expect so but I can't be sure until I've checked."

I couldn't imagine Tony Brown removing all the sacks of food behind the door. He wasn't exactly given to physical exertion but who could tell what had happened since I'd left DLS? Both TB and Robert were angry men and security had obviously been tightened.

"Okay, you check then but promise me you won't go through the wire till the guards are sorted. I don't want you in a scuffle getting hurt. We'll go then to the primate labs. I want you to show me the way again."

As long as we can get inside, I thought. Desperately, I hoped TB hadn't found the unbolted door and I wouldn't let Mark down.

As we set off with the others silently along the lane, he pressed my hand and I knew we were in it together now, that I was as committed as he was, to both our love and the cause.

As we drew near to the DLS compound, we were conscious of much brighter security lights. Erected high on steel frames, they threw the starkness of the Auschwitz chimneys up into the sky, glared over the compound, allowing no shadows, no hiding place. Seeing the burly figures of the guards on their hourly tour with protective helmets and truncheons in their hands, close to the protective ring of barbed wire, I wondered with apprehension how we would ever break in again and succeed.

The lights did not go off this time when the guards returned at ten minutes past two to their hut. All our movements from entry to leaving would be seen. But there were chinks in the armour. The wire previously cut had been re-twisted but cut again unobtrusively by Jake and Mark from the outside making an opening wide enough for us all to enter single file.

As the guards settled in the hut to their TV and cards and silence descended again, one by one Mark, Martin, Pete, Jason, Karl and Steve manoeuvred through the wire onto the compound.

Jenny and Philippa were waiting along the lane with their vans. There were only Gemma and myself left outside.

We watched nervously as the six men, keeping close to the wire, crept cautiously to the cabin. Some thirty feet away, at a signal from Mark, they rushed at the hut, as before, breaking down the door.

From where Gemma and I stood outside the wire, all was confusion then, a skirmish of shifting black figures and helmeted guards fighting in the hut and compound as the group tried to bring the guards down and wrench mobiles and truncheons from their hands. We heard shouts, swearing, a thump and crashing as someone fell backwards into the hut but who it was we had no idea. The fighting went on and on. The guards were outnumbered but stronger and trained. It was more than twenty minutes before they seemed at last subdued. Then, suddenly, one broke free and ran towards us through the opening in the wire.

"We must stop him." Gemma planted herself where Mark had twisted back the wire ready to stand in his way. She was about half his size, tough and resolute in mind but slim and small in frame. As he pushed through the wire, she pulled his arm and stuck out her leg, tripping him onto the long wet grass of the field.

He scrambled to his feet, swearing, a great hulk of a man, and seizing her by the shoulder, punched her in the face. He twisted her arm right back so she gasped in pain and I did the only thing I could think of to stop him and kicked him in the groin. He was about to turn on me when Pete, Martin and Mark, following, caught up with him and at last overwhelmed him, corded his hands and dragged him back to the hut.

Gemma had a terrible nosebleed. There was blood all over her clothes but she insisted on coming to help me check the door at Section 18.

We found the iron door readily enough but it appeared lower, smaller from the outside than I remembered and, as I pushed it, to my dismay, what I feared, happened. It wouldn't budge. I tried pushing again and got Gemma to push but still without effect. Had it been locked again or merely wedged by a sack of food?

"I'll get Pete and Mark," Gemma said.

"No, we'll manage." I needed to prove to Mark I could do it, one of the few things he'd asked me to do without help. "Let's try pushing together."

We both leaned our shoulders against the door and shoved and, to my relief, there was a scraping sound and the door shifted open a few centimetres. By the light of Gemma's torch then we saw that it had been blocked by a torn plastic sack of dried food pellets and the pellets themselves had got wedged in the cracks of the door.

Feeling round the small opening I scooped out some of the dried pellets wedged around the back of the door. I reckoned one of the sacks had slipped down making it impossible to open the door further. We set about then puncturing the sack and scraping out the food until we had created a space big enough to squeeze inside.

While Gemma kept watch and shone her torch for me, I climbed up the sacks of food, then heaved them down to the other side to make a passage through from the door.

There were no sounds from the darkness of the kennel cages just beyond. Most of the fitter dogs, I reminded myself, had already been rescued on our first raid but there were still a number left. I'd been with them, fed them. Were they too ill now even to move or whimper or had they been hidden further away or killed? I had an awful feeling that we were going to be outmanoeuvred or trapped at the last moment.

I pressed on moving the sacks and suddenly was aware of Mark beside me. "You shouldn't be doing this," he said, and he started lifting the heavier sacks out of the way.

Then Pete and Martin came, carrying cages from the

vans parked ready and close to the door. Pete gave me a torch and I went through and switched on the light at the top of the stairs. As I looked down on the familiar neon lit cages, I saw the reason for the silence. There were only four cages now with dogs inside. In the first two the dogs were stretched out stiff and dead on the meagre sawdust. In the third, the beagle was clearly dying. Only in the fourth was there any real sign of movement. Annie was the name I'd given her. I remembered her well for she always cowered in fear at the back of her cage and she was frightened now.

She had one of the great head collars round her neck to stop her scratching the raw sores on her back, the result of Tony B's testing another psoriatic cream.

I suppose I'd become to a degree hardened by this sight but Gemma was crying as she helped Pete lift Annie and carry her into a cage for the van. She barely fitted in with her head collar but we didn't dare take it off for fear of her scratching and infecting the sores on her back. The bandages had all come adrift and her sores were exposed now like salted raw meat. The pain and irritation must have been excruciating. For reasons of cost, Tony B made a point of never giving painkillers to the dogs.

While Pete, Mark and Gemma went to get the dogs from the next unit, I led Mark to the primate section through the maze of Kafkaesque passages and closed doors until we reached, at length, the white door I'd found before leading to the hall of caged macaque monkeys and baboons.

As we pushed open the door and switched on the light, the smell of sickness, urine and faeces was overpowering and the animals seemed even more desperately sad, cowering and cramped in their cages, deprived of all stimulus and expression of their natural instincts and movement. Their eyes followed us with the subdued poignancy of human pleading, uncomprehending. I felt I couldn't bear it. I had to move on.

"These are the main ones to move," I told Mark, "but there may be others in the lab."

"Let's see the others first." Mark pushed the lab door open.

In the centre of the lab was the same steel table I'd seen before. There was no monkey strapped down, no technician torturing and for a moment I hoped we'd found nothing more sinister and could get on with moving the baboons and monkeys from the hall. Then Mark noticed another door leading off the lab and quickly opened it.

The smell that hit us was even worse than in the hall, the smell not only of waste but of blood this time and fatal sickness.

As we switched on the light, we saw this was a second lab with another steel table in the centre but on the wider shelving surrounding it were six large cages each holding a primate, or what had once been a primate, for the animals in these cages were no longer animals as I'd known them.

Two of them, baboons, had huge swellings bulging from their necks. One held the swelling in its hands, its face turned away to the side in a posture of inconsolable misery and despair. The swelling was red and seeping yellow fluid that dripped onto its feet and the floor of the cage. The other baboon slumped against the bars of its cage as if drugged or dying, barely breathing.

In the next two adjoining cages, two monkeys had shaved abdomens with long crudely stitched incision marks, with blood seeping out between the stitches. One had very laboured breathing; the other shook with incipient tremors and as it looked at me, expectant a moment, I could see an expression of bewildered pain in its eyes.

In the other two cages, the two macaque monkeys couldn't see at all for they both had their eyelids stitched down. One had its head clasped in its hands. It looked so human, desolate and bereft, like a child who has trusted and been betrayed. And I knew at that moment that it felt as we do, the same pain and betrayal, the knowledge and awareness of what has been.

I didn't doubt what the swellings were. I'd heard rumours both inside DLS and out of pigs' hearts grafted onto the blood vessels of baboons, the latest craze in xenotransplantation but it didn't take away the horror and I was overwhelmed with a confusion of sadness and anger. We were related to these creatures, to the rest of life, not separate. We shared not only genes but feelings, awareness. Yet, deliberately, people had crushed and ignored the closeness, treated them as objects, not sentient beings at all. They were taking away now the only thing that any creature has finally—its life.

"My God, how could they?" Mark looked round the lab as if he was trapped himself, caged. "Creatures so amazingly agile, intelligent, able to form complex relationships; to be treated like this. The bastards. The bastards!"

"Can we take them away though?"

"We have to, even if they have only a few hours. We can't leave them in this hell hole for more torture."

As his eyes swept around the lab in anger, we noticed two other cages on the ground. In one, a cat with a broken spine was trying to drag itself across the floor of the cage. In the other was a mouse with a huge tumour bulging under its neck so it appeared to have an arrogant, regal expression as it tried to peer over the top.

I felt at that moment a stir in my abdomen, as if Dmitri himself were aware of the grotesqueness and pain. I wanted to be sick only I knew I couldn't be as I hadn't eaten for several hours. But I could feel myself shaking from the effects of wanting to be, of wanting to communicate to the tortured animals that we'd get them out and all would be well. Only I knew it wouldn't. We might get them out but we couldn't change what had happened to them.

Then Mark was holding me, his arm around my shoulder, looking into my eyes, quietly suppressing his anger.

"I'm just going to take some photos, then we'll get them out." From his trouser pocket he took out the instant camera he always carried in case of need for evidence and quickly took some flash photos of the baboons, monkeys, the mouse and cat. He handed me the camera. "Get the film developed and make use of it if I can't. Right, you take the cat and keep watch outside. Ring on the mobile if anyone comes. I'll get Pete and Martin to help with these."

I picked up the cage with the cat while Mark took the two blinded macaques and together we hurried as best we could through the maze of passages to the exit at Section 18. The two large cages were difficult to get through the door but we managed by bending and pushing and soon with the dogs collected, Jenny's van was loaded and Pete and Martin went with Mark to rescue the other monkeys and baboons.

As Jenny drove through the main entrance, I took up a position to the left in a dried-up ditch on the other side of the lane running alongside DLS and at right angles to the road. Sheltered by a hawthorn, I reckoned I'd be able to know immediately what was happening in the road and lane.

For about half an hour it was quiet, even in the guards' hut. I was a little concerned about the delay in Philippa's first load leaving. Realistically, I realised with all the passages to cover, Mark, Pete and Gemma couldn't have got the cages out any faster. When Philippa did leave with her first load the van's exhaust was quite noisy and I was worried people in houses on the other side of the road might have heard. It was deep in the night and they weren't that close but there was a light in one of the upstairs windows. As Jenny drove back again with an empty van to Section 18, I found the waiting getting on my nerves. It was important to keep watch and Mark was right in trying to protect me from straining myself and losing Dimitri, but I'd rather have been involved in some action with Mark.

It seemed ages waiting for Jenny's van to be re-loaded. But at last she was away along the road to her parents' house, where the monkeys and baboons would be delivered discretely to different zoos and reserves.

She was just out of sight when Steve came through the main gate and walked in my direction. I heard him quietly calling my name.

"I'm here." I stood and he joined me.

"Mark rang," he said," wanting to know if you were okay."

"I'm fine," I said, "and you? How are the guards?"

"Obnoxious."

"But tamed?"

"For the moment but I'm sure they're planning something. There's been no sign of the police?"

"Not yet."

"Anyone else?"

"Not so far."

"I'd better get back. I'll see you later at the lay-by."

Steve was about to climb out of the ditch when we heard voices in the field behind us, coming closer.

It took me a few minutes to get attuned. The voices, both male, were deliberately quiet and for a while I couldn't distinguish them. Then, as I strained to listen, with a chill I realised they were the voices of the two men who most hated Mark, Craig, the hunter and Robert. Craig's voice held a triumphant sneer.

"What did I tell you? They didn't waste any time."

Robert sounded nonplussed, on edge. "How the devil could they have got in? We changed the code, repaired the wire."

"Obviously not well enough. They're cunning, no mistake."

"But the guards should have had time to warn us."

"Not if Stanton's planned this. He's probably knifed them by now."

"You think they got through the wire again?"

"And cracked the code. You'd better get the police straightaway. They're not so quick off the mark nowadays. I'll scout around and find a good spot to get Stanton."

We crouched as low as we could in the ditch, hearing a movement quite close as the voices ceased and Craig and Robert pushed through the hedge onto the lane.

I looked out of the ditch and saw Robert walking towards the main road where, presumably, he had his car. Craig, meanwhile, paused then began walking purposefully towards the main gate. It was then as the security lights caught him in their glare I saw he had a rifle in his hand.

For a moment I just stared, unable to comprehend, to take in his intent. Then his words swept back at me and I knew from his steady, determined pace and the way he was holding his rifle ready that he intended to do what he'd always wanted. He was going to exact revenge and kill Mark.

I trembled with panic and clutched at Steve.

"You warn Mark and I'll follow him," Steve said.

It seemed an eternity before Mark answered and I could hardly get the words out, "Mark, please get quickly into the van and away. Craig's just entered the compound with a rifle. He's after you. You've got to get away without his seeing you."

"Where is he, exactly?" Mark asked.

"By the main gate. Steve's following."

"We've just three more cages to load. Then we'll go."

"Let someone else do it."

"There's no one else. Pete and Martin are searching the records now. Don't worry. He won't get me. I'll watch out for him."

Dear Mark, it was typical of him to put the animals before his own safety and he sounded so calm, so unconcerned, I wanted to scream with exasperation. I started pleading with him but the phone was dead and I couldn't get through again. I ran after Steve.

He was skirting the main office block as I entered the main gate but I couldn't see Craig. Then I noticed Steve quickening his pace close to the first kennel section and I ran as fast as I could to keep up with him.

At Section 10 I saw Craig just ahead of him, pressing on, unaware. Then suddenly he was aware and spun round in anger, pointing the rifle at Steve.

"Bugger off or you'll get one too," he hissed.

If it hadn't made a noise, I'm sure he would have shouted at Steve but he had another target in mind.

Steve had no choice then but to wait until Craig was out of sight again. Bravely he pressed on, keeping Craig always one shed ahead of him, with me trailing behind.

At the corner of Section 17 Craig slowed down and manoeuvred himself into a doorway opposite the unbolted door of Section 18. Philippa's van was outside with the back door open where Philippa herself was carefully trying to fit in the cage of one of the transplant baboons.

It was an operation of care and dedication but this didn't count with Craig.

As Mark appeared in the doorway of 18, carrying the last cage with the baboon still holding the terrible swelling in its neck, Craig knelt, steadying his rifle and took aim.

In that moment of fear, of silence, I felt as if my heart had stopped beating. I ran forward to try to reach Craig but I was too slow, too far off.

Then suddenly, risking his life, Steve, ahead of me, threw himself at Craig, knocking the rifle out of his hands. There was a loud bang as a bullet shot out along the concrete towards the van, narrowly missing the back near side wheel.

There was a stunned silence as Mark and Philippa looked out from the van to where Craig was still bent on one knee. As he reached out to get hold of the rifle again, Steve kicked it out of his way. Bending down then himself, Steve picked up the rifle and pointed it at Craig.

"Get out or you'll be meat like the creatures you've hunted."

Craig didn't wait. Like the coward he was without his weapon, he ran in fear and I'd have done anything at that moment to set some hounds on him.

But other events were catching up on us. Scarcely had Craig bolted that we heard an explosion in the main office block. As Philippa closed the door of the van and drove out of the main entrance, Mark, Steve and I hurried across the compound past the sheds to find the entrance to the office block now shattered with jagged pieces of glass hanging dangerously over a gap where the door had been. There was no sign of Jake, but we didn't doubt it was his handiwork and he'd gone inside now to complete his plans.

Mark looked anxiously towards the main gate and across the road, where several lights now showed in the nearby houses.

"You'd better get Kate out," he urged Steve. "I'll wait for Jake."

But just then with blood dripping from a cut on his hand, Jake ran from the building through the shattered glass.

"Get everyone out," he shouted. "They're timed for seven minutes."

Then he was gone, his long black hair streaming behind him, out through the wire opening, into the darkness of the field beyond.

We were about to follow when suddenly a car, with full headlights, swung around from the lane through the main entrance into the compound to the bottom of the main office steps.

In the glare of the security lights, I recognised at once Robert's BMW, spattered with mud but unmistakable. The near side door opened and slammed and Robert, to my surprise, alone, ran up the steps, his eyes, his whole body intent on getting into the building.

Mark shouted at him, "Don't go in. It's not safe! Come back!"

Robert must have heard but he took no notice, pressing on, ignoring Mark, bent on some purpose of his own, his records, no doubt, and research.

Mark dashed after him then and made a lunge at him at the top of the steps, pulling his sleeve and repeating, "Don't go in. It's dangerous and you won't escape."

I saw Robert punch out at Mark, trying to shake him off, heard him shout in anger, "Do you think I'm going to let you destroy all I've done here, you bastard?"

He kicked out, knocking Mark off balance and down the steps and pressed on through the broken glass at the entrance.

I wanted to shout out to Mark to leave him, let him go, but I knew Mark wouldn't, that he couldn't. Much as he hated Robert and all he stood for, he'd promised both himself and the group that no one would be in the building when Jake's bombs exploded. That had been his condition to Jake and himself.

Within seconds he picked himself up and dashed after Robert into the building. Desperately he clutched at Robert's jacket, trying to drag him out. It was then that we heard the next explosion, followed by a staccato succession of three more.

I saw Robert hesitate, then Mark pulling at him again. He was still pulling when suddenly a great fireball of black smoke and orange flame surged into the hall and over to the entrance. Robert tried to turn but it was too late, too late for them both.

Their figures were like black apocalyptic shadows, caught a moment in the orange light, then the upper storey of DLS came crashing down and their shadows were lost forever in a white intensity of flame.

TWENTY-TWO

DLS collapsed that night literally as ashes into the ground. Nothing remained of its elaborate glass structure, computer heartland and cages of torture. So intense was the heat Jake had created with his explosions, not even the strongest metal bars of support remained.

Jake had achieved what he wanted but he didn't stay around to crow. Mysteriously that night he vanished from the area. Many thought he'd perished by accident in the fire but I knew I'd seen him pushing through the wire into the safety and darkness of the field and Pete confirmed my view.

Fortunately the police were slow off the mark that night and the rest of the group got away. By the time the police cars entered the compound, we were at the lay-by and planning a detour through the lanes. Not that we weren't pursued. They called on us all at our individual houses with questions but they'd no evidence in the end for a case. The guards hadn't seen our faces and the CCTV, which could have helped them, had perished with the rest of the defensive gadgets in the fire.

Of course, Mark was held responsible for the fire, not

Jake, and the papers had a field day totalling misrepresenting what had happened and the sequence of events.

Robert was represented as a hero who had gone into the company building to save vital research for medicine; Mark was the terrorist who'd duly got his desserts. Despite the efforts of Pete and myself anonymously behind the scenes, none of the newspaper accounts told the true story of how he'd tried to save Robert and sacrificed himself for the prime torturer. But then the papers wouldn't, would they?

For all their claims to represent freedom of expression and the truth, most represented the establishment when it came to the point and once they'd decided on a line, they stuck to it, no matter what emerged to contradict or conflict with their views. They'd branded Mark as a terrorist and weren't going to change their minds. He deserved all he got, they reiterated.

But the movement honoured Mark for what he was. Over five hundred people came from the Animal Rights Movement from all over the country for a memorial service for him.

No buildings were involved. There were no promises of an afterlife. It was a simple ceremony; remembering all he'd done, out in the open under a grey sky. But the rain held off and the tributes were the most moving I'd ever heard. The main ones were from his father and from Pete, Martin and Steve.

Pete spoke of Mark's dedication and his selfless devotion to the cause while Martin added more humorous incidents showing how human Mark was, and kind. Steve spoke simply of his friendship and understanding.

Most moving was the tribute from his father as he

269

traced Mark's love of the natural world from his earliest years as a child. I felt I was back then myself as a child, with Mark, rediscovering beetles under fallen logs, butterflies on the buddleia and tadpoles in the pond.

Several times Mr Stanton's voice wavered but he kept going. It struck me as he finished that Mark had known all along this could happen, which was why he'd written the letter to his father and asked me to take his camera and develop the film. I'd brought the letter and handed it to Mr Stanton as the service ended. I noticed him put it absentmindedly in his jacket pocket and wondered if, and when, he'd remember it. He looked shattered standing alone, his whole face drained and grey with grief.

I can't remember what happened in the days and weeks following the service. The service had forced us all to focus and keep going but when it was over, nothing seemed to matter any more. Most of the time I lay in bed, unable to think, to move.

If it hadn't been for Tess needing food and exercise in the garden and Steve calling each day, I don't think I'd have got up at all. I couldn't eat. I didn't want to. I didn't want to live, despite Dmitri. Everything had died with Mark, my purpose and being.

Then gradually the outside world began to impinge again. I had a letter from my doctor about a missed appointment, plus a phone call and woke up to the possibility I could be harming Dmitri. Seeing him on the screen at my next appointment, I realised how thoughtless I'd been, how much in reality I wanted him. The same day I had a letter from Ashmead College saying I could start my part-time teaching post in mid-October after half-term. I could no longer hide away alone in the bedroom.

I gave Mark's film to Martin to have developed by one of his contacts. Then he, Steve and I met to check the edited film I'd taken inside DLS, which Mark and I had already scripted. Martin reckoned his same contact could get it included in an undercover series being produced on Channel Three.

There were still a lot of letters and articles in the press against the ARM depicting us as terrorists for having burnt down DLS. It was vital the horrors of the business were made public if we were to prevent DLS reviving and other organisations like it.

Then Steve, who had been consistently a great support, needed support himself. On Christmas morning when he went in to wake his mother with her Christmas presents and a cup of tea, he found her dead. She had died in her sleep, fortunately without the pain Steve had feared. Although he had long been prepared for her passing, it proved much more of a shock than he'd expected. He'd lived most of his life with his mother and in recent years it had revolved round her, absorbing his energy and time. Now he was alone, at a loss, uncertain what to do about her possessions and the house.

He was certain though he wanted a green funeral for her. It was not quite the funeral her own generation expected, but they accepted it for Steve's sake and she was buried in a quiet woodland burial site with a sapling willow in place of a headstone. There weren't the large numbers that had been at Mark's memorial service but all our neighbours in the road came, including Carol and Alan.

Carol and Alan had had several dates together and I was glad Carol had found someone to help her through the trauma of Robert's death and defection, but I knew I'd never trust Alan again after his betrayal of Mark to the police.

A month or so after Steve's mother's funeral, I had a letter from Mark's father, saying he was sorry for not having written before but had only just remembered the letter I'd given him. He asked me to go over to Youlton and see him.

Steve said he would collect me from my visit when he left work so I took the bus to Youlton Post Office, then walked.

It was an unexpectedly warm, sunny day for January and I was conscious of Dmitri being in evidence as I strolled along the lane to Mr Stanton's cottage.

There was no response to my knocking on the front door so I went to the back garden and there he was, bending over his plants in the greenhouse, in exactly the same position as when I'd first seen him; only he looked much older now, greyer, more bowed, as if the life had gone out of him. He was transplanting some parsley into bigger pots but his movements seemed automatic, without energy, interest.

I felt I'd lost everything when Mark died but realised in those moments before he noticed me that Mr Stanton had lost even more. He'd lost his only son, all he'd hoped for, worked for at an age when it wouldn't be easy to adjust and hope again and my heart went out to him. In response at that moment I felt Dmitri stir inside me, as if already he knew the bond was there, the longing of a father for his son, the son for his father.

I opened the greenhouse door and Mr Stanton looked up. His eyes lighted a moment and he came forward and gripped my hand. We didn't speak. We couldn't speak. It wasn't until we were back in the house and had absorbed, in part, our mutual strangeness, Mr Stanton referred to Mark's letter.

"It's true then," he asked, "you're carrying Mark's child?"

"Yes."

"He asked me in his letter particularly if I'd help you. Did you know?"

"Yes he told me, but I'm not expecting anything. I can manage. I have a part time teaching job now."

"You're independent like his mother was, I see." He looked at me with a brief gleam of humour in his eyes. Then the lines of his face resumed their sadness and he said quietly," But I'd like to help if I can, when you need it."

"Thank you."

"You'll tell me what I can do?"

"I will."

It was like the promise I'd have made to Mark if I'd married him, a promise to them both to continue seeing Mr Stanton and involve him.

In the weeks following I saw him often. Sometimes we just talked while Doris bustled noisily around making tea. Other times, if Doris was shopping or feeding her husband, we would play scrabble or cards. We didn't talk of Mark but he was always behind all we said and thought, a presence drawing us, in his absence, closer.

When Dmitri was born, Mr Stanton was the first to see him. I knew at once from the light in his eyes, he'd taken to him. For Dmitri was just like Mark with his dark, dark hair, his strong features and deep blue eyes. I was overwhelmed with love for him, with gratitude that, through him, Mark could go on in part living with us.

Mark lived, of course, far beyond his actual life through his influence, his work with the ARM. The night of his death was the beginning of the end for organisations like DLS. The combination of the burning, the pressure on shareholders, the endless demos and campaigns, all Mark's efforts in the end paid off. Our film showing what DLS really did on prime time TV clinched things, causing an outburst of protest and anger, as did the pictures Mark had taken of the transplant monkeys and baboons.

As DLS fell, other institutions followed in its wake. As people understood the suffering and cruelty involved for creating and producing mere products unrelated to health, emphasis was given to other forms of testing like computer modelling and cell culture, methods in fact more reliable.

Not that the suffering of animals was by any means at an end. As I became more involved in the ARM, taking over aspects of Mark's role, I became increasingly aware of the terrible abuses in the rearing and slaughter of animals for food, on a scale far more massive than vivisection. There would never be a pause to sit back as far as the suffering of animals was concerned. It was a campaign that would never have an end. The work would always be there to do.

But Mark had started a new awareness of what was going on behind the scenes. He was a catalyst that had woken people from slumber. He'd woken me.

I have Dimitri and, through Dimitri, a part of Mark lives on for me. I have good friends in Mark's father, Pete, Martin, Gemma and above all, Steve. I have Tess who managed to survive her ordeal and lead in the end a reasonably normal life. I have much to be grateful for and, as Pete reminds me, Mark would have been inevitably caught and probably imprisoned for years if he hadn't died, which would have crushed him far more than death could ever do.

But being woken, it is difficult to sleep again. I miss Mark far more than I can ever express in words.

FURTHER
INFORMATION

Campaign against Vivisection

All the characters, the precise setting and the plot in *The Cause* are fictitious. The descriptions, however, of suffering animals and vivisection procedures are based on research into written and undercover film documentation.

Despite recommendations of replacement, reduction and refinement, the suffering and procedures continue. 2.7 million animals were experimented on in the UK in 2003. There were 30 per cent more experiments in 2002 than in 1987. Yet testing on animals has not been validated for drug testing and in the study of human disease. An animal testing study in 1990 showed that animals did not predict 67 per cent of toxicity that occurred in humans.

There are now better options as DNA chip technology and stem cell research, which offers cures for people suffering from neurological illnesses like Parkinson's. Why does animal experimentation continue then? It is essentially because of vested interests and the fact that it is a multibillion business.

Opinion polls have shown that the public want more investment in non animal research but the government has given less than £100,000 to this. We urgently need a national centre now to fast track such non animal research so that we can replace for good the suffering pointlessly inflicted on sentient creatures.

For further information and campaigns in this respect, please visit:

Animal Aid	www.animalaid.org.uk
Dr Hadwen Trust	www.drhadwentrust.org.uk
SHAC	www.shac.net
BUAV	www.buav.org
Green Party	www.greenparty.org.uk
Uncaged	www.uncaged.co.uk

The books of Dr Ray Greek, Director of Europeans for Medical Advancement, give useful information on the science. Two of his books are:

Sacred Cows and Golden Geese published by Continuum with foreword by Jane Goodall

How Genetics and Evolution Reveal Why Medical Research on Animals Harms Humans also published by Continuum.